CHARIOT OF A GOD

A voice crashed in the heavens like the thunder in the distant hills. What it said no man understood. From the radiance a vast noise as of palaces tottering and falling pierced through the people. They stood, motionless, their faces uplifted. From the golden radiance a spot of brighter gold burned, and a form appeared. A form like unto a blazing chariot of gold, drawn by beasts of gold, burning, fires limning the whole in glory and awesome terror, a form flew through the limpid air to land beside the wall and the crumpled naked body of Momi.

The villagers were held petrified in their fear. Only Erek managed to croak hoarsely, "The girl spoke true! She was blessed by a god! By Odan En-Ke! It is true!"

As though their tongues had been unlocked as one, the people sent up a long wavering howl, a mournful cry of terror and obeissance.

"Odan, do not punish us! Odan! Odan En-Ke! We did not know!"

About The Author

Because of prior commitments and contractual options by the author, the publishers are not at liberty to reveal the true identity of Manning Norvil. We can say that, as his realistic account of the first days of human civilization under the tutelage and power of those ancient astronauts known as "gods" shows, Manning Norvil is a learned student of the dawn of culture in the Mediterranean and Mesopotamian basins. He has written extensively of subjects celestial and terrestrial. His books have sold in millions of copies throughout the world and have been translated into many languages. The legend of Odan, offspring of a human mother and a "divine" father, is based upon the extraordinary prevalence of such demigod lore in all the most ancient records and primitive theologies of all races and on all continents.

MANNING NORVIL

DREAM CHARIOTS

DAW BOOKS, INC.
DONALD A. WOLLHEIM, PUBLISHER

1301 Avenue of the Americas
New York, N. Y. 10019

Cover art by Richard Clifton-Dey.

FIRST PRINTING, OCTOBER 1977

1 2 3 4 5 6 7 8 9

DAW sf BOOKS

PRINTED IN U.S.A.

Prologue

This is a story of the days when a mighty River flowed southwards between two seas who rolled their blue waters where today lies the Mediterranean Sea. A lofty procession of kingdoms and empires followed one another in pride and power along the broad curves of The River in the land of Ea and upon the sun-lit shores of the two seas. Many a king looked upon his rich lands and was wantonly not content and coveted the land of his neighbor king. Many a poor laborer looked up from the toil of the fields and saw in the ranks of the king's army a brighter horizon. Many a sorcerer wove a dark spell to bring the heart's desire closer, many a beauteous maid languished for her lost lover, many a hero sought a heroic death in relentless combat against the malefic forces of evil.

The gods lived in the land in those days and walked among their people, and every shining city of The River and the two seas cherished their own god who took sacrifice from the city and returned sacrifice with power and wealth and protection.

Then all this bright tapestry of high living and joyous adventuring and dark sorcery was swept away in the green rushing waters as the two seas joined and the Atlantic swept in to drown a world.

Neither gold nor silver, neither shield nor sword could hold back the dark cold onrush of the waters. Neither the proud curvetting beauty of the chariot horses nor the most potent gramarye of the sorcerers could stem the deluge. A world vanished and the lights of civilization flickered and went out for thousands of years. A few survivors were left to return to scraping an existence with the flint tools of their ancestors.

Lost and forgotten lay that high culture of The River and the two seas, and today there is no record of all that beauty and brilliance and terror—save in the accounts that follow. . . .

Chapter One

How Momi came to Eresh

Before they stoned her to death, the good people of the village desired Momi to repent of her crime.

She supported herself against the whitewashed wall feeling the heat beat back at her as the fat golden sun burned mercilessly down. Tears ran stickily down her soft cheeks. Her mouth felt as dry as the desert beyond the last ditches. She stared in an apathy of terror upon the people, not recognizing them, seeing them only as ravening beasts intent upon her unjust destruction.

"You have sinned, Momi, sinned," said Erek, the headman of the village. "You have sinned grievously. Wadu has paid for his part of the abomination." He threw the brick from hand to hand as he spoke. "Now repent with a full heart before you die."

Momi licked at her lips. Her throat was dry, her heart throbbed like a beaten drum. She stared upon the bricks in the hands of the villagers with fascination and with revulsion. Those sharp edges where the bricks had been broken in half . . . Those bricks, hardened in the sun, what would those jagged edges do to her, to her flesh, to the babe she carried?

Flies clustered in a shining black mass over the corpse of Wadu. He had been staked out yesterday, his eyelids cut off, and he had lasted until past midday. Momi could not look at him. He had always been kind, and although only the son of a laborer in the ditches always had a smile and a song as he went about his work. Now they said . . . And he had not . . . And he was dead because of the lie.

The half-circle of villagers hemming Momi in were people she had known all her life. Now they were strangers. They held their half bricks in lean brown hands and stared at her and at Erek, waiting. Here in the ribbon-narrow strip of irrigation along The River stones existed only when carried at great expense from the mountains so far away, yet ritual executions were always spoken of as a Stoning to Death.

Momi saw the looks on the distorted faces of these strangers who had once been friends. Some there were whose excitement overcontrolled them, others whose tongues licked feverishly at stretched lips, others who kept tossing a half brick from one hand to another. She could look in vain for any who showed shame at what they did here this day.

Yet—"Father!" Erek's second son, Valdo, stepped forward. He threw down his halfbrick into the rich brown dust of the village street. The sun shone upon his black hair. He gestured to Momi and to the thing that had been Wadu, and he said: "Momi was forced. She is betrothed to my brother Ladu and she would never have consented willingly."

"Betrothed!" thundered Erek. His face showed in its lean lines only the intense hatred burning in him. This little village of Idu was his all, and his eldest son, Ladu, meant all of life to him. "Aye, Valdo, my son. You speak well. The harlot was betrothed to my son Ladu who will be headman in his turn, and she betrayed him and her sins have found her out and she must pay the penalty."

"No," whispered Momi. To speak at all was effort. "No. It was not Wadu."

"We do not believe your lies, girl. Your mother was not of us. A barbarian slave wench from the northern hills. From where no man really knows. Yet we took her in and clothed her and fed her and my brother took her as his woman. And you—you harlot! What young man do you seek to destroy by your lies?"

Momi shrank back. They did not understand. Poor Wadu, a thing of glistening rawness and blackened with flies, he had suffered. When they had seized him up Wadu had not understood until they began on him and, screaming and protesting, he had suffered as cruel a fate as any—as the fate Momi was to suffer.

The sharp-edged bricks caught the blaze of sunshine and shards of light splintered into her eyes.

"Die, if you will not repent!" Erek lifted his arm, the sinews and muscles long and corded, ridged, like coiling serpents.

"No!" Momi tried to shout. Surely she would not be left to

die? Not like this. He had promised much, so very much, and she had welcomed him with beating heart and yearning body, opening to him as a flower in the sun. Was this dark ending all there was to be?

She lifted her head, her long pale-brown hair trailing, so stark a contrast to the black hair of the villagers. Her mother's hair had been a bright straw yellow. She pressed her hands back flat against the wall. She could feel the heat in the wall beat at her palms.

"No. It was not Wadu—"

"Tell us your lies, harlot. And then die!"

"Not lies . . . It was not Wadu . . ." She had to go on. If they knew the truth then they would understand and would not stone her to death. He had said it must be a secret. But he would understand—yes, he must understand! He could never mean Momi to die. Not Momi, the most beautiful girl, he had said, not after what he had whispered and what had passed between them. Once the people understood who the father was they would stop their frightful hatred . . . Yes, she must tell them—for the sake of the babe . . .

"No!" Momi pushed herself up against the wall, her pale brown hair streaming in the brilliant sunshine, the tears and dust marking her face, her mouth trembling. "No. It was not Wadu. It was Odan En-ke! Odan! Odan! He visited me in glory—"

They did not let her continue.

Fierce yells beat about her, shrieks of execration, vicious catcalls of derision, and Erek, swinging with all his strength, hurled the first brick.

"No god would consort with you, girl!" Smash went the halfbrick against the wall by Momi's ear. "A slut like you who lies with the ditch boys would be spurned by any god. And Odan En-Ke would have no eyes for your likes." A brick struck Momi in the shoulder. She shrieked and span about and fell. A brick smashed against her arm, bringing bright blood, and another thudded cruelly into the side of her head. She fell in a heap, sprawled, motionless, her hair outflung, the blood bright upon her nude swollen body.

Erek strutted forward, poising a brick. He glared down, all the anger and viciousness twisting his face into the semblance of a devil dancer's mask. "Odan En-Ke!" He spat. "What do we know of gods that are not our own? Odan is an

Old god and there is no city dedicated to Odan that travellers have told us. No, not in all the land of Ea."

He lifted the halfbrick, hard-edged and jagged in the bright sunshine. He poised it high with his black fingernails gripping, ready to bring it down in a final crushing blow on Momi's head.

Into that bright sunshine a greater glow poured radiant gold. A pulsing light burned in the air. The people fell back away from Momi, their mouths open in wonder, their eyes staring. They dropped their cruel bricks. Some screamed, some sank to their knees; but most simply stood, silent and unmoving, stricken with mortal terror. The village of Idu was too small to boast a resident sorcerer. Had it done so, he, too, would have been powerless before this greater power.

The radiance spread and engulfed the heavens. Over the irrigation ditches, across the reed and mud roofs of the houses of Idu, sending a blinding reflection from the broad waters of The River, the brilliance grew into an intolerable flame.

A voice crashed in the heavens like the thunder in the distant hills these people had never heard or seen. What it said no man understood. From the radiance a vast noise as of palaces tottering and falling pierced through the people. They stood, motionless, their faces uplifted. From the golden radiance a spot of brighter gold burned as the forge fires burn brighter when the bellows blow. A form appeared. A form like unto a blazing chariot of gold, drawn by beasts of gold, burning, fires limning the whole in glory and awesome terror, a form flew through the limpid air to land beside the wall and the crumpled naked body of Momi.

The villagers were held petrified in their fear. Only Erek managed to force air through his windpipe, muster words to croak hoarsely: "The girl spoke true! She was blessed by a god! By Odan En-Ke! It is true!"

As though their tongues had been unlocked as one, the people sent up a long wavering howl, a mournful cry of terror and obeisance.

"Odan, do not punish us! Odan! Odan En-ke! We did not know!"

Momi was caught up into the heart of the golden radiance. The chariot lifted into the air, rising like a chariot of dreams, a true dream chariot pouring its brilliant floods of light upon the dust and the water and the houses, painting the people's faces in gilded masks of fear and reverence.

"We will take Momi in," shouted Erek, the headman. "We will give her honor! She shall sit at the right hand of my son, Ladu, who will be headman when I am gone. Hear me, Odan En-ke! Hear the prayers of my people."

The dream chariot rose higher, blazing.

"She is gone, father," said Valdo. "She had been taken away from us by Odan En-ke because we sinned against her. Let us pray that no evil falls on Idu."

High rose the dream chariot, high into the burning air. Borne aloft on wings of flame the golden chariot flew high and fast over the land of Ea.

Momi stirred and moaned. The god touched her and her pains vanished. She looked over the side of the chariot, and cried out. The god who told her his name was Odan comforted her and together they flew westwards from the village of Idu, lost and insignificant on the lower reaches of The River. Over to the east The River emptied through the many mouths of the Delta into The Sweet Sea. The land lay spread out far below. Momi gazed, enraptured. She had heard that the mages of the cities of the plain possessed flying carpets; but she thought that not one could be as fine or as grand as the dream chariot of her lord and master, Odan—Odan En-Ke her god.

"And you are not angry I told them?" she whispered.

The reassuring smile, the nod and the firm arm cradling her told their own story. "My Momi," said the god. "I would have burned their village to ashes—in fact, I may go back there when you are safe and burn them all to dust. It would be fitting."

"No, my lord, no! For they are merely foolish. And Valdo tried to save me—"

"Valdo was in love with you and detested his brother. As for poor Wadu, the dead are dead, Momi. Never forget that."

She was held close, so close she could feel his heart beating. Her own slender body was plumply ripe with his fruit, the first tender curving betraying her. The boy would be the son of a god and of a mortal woman. The prospect both terrified and exalted her.

Below them The River cut through the arid deserts, running in a long succession of wide-sweeping loops southwards from the mountains so far away to the north, those mountains on whose lower southern slopes Momi's mother's people lived as free barbarians. The brilliant green strip of cultivation faithfully followed every curve and bend of The River. From The Salt Sea in the west to The Sweet Sea in the east, the land of Ea stretched on average four hundred miles in width. Beyond those confines, beyond unknown lands, legend said a mighty sea extended to the farthest reaches of the universe.

Far away to the northeast the Mak Sea rolled; but no man would say that of the three seas of the known world any one could match the sheer horror of the unending wastes of water supposed to stretch out to the west beyond the Gardens of Golden Sunset. Yet—and here Momi hugged herself in deep and secret glee—yet the father of her child would know, he would know of the farthest oceans, he would know the mountains to the north and the deserts of the south, he would know the three seas and The River as well as all the land of Ea.

At irregular intervals along the sweeping curves of The River the cities rose. Brilliant in the slanting sunshine with their towers and spires and ziggurats catching the light and flinging back glittering spears, they bejeweled the broad waterway with a string of costly gems. Shagal they passed, and Pera and Persar the twin cities of the Persaran Bend; Galash and Zhorzuppak and Nish passed below.

"Look!" cried Momi, all her fears fled, seized up in the enchantment of this aerial ride through the limpid air. "A wizard on a flying carpet!"

Far below them the carpet sped on. Its fringes rippling in serpentine undulations it upheld in steady flight its occupant, who sat cross-legged in the center wearing robes of blue and white and his cap of potency, and with an unrolled scroll before him on his knees.

"Oh, Odan, my lord! Why does he not see our radiance like a second sun?"

Odan En-Ke laughed with that deep-belled voice that had captivated her so easily on the night he had visited her hut, to speak tenderly and amorously, to win her completely. "To all mortals we gods are invisible when we so choose. The mage below has no more conception of our presence in the sky than the very cows in the water meadows."

Momi shuddered at the latent power behind the words; but the sudder was a delicious reminder that in great measure she shared and was a part of Odan's power.

Following the windings of The River, Odan flew northwards so that Momi might experience the fascination of the scene. As they flew on, swinging boldly from west through north and north east and the lordly procession of cities fled away below so Momi received a vivid impression of the vastness of the world beyond the narrow strip of irrigation chained to The River within the encompassing deserts.

All her fears had left her. How she revelled in this heady onrushing flight through the empty air! Odan held her and she melted to his embrace, feeling the hard strength of him, the limber suppleness, knowing him to be a true god and yet all a girl could require of a man. She smiled up at him and he leaned down and kissed her. Her arms were about his neck. He pulled her close, close, and she shuddered with the delicious feelings she could never explain.

"I shall make all arrangements to take care of you, Momi, you and the child. Always remember, because I am a god I cannot be as a mortal man. But you shall be loved and served and obeyed in the land of Ea. I promise you this. And the boy, too, shall become mighty—if he desires and wills it so."

"He will, Odan, my lord. He will!"

Drawing back he raised himself. He pointed over the forepart of the dream chariot and helped Momi to rise. Ahead the broad ribbon of The River gleamed orange and gold in the last burning embrace of the sun.

"There, Momi, glittering like a lake of fire on the horizon! That is Eresh. That is where you will be safe."

Momi looked ahead as he had commanded. She felt no fear, no apprehension. Below them passed Endal tucked within an island-fringed curve of The River, its wharves and jetties busy with traffic. Fabled Endal, mighty upon The River, Endal whose citizens had raised up a mighty ziggurat to Nirghal En-Theus, the god of Fire. But Momi looked at a spot along The River between the majesty of Endal and the distant burning lake of fire that was Eresh. She cried a small cry of astonishment.

"Odan, my lord—look below. Is that a city?"

"It was a city."

The streets were piled with refuse and rubbish, the towers were all thrown down, the walls slaked, and the roofs had fallen so that the squared city gave the somber impression of a higgledy-piggledy collection of shattered clay boxes. Sand whirled through the doorless gates and whitened bones lay scattered about the shattered walls. The ziggurat had been demolished and had spilled a long drift of rubble through the dead heart of the city.

"Has some divine wrath struck this miserable city of sinners?"

"No. This was Tubal. King Svettu of Endal marched up against them with chariots and spearmen and archers and beseiged them and took their city and destroyed them and all their works utterly. Endal is feeling its power, growing. Their belief in Nirghal is complete. And from The Sweet Sea in the east to Endal is only twenty miles further than along The Golden Road from Shanadul to Eresh."

Momi did not understand what her lord meant. But, clearly, whatever it was must be important. There was a dead city below to prove it.

She nestled closer to Odan En-Ke.

He smoothed her pale brown hair, and smiled.

"Your city will be Eresh. There is where our son will be born."

Momi drew closer to her lord, the god Odan En-Ke, and the dream chariot, blazing with supernal fires, flew on towards the ancient city of proud Eresh.

Chapter Two

Gift of a god

In the last orange sparks of the sunset the richly colored spear-carrying infantry of the walls flanking the great staircase seemed to move and march and carry their faithful spears in full-blooded life. Clattering in his flip-flopping sandals down the marble treads, on his way to an evening meeting with a certain witch from whom he could buy ingredients hard to come by, Kidu, the court wizard, instinctively kept to the balustrade side. He left the full width of each step between himself and the light-and-shadow rippling infantry, for all they were merely enamelled tiles decorating the wall.

From the deeper recesses of King Neb-ayin-Ke's palace the distance-muted sounds of preparations for the evening banquet reached him. The air stifled; but soon the evening breeze would bring a little surcease from the heat of the day. Kidu's long and mournful face sweated only a little, his down-drooping whiskers black against the pallor of his smooth skin. His heavy embroidered robes swirled about his agile figure, for he was still a young man with a full two score years of sorcery before him. He made sure his outer cloak's hood snugged about his face. He had left his cap of potency in his cobwebby chambers. No sense in advertising just who he was when he ventured into the perilous alleyways of Eresh.

A real guard stood immobile at the foot of the great staircase. His bronze scaled armor and crested bronze helmet were exact matches for the enamelled figures. Only his eyes moved as he watched Kidu cross the broad flagged space at the foot of the stairs towards the columns lining the entrance-way.

Footsteps clacked authoritatively on the marble.

"Ah! Master Kidu!"

The court wizard turned convulsively at the words from the man he detested with a whole-hearted detestation second only to one other man in the whole palace.

Mnenon-Ket smirked as he approached, his heavy, blood-flushed features with the red and blue of vein-broken skin clear evidence of the amounts of prime meat he consumed from the sacrifices. This man was dangerous, this man held real power, this was Mnenon-Ket, the high priest of the Great god Zadan, the patron deity of the proud city of Eresh.

"Mnenon-Ket."

"I perceive you sneak out, Master Kidu. Can it be you lack aught for your thaumaturgical practice? Is the king, whose name be praised, to be disappointed this early in his faith in you?"

The ferocious curse that boiled to Kidu's lips was quenched with difficulty. Kurd take the fellow! He had penetrated at once to the heart of the matter, for tonight Neb-ayin-Ke held a sumptuous feast for the neighbor king of Dilpur and his fair daughter Fretti. Everyone expected the young king and the young princess to marry and thus seal a pact between the two cities. And Master Kidu must provide a potent potion to make the king glorious in the sight of the lady. And because he had just been appointed court wizard after the unfortunate death of the previous incumbent, one Unsherbi who now fed the crocodiles, he was not fully provided with all he required for his art.

Now Kidu stared levelly at the high priest.

"Beware lest I blast you with an incantation, Mnenon-Ket—"

The high priest quivered with anger, and then he laughed, his flabby jowls quivering purple, his beringed hand clutching at the blue robe he wore gathered in around his paunch with many golden and jewelled belts.

"You are young, Kidu! You should know by now that all your thaumaturigical arts cannot prevail against the gods."

"You are no god."

"But I am high in their favor. I am high priest to Zadan, a great god, a powerful god, master of the sword! No sorcery you can conjure can harm me, little wizard."

The trouble, as Kidu, by Kurd, knew only too well, was that the fellow was right. The gods looked after their own.

"Eresh is fortunate that the great god Zadan the All Glorious has taken the city under the protection of his wings."

Kidu spoke calmly. But Mnenon-Ket took his meaning, and again he tugged at his costly belts. He saw how Kidu insulted him by not mentioning the good fortune of the city in possessing Mnenon-Ket as high priest of Zadan of the Sword.

In the deepening shadows as the westering sun sank into far desert slaves ran into the entrance hall bearing torches to light the sconces ornately bracketted along the walls. On this night there would be no lack of light, for the king wished to impress his visitors with his wealth and power, and also, as Kidu knew, with his artistic tastes and connoisseurship among the riverine courts of the land of Ea.

Over the pattering rush of naked feet the heavy tramp of bronze-studded sandals told of the guards changing duty. Each man wore a bronze-scaled cuirass over his long brown and yellow robe. Each man carried a stout spear with a bronze leaf-shaped blade balanced by a bronze butt-weight. The straight clean-grained wood of the shafts was almost as much of a marvel as the reckless use of stone and marble here in the Land Between the Two Seas. Long-grained wood and stone were enough to establish the power of King Neb-ayin-Ke among the cities of The River.

The torches gleamed exceptionally brilliantly tonight.

Kidu looked up. Odd. The light appeared to be strengthening from outside. In fact, the torches looked weak and anemic. A shout lifted outside followed at once by a babble of voices and the sound of running feet.

If sorcery was in the air, then Master Kidu would be needed urgently.

A passing guards officer, imposing in his bronze and crimson, shouted at the sentries. Kidu, flinging ceremony to the winds, seized the officer's arm.

"Where is the king?"

The man gazed blankly. "The king? May his name be praised?"

Kidu shook him. "What is it? Where is the king!"

The officer licked his lips. His crimson feathers glowed in the unreal light.

"The sun! Newly set in the west, it rises again in the south!"

"A miracle!" yelled Mnenon-Ket. "I must to the temple! Zadan the All Glorious—"

Everyone ran outside onto the broad terrace flanked by the tall columns. The light ghosted in from the south, as the guards officer had said. People milled. Everyone craned to look to the south, and their cries of wonder aroused the doves who swooped ghostlike through the evening air.

Sure enough, low on the southern horizon a light burned, a light brighter and more golden than any star, a light brazening in glory across the sky, growing and rising and approaching with the swiftness of supernal wings.

Soon the brightness as of noon day swamped the palace and courtyards and terraces with light. The whole of the proud city of Eresh was lit as by the noon day sun.

"The king! The king! May he live for ever!"

The whispers and then the shouts rose. Kidu saw the king step onto the terrace. He wore simple yellow robes and he had not yet donned his regal beard, so that his face appeared merely that of a young and handsome lad, eager for life. With him paced the man who brought the furrows to Kidu's brow, the quick instinctive curl of the lip.

This man, this uncle to the king, this Gabal-ayin, aroused so fierce a revulsion in the wizard that Kidu was forced to draw the flap of his hood about his face. Only his dark eyes showed within the shadow of the hood, bent in full evil intent upon the lord Gabal-ayin, the king's uncle.

Kidu, for all he was a wizard and, by Kurd! although a young wizard one already of great renown so that he had been selected by the young king, knew that he remained always a man. He was a mere mortal. Sometimes the high priest Mnenon-Ket forgot he, too, was a mere mortal in his high junketings with the gods. But Kidu knew with all the powers he owned that great and grotesque ambitions possessed the king's uncle, Gabal-ayin.

The king, Neb-ayin-Ke, passed always in pleasant converse whenever king and uncle met. There appeared no surface rift to cause gossip and speculation. Often since he had arrived in the palace from his eyrie high in Yellow Lotus Street Kidu had watched, waiting for the explosion he felt inevitable. But none came. Yet, even as a mere mortal, his own wizardly instincts told him unmistakably that such an explosion, like a gigantic blast of thunder, must one day rend the palace and all who lived there.

But thunder and lightning and rain were all rare along The River. Old men spoke of the last rain as of a miracle of their fathers' youth. From travellers with their tall tales the stories of the gods shaking the distant mountains might be heard, of the gods striking with spears of light and drenching the world with water. And now, as he stood with the others on the high terrace, Kidu felt that such a new miracle might be afforded them all.

For this was a god.

This great light beating from the night sky could herald only the personal appearance of a god.

Mnenon-Ket and the other priests of Zadan the All Powerful said they were often visited by the gods whilst asleep.

There were other shrines to other gods in the proud city of Eresh. The greatest temple was dedicated to Zadan, and the next to Ke, the Old God, the Great One, He who had created the universe and set the seasons in train. There were other temples.

The people fell to their knees as the light drew near. Kidu followed their example. A flower field of upturned faces awaited the manifestation.

Mnenon-Ket waddled back, strutting importantly, to bend low beside the upright form of the king. It was clear to all that the flaming apparition was bound for the palace and not the temple. Kidu killed instantly his little tickle of delight at the priest's discomfiture.

"A chariot!" People were exclaiming now, some daring ones pointing up. "A chariot of fire!"

"The Dream Chariots of the gods made manifest, oh king!" declared Mnenon-Ket, self-importantly.

The radiance swooped nearer. The burning outlines of a quadriga limned the skies with light. The light coruscated so that the people were forced to shade their eyes or turn their heads away.

Squinting through slit eyelids, tears running down his cheeks, Kidu watched as the god-chariot hovered above the terrace.

The god-voice spoke.

"Good people of Eresh, Zadan the All Glorious and Swordlike's city! People of the city of Zadan of the Sword! Hearken!"

Mnenon-Ket took it upon himself to answer. The king remained motionless. He still stood upright; but his eyes were fast shut.

"We hearken and obey, O mighty god," said Mnenon-Ket. For all his detestation of the high priest, Kidu felt a stab of unwilling admiration for the way he spoke in firm priestly tones. "We are the people who cluster in the hands of Zadan and run for shelter beneath his outspread wings." Mnenon-Ket lifted his voice. "But you, O mighty god, are not Zadan the All Glorious!"

"I am not Zadan of the Sword."

Every priest was required to know the attributes of the gods. Along with reading and writing and numeration, that was a prime requisite for admission to the priesthood. And the land of Ea boasted a profusion of gods, at least five gods to every single day of the year. To know all the plants and animals and fabled beasts and symbols that marked a god was a profound study. Kidu had often cynically assumed that a priest simply learned the attributes of the god to whom he was apprenticed, and those of the gods who shared the same day, and a few others nearby in the calendar. After that—who was to tell?

So now Mnenon-Ket in that rich plummy voice spoke out.

"We of Zadan's city of Eresh salute and greet you, O mighty Odan En-Ke! By your attributes are you recognized and by us are you welcome."

Even then, the high priest did not have the nerve actually to enquire of the god what he wanted. Perhaps it was not a lack of nerve as a knowledge of common sense.

The light sensibly faded. Now Kidu could look at the radiance surrounding the chariot without a whirlpool of color blinding him.

At the king's side his uncle Gabal stirred and sat back from his obeisant crouch. On the other side the King of Dilpur and his daughter sat up, staring with undisguised fascination upon the blazing winged chariot. Now all could see there were two occupants of the car.

"I come to the city of Zadan with his blessing!" The god-voice boomed down, strong and masculine. "I, Odan En-Ke, bring good news to your city."

Kidu made a face. That usually meant trouble for someone. The gods had not been as communicative in these latter days as they had at one time. But there was no doubt they had brought to men, the sons of the sons of Ke, many blessings. They had shown the secrets of tempering bronze, the cunning of the wheel, the leverage of pulley and block, the full-headed wheat that grew where once only thin-eared corn had struggled, the full uddered cows, the taming of onagers, oh, yes, the gods had taught men many things. So what new thing was Odan En-Ke bringing them on this fateful night?

The chariot burned again, suddenly, fiercely, so that faces were hastily turned away. When the voice boomed out once more Kidu could see the chariot rested upon the end of the terrace. On the podium against the eastern colonnade the king and the group about him were reaching forward. Approaching them walked a young girl. Kidu could see her clearly.

He gasped.

Never had he seen a girl as beautiful.

She wore a long white robe of that magical substance the gods could conjure from caterpillars, and she was pregnant. She walked in tiny scarlet slippers, gem-encrusted. Her yellow-brown hair was unbound and fell freely about her shoulders. And her face! Wizards were men, and understood the sexual drives of ordinary mortals. Kidu repressed his instinctive hungry thoughts. Such beauty of form, such purity of face, belonged, he felt sure, to a goddess.

But no . . .

"This is Momi, beloved of Odan En-Ke. You will care for her, king, care for her as though she were your own wife. All that is needful for her will be done. The child will be called Odan. I shall not speak to you again. But I shall know. Remember what I have said, King Neb-ayin-Ke. Ponder on my words. Tremble at my anger. Momi is the mother of Odan, and yet is she a mortal woman."

The chariot of fire lifted. The light coruscated down. The words beat about their heads with the same supernal force.

"I am well-pleased in Momi and in her child, Odan. She is as a queen, king. As your throne and head and guts depend on it, see you keep this covenant."

The quadriga soared upwards, the light growing as it rose, so that the whole heavens were one sheet of orange and gold.

Then, like a rushlight extinguished in a bat-cavern of the far hills, the radiance faded and vanished.

The darkness crashed back in solid walls of blackness.

Presently tiny lights pricked the gloom. The torches shone out anew. But there would be some few clepsydra cycles to pass before eyes would see again as normally.

The king spoke imperiously to Mnenon-Ket.

"Send for the high priest of Odan En-Ke."

A thin and trembling figure was half-pushed half-assisted

up to the podium. His sparse white hair glinted in the gaining torchlight. He carried a great twisted olive stave and he used the staff to support himself as he faced the king. His lined and careworn face with the faded brown eyes showed all the marks of resignation, of contumely and of disregard.

"Your god had seen fit to pay us a visit, Nabozinadas."

"Yes, king, live for ever. I am glad I am alive this day."

Mnenon-Ket bristled and would have spoken; but the king held up a slender hand on which the two great rings glittered.

"You have heard what he asked us—"

Nabozinadas thrust the marble with his olive stave, trembling, holding himself up. "Commanded, oh king!"

King Neb-ayin-Ke nodded. He was young; and he still clung to ideals his father had shown him. "Yes, Nabozinadas. He did so command us. And he came to Eresh, the city of Zadan, because we also honor Odan En-ke and preserve a temple to him within our walls."

The king turned to Momi, who stood still with the radiance clinging about her, her face uplifted, staring at the stars.

From the king's side Fretti, the daughter of the King of Dilpur, stepped forward. She took Momi's hand. The coolness of the touch surprised her, for she had expected the lightning bolt of godlike heat. She turned to the king.

"We must take the girl in, Neb-Ke. She—"

"She is near her time?"

Fretti smiled. She was a charming girl. "No, Neb-Ke. Her belly is only just beginning to swell. A week ago you would scarcely have known. But she needs rest, refreshment—"

The king, who permitted the ayin to be dropped from his name among familiars, beckoned, and at once female slaves took Momi away. Fretti, with a delightful sidelong glance at her father, went with them.

Her father, King Norgash of Dilpur, stroked his beard. It was a real beard, threaded with gold and silver and pearls.

Softly, so that no one else on the podium could hear, he said: "You would be wise to see to the girl, king. We have no shrine to Odan—he is an old god but almost forgotten now—and I feel relief at that." Norgash of Dilpur fastened his pouched eyes upon the young king. "But you would do well to wed my daughter at once. I do not like what may befall."

King Neb-ayin-Ke laughed. The laugh rang shrill, not quite genuine and yet not a false laugh, either.

"There is time, king, there is time. We have a feast tonight. Then we may talk."

"The alliance between us is vital. I can hardly hold the north alone, and from the south you have Endal encroaching. Would you wish the fate of Tubal upon Eresh?"

"There is time, king. Let us dress and make ready for the feast. By Turbash! Shall we ever forget the chariot of the gods! A Dream Chariot made manifest!" He swung sharply about and lifted his voice, shouting to old Narpul the Staff, the court chamberlain. "Remember to have gifts sent to the Temple of Odan. Let it be known in the streets that Zadan and Odan, gods glorious and ever to be revered, have blessed our city of Eresh."

As the court chamberlain bowed deeply, jangling his keys of office and clanging his bronze shod staff upon the marble, the king and his party took their way within to prepare for the feast.

Among the throng Kidu pulled his hood closer and slipped out, hastening to the witch. Now more than ever the king would wish to appear glorious in the lady's sight.

For Kidu, and not for him alone, the question now was: Which lady?

Chapter Three

Of a double wedding in Proud Eresh

"I do not really understand, Neb-Ke. Not really. I thought you loved me."

"I thought so too, Fretti. I did, truly. But now—"

King Neb-ayin-Ke spread his hands. There were dark circles about his eyes and he wore a haunted look. He stroked his bare chin in a nervous habit, and strode about the tall room within the Alabaster Tower, picking at rugs and tapestries, looking at ivories and fans and jars, fidgeting. He would not look at Fretti, who sat slumped forward on the couch, her white gown trailing about her legs, the flowers in her hair wilting.

"You do love me, Neb-Ke. You do!"

"Yes—yes, that is true. But I love Momi more."

The quick hurt in the girl's face touched Neb-Ke. He could not, after all, not look at her. A quick stride brought him to stand at her side and he touched her shoulder gently. She began to cry.

"What will father say? And those horrid people of Sennapur! They mock us and charge exorbitant tolls for our ships. And you have the King of Endal raving and ready to march upon your fine city—what you are doing is madness, my love, madness."

"I cannot stop myself. And I hate myself because I hurt you."

"Is this Momi then so beautiful? She is with child and not by you."

"I—" Neb-Ke stroked Fretti's shoulder and stared numbly at the tapestry nearest, quite without seeing it. If only Odan En-Ke had not chosen Eresh because they gave some little honor to his shrine! The place was old and decrepit and near to falling down. But many people were flocking there and builders were giving their time and materials free, and the largest herd of bullocks seen in that quarter of the city in years had been driven up for sacrifice. Yes, Odan had quite caught the fancy of the crowd of Zadan's city.

Then an idea struck Neb-Ke and he found he was smiling.

"Listen, Fretti. I see a way. I must wed Momi because I do love her and because she will bear the son of a god. That will be of enormous value to my city. But, Fretti! I will wed you also! I may wed four wives in all honor. This will be—"

"Oh, that is a man's way out! I shall not be your *first* wife! I knew I could always marry you, with three others. But, Neb-Ke, my only love—I want to be the first!"

With a gentleness he had not thought himself capable of, Neb-ayin-Ke talked persuasively. All women could understand that a man could love and cherish four wives. That was a mere part of normal life. But he had to persuade Fretti that Momi must, because of the god-child, be the first.

In the end, hardly convinced, she went away to cry for a long and miserable space before she aroused herself to fresh thoughts for her future. Not quite empty-headed, Fretti, the princess of Dilpur, not quite overcome by flattery and adulation and the fulfillment of every whim. She was accounted a girl of equable temperament, sweet in her way, kind to her slaves, undemanding save in pursuits of great moment. No thought of conspiracy entered her head. She loved Neb-Ke from the moment she had first seen him. She would not go against him. He was just twenty years old, and she but seventeen, and this Momi creature not more than sixteen. Well, they all had their lives before them. Let the gods decide—and then she started weeping again, copious floods of tears as she realized that the gods would surely favor a girl who bore a god-child in her womb.

She had always been a good girl, her father had always said so. Her elder brother had fallen in The River and been eaten by crocodiles, and she had only a younger sister who ate honeyed dates all day long and who was pouting and fat and sweaty, and of no hope. So Fretti must wrack her brains for answers to her problems, and remember that she was a princess, and try to remember, also, the lessons the priestesses of Lufali had taught her.

So it was that in due time the twin marriage ceremonies

were held in the palace. The king had thought it imprudent to hold the one marriage ceremony with Momi in the temple of Zadan; and the temple of Odan, despite all the work newly lavished upon the ancient structure, was far too poor and mean a place for so great a king's marriage. So as one marriage was to be solemnized within the palace, the other, which must follow at once, should be held there also.

The high priest of Zadan, Mnenon-Ket, took this ill.

"It may well be that Zadan holds some affection for Odan, although this has never been vouchsafed us," he grumbled to the grey-haired vicar of the temple as they donned their vestments in the spacious quarters assigned them by Narpul the Staff.

"Yet did Odan say so himself, your reverence."

"He did so say. And I would not dispute with a god unless I were on very firm ground indeed. But Zadan has not visited me lately, not even in a dream."

The vicar looked at the ground. He understood what Mnenon-Ket meant. The chief priest was attempting to infer that he usually conferred with Zadan the All Glorious in person, and that a dream audience was unusual, and obviously when the god must consult Mnenon-Ket upon some unusually urgent matter. That the converse was true made no difference. At least, Zadan had put in a personal appearance when Mnenon-Ket had been ordained high priest. No one could doubt that.

"Had Zadan been opposed to the match he would surely have made his displeasure known." The vicar spoke soothingly.

"Yes. That would appear to be true. Now, in the sweet name of our master help me with this confounded cope. The thing is so stiff with gems it has a life of its own."

In his suite of apartments in the Tower of Relicts Kidu sat in conference with four fellow-sorcerers of the city.

In a corner a golden bowl resting upon a golden tripod sent up a thin spear of dull greenish smoke. The atmosphere was oppressive. The walls of the room had been tastefully furnished with skulls, parchments, hieroglyphs, mummified crocodiles and foetuses, alembics and mystical instruments that the art required. Each wizard wore his finest robes. The glitter of gems rivalled that of the richest kings; but only the wizards knew which stones were genuine and which the result of their occult art.

The servant who handed around tiny ivory bowls of wine had been inherited by Kidu from his predecessor, Unsherbi, who had served to fatten up the unholy crocodiles, and she presented a macabre appearance even to the mages gathered here in conclave.

At one time she must have been a young and beautiful girl, nubile, with long slender legs and a delightful figure. But now instead of a gorgeous face with full red lips and sparkling eyes and a strong straight nose, with the bloom of roses of Artamon in her cheeks, her head was a mere monstrosity. Her long lustrous black hair, that lovely face, had all gone.

Instead, balanced on those shapely shoulders surmounting that delectable body perched a grotesque and blasphemous head, a thing of wrinkled green skin and scarlet eyes, dewlaps and grey coarse strands of hair, with the jagged glint of uneven black teeth catching slobbering brown lips. Unsherbi, frustrated by the girl's unsuspected lusty resistance to his own lust, had in a peevish fit of temper cast a spell and so changed her beauty into this ghastly monstrosity.

As she served the wizards wine her scarlet eyes rested on Kidu with a mute beseeching supplication, for of tongue she possessed neither flesh nor root. Kidu had promised to recant the spell as soon as he could. But all his efforts had proved unavailing. He was still searching through the musty tomes in the wizard's private library, hoping to stumble upon the necessary incantation. Then he could begin the process of reversal.

But it was not to return poor Littly to her proper form that the mages were here gathered.

Kidu took up his ivory cup of wine and looked from one to the other of the four.

"We are agreed, then, brothers? All hostility is to cease between us from the rising of the sun until the rising of the sun on the day following the king's wedding."

One by one, they nodded, each in his fashion, and drained the cups.

Of course, that spiteful and yet often delightful little wicked voice echoed in Kidu's head. Of course, he could have poisoned the wine and so rid himself of all opposition here in proud Eresh. But, no, he would not wish to dispose of old

Master Asshurnax, the too-tender thaumaturge who had taken over Kidu's old premises in Yellow Lotus Street.

All the wizards had met him here well-protected by spells and with their familiars handy to call, yet Kidu suspected that of them all old Master Asshurnax would have made the least preparation for treachery. No, by Kurd! Not suspected—Kidu knew old Asshurnax would come here with the minimum of protection, depending on the affection he felt for Kidu and in no way expecting anything other than affection from the new court wizard.

The case was quite the reverse for Master Chaimbal. As Kidu involuntarily glanced at the gaunt hunched shape of the powerful necromancer, he felt again that perhaps he had not taken quite enough precautions against Chaimbal as he ought to have done, here in an outer reception room of his own suite in the royal palace. Chaimbal was quite capable of breaking the truce for the king's wedding and of spelling Kidu where he sat, turning him, for instance, into a little lizard that might run with wriggling tail to be trodden on by the first bronze-studded sandal to come through the door.

The other two sorcerers, men of immense learning and moderate attainments, quaffed their wine, agreeing to the truce. Chaimbal hesitated, staring with hooded eyes at Kidu, and then, deliberately, lifting the cup. Kidu used a minor grifting to peer down over Chaimbal's shoulder from an invisible point in the air. In his own chambers he felt sure Chaimbal would not be aware of the power used in the grifting. The cup was empty. Chaimbal had drunk. Now he could not break his word, for to do so would imperil his status with his familiars, who would feel they could not trust him hereafter.

The voluptuous body of Littly with that grotesque and obscene head passed before Kidu's grifting-view, and with a sigh he withdrew to his own eyes, and so stared out from his proper place. Poor Littly. And, even with that head, as she passed Chaimbal the necromancer reached out one hand like a claw and stroked her flank. She appeared not to notice. Poor girl! Perhaps she welcomed the attention. Perhaps she felt it reassured her own feelings of womanliness. Kidu, gorge rising, forced himself to take no notice and to proceed.

"It is now necessary for us to ensure good auguries for the king in his double wedding. As the king's wizard—"

At this Chaimbal barked a harsh laugh. Asshurnax looked

up, and shook his head, and went back to stroking the tiny ginger cat in his sleeve. The animal had been immediately tested by all the sorcerers the instant Asshurnax had entered. The ginger cat was just that—a ginger cat.

"The king's wizard!" said Chaimbal. He would have gone on, but Dorhutinax, the wizard who specialised in the moods of The River, cleared his throat and spoke loudly.

"We have drunk to the pact, Chaimbal. We all know you considered yourself to be the natural choice for court wizard. But the king, whose name be praised, thought otherwise." He looked around the table with the habitual and unthinking arrogance of almost all wizards. "Although why he should have chosen Master Kidu when I was available I cannot understand. But it is a thing done and written, and the tablets have been baked."

"The tablets may be broken," growled Chaimbal.

"Assuredly," said Kidu. "But Master Dorhutinax is right. The truce operates now. We must work together to further the prospects of the king."

And as he spoke so Kidu decided that he must be very very careful with respect to Master Chaimbal. The fellow had been pushed very hard by the king's uncle, that bastard Gabal-ayin, may his bones turn to slime, and Gabal-ayin and Chaimbal between them formed an unholy pair and a pair to watch with eyes both physical and occult.

Of the ceremony itself those jam-packed into the overlarge Hall of Offerings situated just within the outer court of the palace could see little. Truth to tell, as Kidu mumbled away crossly to himself, there was little of sense in the whole proceeding. Mumbo-jumbo, that was all it was. Ancient tongues and ancient mysticisms and ancient rites, wands and scepters and crowns, branches of trees, cups of wine, rings, and, a final gross intrusion, the little bronze knives to nick the skin so that blood might be blended.

The king was so covered in stiff robes that he became a mere object, a rigidly strutting popinjay among a host of other popinjays. His clothes weighed him down and made the sweat run and what it would be like next to his skin Kidu, for one, did not wish to know.

Slaves wearing tissue-of-gold for the occasion swung ostrich-feather fans, plunking them up and down and back and forth and so stirring the soupy atmosphere into sluggish motion.

As for the incense—Kidu's nose as a sensitive adjunct to civilized living had never accustomed itself to the coarse putrefactions of incense. He wrinkled up his nose and suffered. During his own incantations where the use of magical smoke was a necessity he used carefully scented sticks so that at least the proprieties might be observed.

The priests went through their dirges and hymns and solemn chantings, and occasionally a huge priest clad all in bright feathers would leap up, over the heads of the others, and emit a huge brilliant bellow.

On this signal the congregation would let out a rapt 'Ahmeen' and so feel they were taking a part in the marriage of their king.

As for Momi—here all the indignation welled up within Kidu. She went through all her part of the grotesque proceedings with a simple grace he found moving. But he could understand a little of her feelings. Thrust from the flaming chariot of a god, pregnant by that god, now she was bowing and kneeling, rising and singing, answering this question and that question, all so that she might marry the king and thus legitimize the god's offspring to the greater power and glory of the king.

He caught a glimpse of her pale face, sheened in sweat, and saw the creases between her eyebrows beneath the heavy circlet of gold, saw the wrinkle of her tiny nose as incense stank into the overheated air.

Surreptitiously, Kidu performed certain slender movements with his hands, moving his lips just enough to part the air and so form the necessary spell.

He watched Momi closely.

She looked fresher at once. The creases over her nose disappeared. Her eyes brightened. She walked with a lighter step to the altar, and she knelt and was sprinkled—the foul ceremony called for bullock's and sheep's blood to spatter her finery in indication that she would inherit the fat of the land—and she rose and moved gracefully in the weight of the cage of golden clothes encumbering her. Well, at least he could perform that small service for his queen.

Finally, after an age, the deed was done.

"No," said Neb-ayin-Ke, firmly, with whitened nostrils.

"No. There must be a space. I will wed Fretti this afternoon."

Few there were there who could blame him. But King Norgash of Dilpur fingered his gold-encrusted sword-hilt, and scowled. Who knew what disaster could strike in the time Zamaz, the sun, took to cross from the east to the west of The River?

The various instruments which had been creating a bedlam of sound throughout the proceedings fell silent. The incense cloud wafted away to foul the down-wind sections of Eresh.

The king withdrew to relieve himself of his vestments and to drink a whole pint of clear water down in a single draught. Momi was escorted to the sumptuous chambers newly furnished for her use. She did not see Fretti, and Fretti did not see her.

In the afternoon when everyone had fortified themselves for the ordeal, the whole ludicrous business was gone through again. King Norgash would make very sure that no single potent point, no important item, would be missed. He had raged, he had sworn, he had flown into a tantrum; but, in the end, he had agreed. The reivers took a heavy toll of his shipping along the great arm of The River running westward from his city. An alliance with Eresh would serve to relieve that burden. His coffers were empty. Trade had dwindled away as the power of Eresh had grown. That was geography and economy and man's natural cupidity against which even the gods might tussle in vain.

When, at last, at long and thankfully last, the king was safely wedded to Fretti as well as Momi, everyone went off to drink themselves stupid.

The whole of Eresh resounded with the uproar. Had the nomads of the deserts chosen that moment to ride in they would have been weary of arm and wrist from killing, weary of back from carrying off plunder. But the auguries had proven fair and the wizards had spied on the nomads and knew they had congregated for a great dhiljazl of their own at the Oasis of Enferontes, miles to the west.

The monstrous dhiljazl going on in Eresh ought to have been more civilised. If anything, having regard to the greater varieties of wine and beer available in the city, the party turned out to be the biggest riot anyone had known in their lifetime—and in the lifetimes of their fathers and mothers, also, if they happened to have known those folk. The old king, Neb-ayin-Ke's father, had not put on anything like this spread.

Kidu wandered the streets for a space, splashed with wine at every corner, dodging thrown fruit rinds, crusts of bread, half-gnawed legs of chicken, partially stripped lamb bones.

The king provided this day and night and it behooved a man to stoke up for the leaner days to come.

He was accosted a number of times with intent by the girls; but he shook them off, forcing a laugh, and so wended his way from gate to gate, just to make sure. The guards officers were as incapable as their men. The vision the wizards had agreed on had been sure. The nomads were miles away. But—but, just in case, Kidu stalked the streets and visited each gate and stared out across the moon-glimmering irrigations to the far undulating line of the desert.

As for the king and his two wives; they made the most of the situation and went to sleep, at last, most satisfied.

When the sun rose again from the eastern desert, striking down upon the dunes of level golden sand, Kidu was safely back in his eyrie in the Tower of Relicts.

He set a triply-strong spell on all the apertures, told Littly to go back to bed, summoned Kjarmer and Nel-abon to stand guard, and stretched out on his pallet. He was asleep in an instant, and he would never remember his dreams.

Chapter Four

Being born, Odan the Half-god creates trouble

In due time Odan the Half-god was born.

He came wriggling and struggling into the world in a caul and with a thick shock of brown hair.

Everyone in the city understood the deep significance that Momi his mother had produced him on Odan's day, which was also Zadan's day. This was a further sign of the god's pleasure.

When the midwives had performed their duties and Momi once more looked superbly beautiful, the king was summoned.

With due regard to the proprieties and with many sacrifices, with guards physical at the doors—a company of the king's spearmen—and guards spiritual in the ante-rooms—Mnenon-Ket and Nabozinadas and priests of all the gods honored in Eresh—and guards thaumaturgical in the eyrie in the Tower of Relicts—Master Kidu and his famulus and Master Asshurnax—the king entered.

He took a single long loving look at Momi, for he had come to love her with a surpassing passion over these last months, and then strode to look down at the face of the god's son.

"So this is Odan the Half-god," he said. And he smiled.

"You have been good to me, Neb-Ke."

"You have seen nothing, my love. I shall be better. You must get well soon. All that can be done for the boy will be done."

"I know. And—and I love you for it."

"And Odan En-Ke?"

"He is a god. You are a man."

"For your sake I would be a god."

"No!" She stretched her arms to him. "Do not say that, my heart. Odan En-Ke stormed me, and I trembled and, and felt all my foolish virginal pride tumbled in glorious confusion—but you, my love, you are a man, and you storm me with different weapons. How can one compare the tempest of the distant hills with the strong flood of The River?"

He sat on the bed and took her hands and bent and kissed her. He was very gentle—for a king.

"You say your mother was from the northern hills? That is where your yellow hair comes from. But the babe's is brown, a glorious glinting brown—what little I can see beneath the swaddling bands."

"My mother was taken as a slave from her own people. She would never tell me what her station had been. But in the village the headman's brother took her to wife right gladly, and the headman's son, Ladu, pestered and pestered to marry me—It was a terrible thing they did to poor Wadu—He was kind—"

"Hush, hush."

Neb-ayin-ke released her hands and smoothed her hair. He kissed her again, on the forehead, and whispered: "Now you must sleep."

As he withdrew and half rose her eyes opened. She stared up at the king with great meaning.

"And you will treat him as your son?"

There was no hesitation in the reply.

"He *is* my son!"

She sank back on the pillows, smiling, content.

Odan the Half-god was thus born all unknowing into a life of enormous wealth and power and prestige. Thousands of slaves there were who scuttled in mortal terror to do the bidding of their overseers, who in their turn ran terrified to obey the commands of their masters, who listened with great respect and considerable trepidation to the orders of their lords, who all, every one, turned for light and life and sustenance to the countenance of the king.

Every whim conceived by Odan was instantly gratified, no matter how small, no matter how large. He was fobbed off with an enormous silver bowl when he asked for the Moon, and was assured solemnly that the orb of light he could see riding the night sky was merely a poor copy manufactured by the slaves and craftsmen down in Silversmith Souk at the orders of his father, the king, may he live for ever, and hurled high by a giant catapult from the encircling walls of proud Eresh.

In the fullness of time, when Odan was running everywhere and tripping servant girls and throwing glass and pottery, upsetting the pet animals, chasing birds, his mother Momi presented him with a sister, the true daughter of Neb-ayin-Ke.

Odan, forceful, passionate, strong-tempered and utterly selfish, viewed this new squawling red mite of humanity with mixed feelings. No longer could he summon Momi instantly, so that she would come running to him. Now one or other of the nurses would soothe him, and attempt to divert him with some tale or other. He was strong-willed. He broke into the lying-in room past an appalled guard who stood, spear shaking, knees knocking, knowing his head would roll for this, burst in and threw himself on his mother, yelling for her to come—at once!—and play.

Then his sister Zenara claimed his attention by burping loudly.

"Don't like her," Odan announced. He tried to push the cot over, to show his displeasure, and Momi's cry, her outstretched hand, drew him back to her. "I love you, Momi. You must come and play."

The sentry, still shaken, had summoned the guard commander. In a mood of sad resignation—to lose his head over a spoiled brat!—the guard captain was informed. The lord of the body guard on duty was playing knucklebones with a pair of strumpets in his chambers high over the main gate. He cursed with a rapid and fluent tongue; but his exit was even more rapid.

So the lord of the bodyguard on duty summoned Narpul the Staff, and the chamberlain found the king poring over the tablets just brought in regarding the figures for oxhides and sheepskins passed through the city over the last quarter. As soon as Neb-ayin-Ke brought his mind back from commerce to domesticity his brow darkened. He picked up a thin rod of suppleness remarkable as he followed Narpul the Staff to the chambers of his premier wife.

The scene that met him struck him as grotesque and also as highly comical in the entourage of a powerful and formidable king.

The nurses and handmaidens and female companions clustered in a horrified group below the open windows. They, of course, were useless. No mere woman could ever be allowed to strike a man, particularly not a young man of two years old who was the Prince of Eresh. Momi, herself, the mother of Odan, knew that she might not strike him without the express permission of her lord, and that would be sparingly given.

Odan had half-pulled Momi from the bed and was making her play knucklebones with him on the carpeted marble floor.

"Odan!" bellowed the king.

Odan looked up, his chubby face excited, his thick brown hair tousled, the glint of victory in his eyes.

"Father! I can beat you, too, if you play like Momi."

Neb-ayin-Ke forced down all fatherly virtues, and thought and acted like a king. The switch of remarkable suppleness rose and fell.

The scene that followed left Momi crying, the female servants bustled shrieking from the chamber, the king panting and most red of face, and Odan standing stock still, his hands to his rear, his mouth so far open he appeared to be swallowing his private property, the Moon. Somewhere or other a new idea percolated into Odan's mind. He could not understand, not completely; but something in the world he knew had changed.

He determined, with the passionate will-power he felt even then within him as a deep and dark force, that he would set himself to discovering what had caused the change.

After that he would decide what to do about what he discovered.

These thoughts were not coherent, not connected, they formed no hard and definite course of future action. Rather they swamped him in a sea of red. They filled him with feeling. They existed. And perhaps he would never rid himself of that scarlet and yet black inchoate groping, that universe-filling and yet minutely perceived sense of desperate incomprehension battling against the darkness.

During this period of his life Odan was aware only of self and Momi, and his father as a giant who strode the sky, glittering.

The numbers of maids and nurses and servants was so great no single one came to mean anything to him. Only Momi counted. He even came to accept Zenara when she could crawl and he found he was allowed to play with her for a turn of the clepsydra during a day. He desperately wished to play with her for longer; but he would be caught up by his father and hauled off under an arm, legs kicking.

"When you learn to treat her as a sister, then you may play with her, young prince," said his father, and that was that.

Something in the world was denied to Odan the Half-god.

During this period also the king of Dilpur visited his daughter in Eresh often. The alliance had proven beneficial to Dilpur, for now the cities west along The River had to accept Dilpurian shipping at the same rates as those for the vessels of Eresh. Each city was ruled by a king and each city-state was free and independent, and each made what it could out of the commerce of The River between the seas. As for the reivers, a single sharp encounter, in which the spearmen and archers of Eresh and Dilpur had stood in line together, and the cities' combined chariotry had thundered onwards in riven dust, had served to tumble the reivers back in shattered confusion. The lines of communication were open and safe—at least for a time.

The main burden of King Norgash of Dilpur was summed up in the few bitter words he spoke to his daughter Fretti as they stood on a narrow terrace-balcony high on the western wall of the palace's Tower of Pearls. Away across the irrigation the sun sank splendidly into the desert sands. The golden and orange light splashed everything with a warm glow. But the words of King Norgash reached Fretti hard and cold, knife-blades cutting through the sunset flame.

"And more than three years have gone by. There is this Odan, the Half-god. And there is a daughter, Zenara. And you, princess of Dilpur, second queen of Eresh. And are you barren? Have you not striven? Where is the grandson I must have?"

"I have striven," said Fretti. She did not say, as she wished to burst out with: 'And I joy in the striving!' for that had nothing to do with the question. "I have prayed. I have sacrificed. Moons I have spent in the temples." She did not cry; but she felt the prickle at the back of her eyes.

"I, too, have made heavy sacrifices to Redul of the Oxen, whose name be praised, the god of our fathers and our city. Many choice oxen have been sent to please him. But even he does not answer my prayers." Norgash did not look at his daughter. He stared across the balcony rail to the far western desert, and his mind was engaged with the needs of kingliness and of commerce, and of the necessity of a strong grandson to ensure that Dilpur should not perish. "I have prayed and Redul does not answer. I fear the sin is with you, Fretti, daughter of your mother. In you lies the barrenness."

Now Fretti did cry. She could not stop herself. What her father said was true. The proof lay with Momi, with whom Fretti found always that she must fight against a genuine and spontaneous liking, for had not this witch woman stolen her lord:

"You have three more moons, Fretti, my daughter. Three moons only. Then I shall take a different hand and bring this business to fruition in a different way."

Fretti had no idea what her father meant.

Whatever it was, it boded little good for her, and none at all for her lord, the king Neb-ayin-Ke.

"By Turbash! Master Kidu—my guts ache."

The king groaned and leaned forward, fist pressed into his stomach, his face turning green. Spittle dripped from his lips. The small and private chamber in the deepest recesses of the palace held the close secret stink of conspiracy. The white-washed walls writhed with colored paintings of birds and animals, of scenes of hunting and of sacrifice, with the smoke rising from the altars so real one could almost smell the stink. Many hieroglyphs and cartouches of the names of gods from the earlier writing of the land of Ea adorned the walls. Here came the king when he wished to pray in secrecy, away from the prying gaze of the priests, away from the glaring light of public attention that rested upon his lightest doings.

"You are sure, Kidu?" he managed to gasp out. "You have sealed me well?"

"This is no evil spell, king, no secret grifting." Kidu had gained in stature since those first uneasy days as court wizard. Neb-ayin-Ke had chosen well. Now he spoke with a brisk firmness he judged best suited to the situation. "I have tripled all the sealings, although that was not necessary. No wizard can strike at you or your wives or your son or daughter. This is so." Kidu kept the wrinkle-line out of his lips. What he had to tell the king now was a grave matter in so exalted a personage. "My king, you have a real gut-ache."

"Then Mnenon-Ket was wrong. He claimed a wizard whose name is of no importance from Endal sought to lay me low."

"They have tried, those devils in Endal. They fail. But, my king, it is of great importance that the name be known. Names carry vast powers, mysterious sorceries—I must question the high priest on his knowledge—aye, and how he came by it."

"My guts!" Neb-ayin-Ke groaned again and Kidu reached for the golden bowl filled with warmed wine. Later he handed the king the fine linen towels. "Cannot all your arts dispel this agony, Master Kidu?"

"If the doctors have failed you, then I will do what I can. But in an organic matter the arts are often drastic. With all due respect, my king, my master, the Sage Kidu, whose name be reverenced and who named me in his stead, taught me well. If the doctors fail you then I will do my part."

Neb-ayin-Ke had had enough experience of mages to know he would get nothing further from his court wizard. Anyway, he'd eaten so vastly last night and Fretti had been so demanding that it was a miracle he had nothing else besides a gut-ache. He rose, groaning, and Kidu stepped respectfully back. Between king and wizard, now, a sincere relationship had built up that could do away with the exaggerated forms of genuflection and near idolatry requisite in public.

"You guard me well, Kidu, and in that I am grateful—as you know. Tell me, your servant, Littly?"

Kidu shook his head. "Nothing works, my king."

"A tragedy. A body like that—and a head."

"Master Bitori of the ivory-workers, and his friends of other guilds—the potters, the silversmiths, the weavers,—are fashioning for me a mask. It will be a mask of a beautiful girl. When it is finished I will animate it with a grifting known to few. I think Littly will have a better life thereafter until I can release her from her spell."

"Have you kissed her?"

"Once."

"Well, you cannot trust the old stories all the time."

In the topmost chamber of the squat ebon tower set in its own gardens, unkempt, rank gardens of luxuriant loathsome growths, the tower known with a shudder as the Abode of the

Bats, Master Chaimbal drew back trembling and with the sweat running down his gaunt features.

"You have failed again?"

The king's uncle, Gabal-ayin, spoke with a vicious roughness that thickened his words. The blood rushed to his face. His eyes glared madly upon the crouched form of the necromancer, and his fists gripped down hard upon the hilt of his bronze sword.

Chaimbal took a whooping draught of the cleaner air outside the pentacle.

"I did not raise the spirit of Ghor-No-Ter, my lord. It has been previously charmed and resists the summoning—"

"Charmed by that bastard Kidu, I'll swear!"

"Yes. Nothing we have done so far has penetrated his defenses. The king and his family are guarded well."

The stink of incense wafted about the two men in that ebon tower, incense and another, subtler, muskier smell redolent of nameless things. Gabal had no fear of the awful mysteries of necromancy when with Chaimbal, for Chaimbal knew his lifting of the veil would threaten the lifter. And, anyway, any treachery would be punished by the instant stroke of a blade. Chaimbal knew his life hung by as slender a thread as that which drew forth the spirits of the dead.

Chaimbal drew back and seated himself on his black carven chair. His claw-like hand lifted the silver goblet of warmed wine that had all run cold. He said: "Your own grifting still holds, my lord. I can sense the thrill of it, clearly, here in my own tower."

"The spell of defense was sold to me by Unsherbi, before the fool had himself fed to the crocodiles. It will hold."

"Yet will a bronzen knife blade pierce through—" said Chaimbal, adding: "My lord."

Gabal glared at the wizard with a ferocity that had caused many a brave warrior heart to quail.

"That is true. But I have yet to meet the man to wield that blade."

Gabal was the younger son of the old king and, as primogeniture operated in Eresh, his elder brother took the throne. On his death his son, Neb-ayin-Ke, had become king. But Gabal had never relinquished his hopes. He had failed to destroy his brother and so far he had failed to dispose of his nephew. But he kept always casting about for fresh tools. Kidu, the fool, had fatally refused to co-operate, and Gabal had left the wizard's quarters, where he then was, in Yellow Lotus Street, with a nasty scarlet rash and a powerful itch between his legs he could not positively blame the mage for grifting upon him.

Now he had a son of his own, young Galad-ayin. The boy was a very devil, a few years younger than the king, and Gabal had sent him to the shores of The Salt Sea to gain experience and keep him out of the way. The boy's mother—ah! Vashti had been a devastating experience in any man's life. She was the older sister of Neb-ayin-Ke's mother. Although there was no proof of the deed, reputable rumor had it that when she had seen her younger sister wed the king she had incontinently poisoned her own husband and then set to and married the king's younger brother, Gabal. Whatever the truth of it, she was dead now, and the king's father and mother were dead, and so this generation played one against another for the fortunes of their children.

These twists of fate drove Gabal-ayin on. He would not rest until he ascended the Crocodile Throne and lorded it as king over Eresh. Even those devils of Endal could be used as tools until he had gained his ambition. Then he would turn on them and rend them. It seemed to him that the king paid no heed at all to what had happened to Tubal. This alliance with Dilpur was a weak thing at best. At worst it alienated the strong cities along The River to the west. And that was where the shipping must go to carry trade from The Sweet Sea in the east to The Salt Sea in the west. As for the Mak Sea in the far north east, that was seldom included in the calculations of the Land Between the Two Seas.

"So it is to be a bronzen blade, then."

At Gabal's harsh words, Chaimbal looked up quickly, then away, and sipped his wine, although it was cold. The look on the lord's face reminded the necromancer of that spirit he had conjured last week, when it writhed under his enchantments.

"If I can be of assistance, my lord . . ."

Chaimbal was too shrewd and too frightened to suggest the lord had finished with his help.

"Prepare me a grifting that will bring instant sleep, one that I may carry and fling upon those I wish to deceive. I will send for it tomorrow night."

"As my lord commands."

Shadows writhed upon the ebon walls and the spider's webs

shook. Urt, the seeming-spider, looked out, and grumbled that this puissant lord had not taken himself off so that Chaimbal might bring in his dish of fat flies.

Gabal-ayin threw gold upon the cluttered table, and a coin rolled into the gap-jaws of a naked skull. "Tomorrow night, then." He spoke thickly, his jaw muscles ridged. "And on the night after that. . . ."

As he went out with a swirl of black cloak even Urt, the seeming-spider, shuddered so that his webs shook.

Chapter Five

Odan enters upon his inheritance

"No, no, Odan! Not like that! You five-thumbed bungling idiot!" Bluff Seljak bellowed with a face so scarlet and bursting his eyes bulged like chariot knobs. Then he remembered. "My lord! Your highness! Your most puissant prince!"

Odan stumbled back in the dust of the practice ring, slipping in the heat and sweat of action, the sting of Seljak's wooden sword across his chest.

"I'll have you strung up and your tongue burned out, Seljak, the Mighty Warrior!"

"If you fight like that you'll never live to see the day—my most puissant prince, my lord!"

Momi clapped her hands together. She did not know if she should laugh or cry out in alarm. Odan was so forceful. And although she knew well enough her beloved Neb-Ke would never order the Mighty Warrior, Bluff Seljak, punished, the ways of men with edged weapons were passing strange.

Bluff Seljak, now, used to swear and blaspheme and insult the king most horribly as they sweated and bashed each other with their wooden swords. And Odan must learn likewise. In any other place but the practice ring then Seljak was a submissive and obedient servant to the king and his family. But—Odan the Half-God was a little boy only four years old. He spoke very well and he was bright and intelligent. But—he was only four.

"He is too young, my love, thus to bash about with a great wooden sword!"

"Nonsense, my Momi! He must learn to defend himself. If he does not any whipper-snapper from the desert may ride in when he is king and wrest the kingdom and all Eresh from him."

"But he is only four!"

"When I was three I could have beaten him, two out of three."

"My lord!"

Neb-ayin-Ke gazed with fond delight upon Odan. The boy was the son of a god; but as far as Neb-Ke was concerned, Odan was his. He loved the boy's mother and he was certain sure she loved him. Odan En-Ke, the old god, had put in no further appearance since he had delivered Momi to Eresh. He had not even showed up at the birth or at the naming. So Neb-ayin-Ke, father to Zenara, regarded Odan as his rightful heir.

To prove that, the great ceremony of ritual inheritance would soon be performed. Perhaps Odan En-Ke might turn up then.

On the day appointed Odan would have to his name of Odan-ayin, the regal, lineal and jealously guarded name of Ke added. Ke—the Great Old One, the Great God, the creator of all things, whose sons fathered the race of men through their sons, yes, Eresh basked in the sure protection of Zadan the Sword, and of Ke, the Great Old One. And the name of Ke was ritually added to all those who would be king.

Once that had been done, Odan would be king in his time.

If that was not done—well, and here Neb-ayin-Ke curled his lips a little—well, he fancied the boy would have a word or three to say on the matter later on.

"Take that, Bluff Seljak—and I hope it hurts!" Here Odan drove in with his wooden sword held stiffly before him, his small frantic figure demoniac with rage and fury. Seljak shifted his wooden wand a fraction, Odan's wooden blade skittered past and as he went so Seljak pivoted and slapped the wand across Odan's rump.

"Hai! And you are very dead, Odan, the great prince."

"I'll—I'll mutismistacateyou, Seljak!"

Momi laughed. "Whatever that is, my love, it sounds horrendous!"

"He will make a fine prince." Neb-ayin-Ke stroked his chin.

"Aye, my heart, and a fine king—but not for years and years, when you and I are both with Ke and Zadan and—"

She stopped.

Neb-Ke affected not to notice and walked over to Odan, picking him up, knocking the dust off with his regal hands.

"You must learn to fight, my son, or you will, as Bluff Seljak, the Mighty Warrior, so truthfully says, be dead."

"I'll get him the nextish time!"

"I'm sure you will. And Seljak will teach you more. Now you must go with Momi. Your lessons await."

Nothing that Odan could say or do could deflect the king from the dedication with which he forced Odan to learn to read and write and number. He learned with the priests. As for the attributes of the gods, during these periods Odan would draw wonderful squiggles on his clay tablet, and run the wooden spatula over them and squiggle some more with the cut reed.

They'd let him try a reed pen on papyrus; but the result had been simply to return him to his clay tablet.

There were more and more things in this bewildering life Odan was finding a prince and the son of a god might not do.

The day wended itself on as any other normal day. There were no great ceremonies, no processions, the ziggurat of Zadan remained comparatively quiet save for the bleatings of the sacrifices, abruptly terminated, and the smoke which rose wafted away on the light breeze.

Eresh appeared to slumber in the sunshine. No great caravans came in from The Sweet Sea and only four medium-sized sailing barges ploughed their way upriver into the docks where they would be unloaded and await the next out-going caravan to far Shanadul on the coast of The Sweet Sea. There were two smaller sailing vessels which went upstream to the north and west, but they carried slaves captured from the desert tribes to the south and aroused no comment.

After his evening meal and the observances to Zadan, and, because of his name and ancestry, to Odan also, Odan was packed off to bed. He slept in an airy chamber with wide latticed windows. Two slave handmaids slept on pallets in the room, and a guard detail remained at all times outside the folding doors of ebony and ivory. Odan sprawled, mouth open, and slept.

Much later, walking back from their last meal of the day, the king and his uncle traversed the tessellated pavements and passed under the brick arcades towards their own apartments. The king appeared tired. He complained of a gut ache.

"I shall seek out Fretti this night," said Neb-ayin-Ke, rubbing his stomach.

"The king is a fortunate husband," said Gabal-ayin. He had ascertained a fact he had to know. Fretti. So he could dispose of the witch Momi and her brats after he had destroyed his nephew. It would all work out well . . .

They parted at the first landing encircling the Hall of Retreat and, lighted by slaves carrying torches, took themselves their different ways. Fretti expected her lord, and had decked herself in her bravest finery, sensuous gold-tissue vestments, tiny tinkling bells, kohl and rouge and scents to please a man and inflame his senses. Her father grew no more impatient than she herself for the quickening of her womb.

When the king had been disrobed and could stand in a long god-given caterpillar-thread gown before her, shimmering and running miracles of torchlight within its fabric, he smiled and held out his hands.

"Come to me, my Fretti, and tell me what you have been doing this day—"

The king's face screwed up. He let out a surprised exclamation. His hands flew to his stomach, and pressed, agonizingly.

"By Turbash! I burn! I am assailed by all the devils of hell!"

"My lord! My love!" Fretti ran to him in consternation, screaming for her servants.

"No, no, Fretti, my love. Help me walk. Help me to go to Momi. She has a certain balm—it may help—help me, my love."

No incongruity in the situation touched Fretti. Her lord was in pain and it was well-known the witch woman, Momi, had a balm. Nothing was more natural than that she should help the king even if that meant going to the woman who had been her rival. Momi and Fretti had reached a tacit understanding in these latter days.

Through the dusky corridors the two walked as fast as the king could stagger, and a few slaves ran with lights and others helped support the king. Fretti did not let him go, and so the little procession burst into Momi's room. She sat up with a quick intuitive understanding and before the king collapsed on her bed she had opened the pearl and ivory cabinet and was busily mixing the potion.

"Send for the doctors," she commanded the slaves. "And fetch Narpul the Staff. Hurry!"

The bustle claimed everyone's attention.

The guards from both Fretti's and the king's chambers stood by the doors, talking in low tones to Momi's guards.

Kidu the court wizard arrived before the doctors. He took the king's wrist in his hand and looked down. His long face still wore his habitual mournful look; but he had fleshed out a trifle since his first days in the palace. Littly took a deal of the blame for that, for she insisted he eat well, anxious for him to keep healthy and find the spell binding her.

"The doctors—" gasped the king. "Useless. They jabber and use words culled from the Worm-men. Grift me, Kidu! As your king, I command you."

"As you command, my king. But the pain will be intense at first. Send these chattering people away. Momi the queen and Fretti the queen should stay, for they are good influences."

So it was that as Gabal-ayin, the king's uncle who would be king at all cost, stalked towards the chambers of Fretti, the queen, he found them empty and a frightened babble of people screaming that the king was dead.

Gabal halted his body of ruffians, his own men, men who might be trusted if he continued to pay them enough gold. He grabbed a half-naked water-wench and shook her.

"What of the king?"

"Lord! Lord—they say he is dead. Seized by a demon in his guts—lord—"

Gabal tossed her aside. If the king was truly dead then his work was half-done. Now he must send Odan on the same trail.

With a curt command to his men he led on. He went by circumspect routes. The king might be dead; but the king's uncle must never be seen going to the next king's apartments when that king-to-be would be found dead. He must execute his plan. The prince must not be found. With his disappearance a far greater stir would be caused, the act would be put down to the displeasure of Zadan, than if he was merely found with his throat slit.

Gabal's men advanced boldly along the last corridor where the torches smoked just a little, indication that the trimmers had not been along recently. The guards at Odan's door stiffened.

"Halt! Declare yourself in the name of the king!"

Before the guard ceased speaking a spear transfixed him through the throat. It had been a fine cast. Two more spears flew; but the guards snapped their long oval shields up. Their spears lifted and flew. A man in front of Gabal choked, and doubled forward. The thick bronze spear-head stood out from the back of his neck.

"Get them! Get them you idiots!"

For an instant the corridor rang with the clash of bronze blades. After that first flurried exchange of javelins when the spears flew like the whirring birds of the delta far to the south, the guards and Gabal's rowdies took to their spears and swords.

Gabal-ayin hung back. This was no work for him. He clenched his left hand on the vial brought from Chaimbal.

Once he cast that and the grifting took hold, he would spell all whom it touched to sleep. But once thrown it was gone. He had use for that elsewhere, not here, where his bully boys should finish the job with the speed of Loti's arrow.

Odan's guard fought well. But they were overmatched for numbers. Their shouts failed to bring any response, for all the palace was alive with lights and the sound of running feet and every effort bent towards the apartments of Momi where the king lay grievously ill.

The last guard died with a gurgle as a blade slid past his cuirass and withdrew, sticky with blood. His body fell and Gabal thrust past and smashed the door open.

The sight that greeted his eyes was completely unexpected.

Holding the wildly struggling form of Odan who wielded a dagger with murderous intent, the portly and dignified form of the high priest of Zadan, Mnenon-Ket, confronted the king's uncle.

"I know why you are here, Gabal-ayin!" boomed Mnenon-Ket in his fruity voice. "Beware lest the doom of Zadan strike you where you stand!"

"Out of the way, priest!"

"I am the high servant of Zadan of the Sword." Here Mnenon-Ket had to take a fresh grip on Odan. The boy writhed and struggled to break free and hurl himself and his dagger upon these crude intruders.

The two slave handmaids were efficiently caught by Gabal's men, not without much bawdy talk and heavy handling, and tied up in strips torn from the drapes. Still Mnenon-Ket grasped the young prince and confronted the tempestuous form of Gabal.

"Zadan!" intoned the high priest. "Zadan the All Glorious! I beseech thee to send down thy wrath upon this desecrator—"

Gabal uncorked the crystal vial and threw the invisible contents.

One of his men who had been rummaging about with his spear under the bed stiffened, twisted about like a scarecrow at the onset of a storm, and fell rigid across the bed.

Mnenon-Ket sneered with his heavy purple face, his eyes vicious and gloating upon Gabal.

"Your puny griftings cannot harm a high priest of Zadan! And the boy is half a god! You are undone, Gabal-ayin, a traitor to your king and city. Lay down your arms and resign yourself to the mercy of the king, may he live forever."

"The king is dead," snarled Gabal, and whipped out his sword and charged.

Mnenon-Ket skipped aside, quick for so heavy a man. Gabal ran on, halted, and turned, breathing with a white fury.

"Dead?" said Mnenon-Ket. "If this is true still I cannot allow you to slay the prince—stand back, stand back!" And he lifted his voice again. "Zadan! Zadan the Sword!" And this time there was more desperation, more pleading in his voice.

In that twinkling of an instant Odan broke free.

Unhesitatingly he ran at his uncle. He had never liked the man, gross and smelly, and always patting his head with a heavy hand and a sickly smile on his face. Even at four years old Odan sensed the chicanery in the man, the falseness.

The king was his father. If he was dead then this smelly uncle had killed him, as Odan had seen him kill a stubborn horse when the poor beast baulked at backing into the chariot ring.

The bronze dagger lifted high in Odan's fist as he ran.

He shouted in his shrill small boy's voice.

"I'll kill you, uncle!"

Forgotten were the lessons so painstakingly hammered home by the Mighty Warrior, Bluff Seljak. No finesse here, no thrusting point, just a wild angry swing of the blade.

Gabal swung, kicked out neatly, sent the dagger flying.

Odan staggered on, towards the window.

He swung back, his little face inflamed, near to bellowing

those words he had heard the stable-boys use and did not understand and remembered being told with great sorrow by Momi that little princes did not use.

Passions flared with ugly viciousness in the bed chamber.

"Strike down the priest, dogs!" bellowed Gabal.

His men hung back. To slay a priest of Zadan! Surely then the light of Zadan the All-Glorious would be withdrawn from them, and then they would be finished in Eresh. No, no they would not interfere.

"You fools!" shouted Gabal. The sword in his fist snouted up as Mnenon-Ket, determinedly, advanced. The priest had drawn a sword from beneath his robes, a glittering blade that shone with an icy fire in the torch glow. Gabal recognized the metal, saw the sword for what it was, saw the metal run with blue-white shimmers.

"You will surely die for your impiety, Gabal-ayin!"

"I do not serve Zadan, the god of donkeys! I serve Nirghal, the god of fire! I do not fear you, Mnenon-Ket, nor your sword!"

"Die, blasphemer!"

Shrieking with the passion of outrage, Mnenon-Ket leaped for Gabal. The priest's bulky body moved with a swiftness that completely deceived the king's uncle. The blades clashed. Hacking with a monstrous fury, Gabal saw his blade crash against the grey sword in Mnenon-Ket's grasp, saw the edge buckle and curve back in a v-shaped notch. Not a sign of a dent appeared in the blue-white sword. Mnenon-Ket roared and drove on, and Gabal was forced back toward the window.

Odan skipped in from the side and grabbed Gabal's ankle. He hung on as the men battled across the chamber, hampering Gabal. The priest was no match as a swordsman for the lord.

A slash appeared on Gabal's robe over his shoulder. But through the rent the dull gleam of bronze showed.

Gabal cursed. The priest besides his sword of grey metal wore a cuirass or a jack of bronze.

With a sudden vicious leap back, Gabal cleared the reach of the impervious sword. He swung his own blade down towards Odan still hanging on and biting his calf. The boy saw the blow coming and tried to dodge. The flat of the blade laid alongside his head.

Over backwards went Odan the Half-god. Tumbled into a

sprawling heap went the prince of Eresh. He did not even cry out. He lay there, crumpled, unmoving.

"Now you are a man doomed!" screeched Mnenon-Ket. "The king placed his trust in me! I am Mnenon-Ket, high priest of Zadan the Sword! Die, traitor!"

Roaring with fury the priest launched himself at Gabal, the sword of Zadan whirling about his head.

Gabal fenced him off desperately, all his arts of swordplay brought into brilliant fruition. He saved his own life. He staggered back under the very violence of that onslaught.

His foot caught against the sill.

Still Mnenon-Ket drove on, the sword high.

Even as Gabal stumbled back and Mnenon-Ket hurled his gross body on for the final blow, so Gabal, the master swordsman, thrust deep and upwards, finding the exposed lower edge of the corselet.

Mnenon-Ket staggered back, a look of the utmost surprise on his bloated face.

He put his left hand to his belly. The fingers came away red and sticky with his life's blood.

And, with a despairing shriek, Gabal toppled out of the window. Arms wideflung he fell to the ground. He struck with a flat and solid shock, on his back. He lay there and all the stars of all the constellations pulsed through his head and danced before his eyes.

In the bedchamber Mnenon-Ket sank to his knees. The great grey-white sword of Zadan slipped from his nerveless fingers. Gabal's thrust had gone deep. Mnenon-Ket knew he had only moments to live.

He lifted his head and peered through the gathering mists at the pack of Gabal's men, clustered, uneasy, fingering their weapons, unsure what to do.

"You had best," said Mnenon-Ket. "Not—kill the boy. He is the prince. It—would go hard with you."

He gasped. He knew he was dying.

One of the bully boys, a fellow with a huge black-haired brown wart on the back of his left hand, took half a step forward.

"Do not slay the boy." Mnenon-Ket saw the darkness creeping in upon him as the ink spread from a spilled inkpot. How often he had been in scrapes when he had been a boy, and learning all that a priest needed to know! The broken tablets, the spilled inkpots, the canings—but he had learned.

He had worked. He was the high priest of Zadan the All Glorious. "I am Mnenon-Ket! I am the high priest of Zadan of the Sword—"

The last words he said were: "I have kept faith with the king and with my lord Zadan."

The roughs looked down on the body.

Not one ventured to touch the grey sword of Zadan, although it would be valued at a hundred or more bronze swords.

A thousand bronze swords, in some cities, that blue-grey sword of Zadan would fetch.

"What do we do?" asked a fellow with an unbound shock of black hair where his headband had been sliced through by a wild blow from a guard.

"Kill the bastard!" said the man with the wart.

"No—we must see to the lord. He may not be dead."

"Fetch the boy. Bundle him in the carpet and bring him. And for the sake of Taxadrun, go quietly and with speed!"

Outside they clustered around Gabal.

He looked up. His face had changed. The mouth had thinned to a slit, the eyes had sunk and looked feverish.

"Take me up, you dogs," said the king's uncle. "Take me home. My backbone is broken through."

From the far side of the palace the noise consequent on the king's illness and necessary hurly-burly went on. Lights flickered. His men took up Gabal and laid him upon a gate roughly torn down and bore him off. He saw the carpet.

"We thought—" began the man with the wart.

"I think. You do." To speak was an effort. Gabal gasped and his lips thinned until only a blue slit showed. "Slay him and have done."

"But—"

The man with the broken headband caught up his black hair in a twist of a leaf torn from a bush. He nodded to the four carrying Gabal.

"Take the lord to his apartments. Treat him gently. If he asks, say the boy is dead."

The man with the wart nodded, eagerly.

"And there will be a gold piece in it for us."

Gabal was carried off, fainting, hardly knowing where he was or what was taking place. He was crippled for sure. That at the least he did know and understand.

Wrapped in his carpet Odan was taken down to the waterfront. Here the men quickly made arrangements with the master of a vessel travelling northwards. Odan was inspected. He was still alive.

"Reasonable merchandise," said the slavemaster. "But if you think he will fetch a gold piece you are vastly mistaken."

They bargained over the still form of Odan. At length he was sold for seventy pieces of silver. They sold the carpet for seventy five. Long before full day the slave vessel shoved off from the wharf at Eresh and began her journey upriver.

So Odan the Half-god entered upon his inheritance.

Chapter Six

A dagger-tooth lion hunts in the hills of Zumer

Odan crouched in the withy hide and felt as miserable as he'd ever remembered. No thought of failure in the ritual tests entered his head; he would sit crouched all night as was ordered by the tribal elders and shamans and then he would use his flint-headed spear to kill his food for the day. He must slay a tusker, and a tusker only. The various birds, the antelopes, the mountain goats, all must be left alone. The ritual tests demanded that on this day he kill a tusker for food. To the south the mountains lifted in tier upon tier, until their peaks caught on their snowy summits the first glint of dawn sparkling through the cool clear air.

Odan rose. He rose lithely and easily even after the night in the withy hide. He was accounted a big younker among the boys of the tribe. He had been with the Hekeu for ten winters. He was big enough to undergo the rituals that would transform him miraculously from a boy into a warrior.

The Hekeu were renowned among the Zumen of the mountains and high plateaus for the savagery and inhuman ferocity of their initiation rituals. Never in any warrior's memory lay the thought of a year in which all the young aspirants had succeeded. Every time some died. The harshness of the tests based on the years of training from the time a boy could first walk were designed deliberately. No weaklings could live among the high mountains or the northern plateaus.

Game was often plentiful—but often it was not. During those periods of scarcity only the best men would survive. And with their survival they would ensure the survival of their women and children, the continuance of the tribe of

Hekeu, the dagger-toothed lion totem, proud and defiant, truculent among the mountains.

So as Odan trod noiselessly downslope his nostrils flared as he tested the scents borne on the breeze. The other boys laughed at the dullness of his sense of smell. Somehow they were closer to nature than he was. He had been captured in a raid. They had told him that. He had been, as they judged a man's size, six winters, although in all truth Odan had been but four years old when he'd been passed from hand to hand up The River, to be snatched by the yellow-haired barbarians of the southern slopes of the mountains. When the Hekeu had taken him from the barbarians for whom they held the contempt of free mountain men for dogs who lived in wooden cages, he had been accepted into the tribe as a fine gift from Ke himself, a half-grown boy to swell their depleted ranks.

A full half a wild bird had been sacrificed to Ke, in the name of Hekeu the dagger-toothed lion, to give thanks.

Much effort and toil and sheer agony had passed over Odan and changed him from the spoilt princeling brat into a primitive warrior and hunting man, at home among the hills and plateaus, harder than bronze, faster than a lion, harsher than a crocodile, more cunning than a snake.

But, even as he systematically went about running down a tusker and thrusting the flint-headed spear through just beneath the ribs, the misery would not leave Odan.

At fourteen he was large for his years, competing against boys of sixteen and seventeen who were his size or smaller.

They had a way with them. They knew that once they had been initiated into the fighting men of the tribe they might take their girls to wife. Each boy and each girl came to half-spoken, dim, tacit understandings. Odan had essayed and had lost an understanding with Ishti. Ishti was quick-silver, a brown-eyed sprite, laughing, mocking, teasing. Ishti was life and laughter and love. Ishti was the daughter of the chief and Ishti was not for Odan, accepted by the Hekeu but still a stranger.

The way in which Odan thrust the spear into the tusker revealed the depths of his passions.

Blood spouted, warm and alive in the early morning. The air carried still the chill of the high mountains. Odan twisted and dragged the tusker down, and so drew his flint knife and, kneeling on the squealing grunting animal, deftly slit its throat.

Now he had food for many days. The Hekeu could live on provender that would not last a barbarian or a man of the cities half a day.

Slinging his food supply over his shoulder and taking up his spear, Odan set off for the ordeal. His body did not bulge with muscle, rather the sense of immense sinewy power sliding and roping beneath his skin conveyed an impression of enormous strength in muscles tuned to carry him tirelessly for mile after mile, to sustain him through days and nights without sleep, and then to enable him to fling himself upon an aurochs and break the massive neck with a single savage burst of strength. The proud, savage black aurochs roamed the hills and the primitive men of the mountains, the Zumen, did not seek to tame the great beast to domesticity. For, then, where would the joy and mysticism of the hunt lie?

Wild and savage and primordial in his strength and fleetness Odan returned to the camp and flung down the tusker. The painted shamans regarded him gravely, their eyes burning behind their grotesque masks. They did not speak. Commands were given by waving a wand in secret signals long-learned and vital to success in the silent stalk and the sudden kill.

The Zumen made no permanent homes. They wandered from hunting ground to hunting ground. When tribes met they fought.

Four boys lay staked out, wrists and ankles thonged to heavy stakes driven deeply into the ground. They would stay like that all night and day. On the next night they would be released and run twenty miles to a hide, where they would sit up all night, awake, and on the morrow make their kill, and then return.

Odan had completed that.

The next sections of the initiation rituals proved more difficult.

Yet only a few of the tests bore no relation to the life the wild men must lead among the mountains and plateaus. Only a very few tests had become ossified by long usage and mere appendages to survival. The ritual paintings of the body, the achievement of a skin breechclout, the daubing of a spear to impart magical powers. These were possibly superfluous.

Paint held at bay the monstrous legions of the night, and

struck terror into the hearts of the foe. But Hekeu the dagger-tooth lion extended his mighty protection over all the members of his totem tribe, and his aweful countenance and dread presence cowed all who opposed him.

A skin breechclout was a mere gawdy tinsel. Any Zumen could run and fight and exist stark naked as he had been born, warm on the coldest night, using the secret processes of his own body to sustain him, at one with nature rather than struggling against nature.

A spear would kill through the skill of the hand that wielded it, although, to be sure, a little magical help was not lightly to be disregarded. But, for the savage primitives of the high mountains, a spear was a luxury, an adjunct, a powerful extra help in killing. The hands, the feet, the teeth—these were the weapons of the Zumen.

As Hekeu the dagger-tooth lion imparted his own strength and help to his tribe, so he had given them the bow and arrow. For these weapons the Zumen were grateful, for they could discharge a straight arrow and kill at a distance far longer than they could throw a spear or a knife or a stone. In the arrow, symbol of the straight death, Odan sought his greatest help—although he was already accounted the finest among all the tribe, even among the grown warriors, at hurling the heavy hunting spear.

When Odan hurled a spear, he hit what he aimed at, and the spear's keenness and weight would kill what he hit.

So the shamans gave him only a small, light spear, and told him what he must do next by magical signs from their painted wands.

The initiation tests would continue for a whole Moon. Then the ceremonies would take place. Then, once the boy was a man, he would be introduced to the other side of manhood, and learn the reasons for the existence of girls. Despite the well-understood but never-spoken understandings between boy and girl, fostered by parents, the two sexes rarely played together and were rigidly segregated. That girls were skinnier than boys, lacking appendages and with odd lumps upon their chests, was obvious to Odan. But, he knew, there was much more to be learned about them.

All the torture through which he went did not apply to survival. Some of it related to the mysteries of women.

So the misery engulfing him when he thought of Ishti and his own negation came from many areas of self-consciousness and feelings of insufficiency and from a suffocating sense that he would miss something that, if he only knew what it was, he would move the very mountains themselves to obtain.

Odan stooped as he loped tirelessly on the spoor of the wolves.

His height made him stoop so as to put his brown shock of hair on a level with the darker polls of his companions.

Each boy must stalk and slay a wolf, skin it, and return safely. If a boy did not return, then the matter was decided. The shamans would scrutinize the pelts brought in by those who did return, and they would muse and decide. No boy doubted that the shamans were able to watch them at all times. If the pelt was found not acceptable the boy had another chance; but then he must go up against the wolf pack alone.

Odan understood nothing of politics. Life was survival. Self-reliance was the highest aim, encouraged and demanded by the elders and the shamans. He could not see why his wolf pelt, when he brought it in, was inferior to any of the others. But the shamans moved their magical painted wands, and so Odan took to the hills again, seeking the wolves, alone.

From the downwind position hugging the grey lichened rocks Odan watched the wolfpack. They behaved as one would expect, their sentinels out on their haunches, watching, the pack peacefully resting.

He screwed his head around and surveyed his back trail and the ridges beyond. If anything was downwind of him he wanted to know before he committed himself. Once he had almost been taken by a yeti and only his spear-throwing arm had saved him. Nothing stirred. Odan waited. Patience equated with survival.

The wolves were moving. Their lean grey bodies stretched as they rose. The lick of their tongues was very red against the white of fang.

Odan's spear lifted soundlessly, as though the magical paint caressed it with power. He poised and threw. The action was begun and completed in a smooth eruption of muscled strength.

The nearest sentinel span once, trying to snap at the shaft, and then rolled over. The cast had not been perfect. He must have merely nicked the heart instead of bursting clean through. But the wolf was dead and the others were sniffling and snarling and looking about, and some were breaking away in a trail upwind. Warily, watching, Odan saw them go. He would wait until they were gone before he moved. If they saw him they might well decide to charge. He had no fear of a single wolf, even of two. But a whole pack equated with non-survival.

At last, a painted primordial savage, Odan rose from his place of concealment.

He felt no exultation, so sense of being master of the terrain, as he started down towards the wolf carcass. Every sense alert he stooped over the dead beast and drew his flint knife.

That extra sense ingrained into him by the Zumen of the mountains, that primitive beastlike awareness, saved him.

Without looking, without hesitation, he hurled himself sideways and rolled twenty feet among the grass and boulders.

The dagger-tooth lion's spring landed where Odan had crouched above the dead wolf.

Snarling, spitting, the enormous beast sprang ten feet towards him, and stopped. Its tufted tail stood straight. Its cavernous mouth gaped, and the twin daggers of bone glinted in the sun. A few ragged clouds passed, a scatter of birds crossed like driven leaves, and the dagger-tooth lion regarded him from yellow eyes.

Totem animal or no totem animal, this Hekeu would slay and eat him if he gave the fellow the chance.

Odan spoke.

"Now, Hekeu! I am one of your tribe! You are our great totem, to you we offer sacrifice, to you we give our allegiance among the hills."

The lion moved his head from side to side, slowly.

"We have no dealings with the aurochs totem, or the eagle. And we detest the dragon totem. The Hekeu! Hai! We are the Hekeu!"

Still the enormous lion regarded him. It dripped a little spittle from its black lips, its tongue flicked. The two long dagger-like teeth glinted. The lower jaw hung free.

"Let me pass in peace, Hekeu, and we will sing your praises tonight—"

Odan stopped speaking, leaped to the side as the lion sprang.

In a flurry of dust among the dry boulders and sparse grass man and beast once more faced each other, waiting, quiet, yellow eye and brown eye fixed and glaring.

"I do not want to slay you, Hekeu—go away—go away before I must!"

The black tufted tail flicked from side to side.

Again the spring, again the lithe leaping avoidance, again the stalemate.

But Odan had worked his way back down the boulder-strewn slope. The wolf's carcass lay half a dozen long paces away. The spear showed, bloodied, sticking in the grey pelt.

"Go away, Hekeu! I am Odan—Odan—and I am a mighty hunter in the hills."

That was definitely a premature claim for a lad who had not passed the initiation ceremonies. As for Odan—once, he felt sure, he had another name. But that was gone, swept away by time and all one with vague dreams of sparkling lights and a soft face and voice, and a dream time which he could never focus in his head.

The lion sprang again and Odan, not taking a risk so much as a gamble, leaped towards the wolf. The lion caught him across the shoulder blade with a single claw. The pain meant nothing. The feel of blood meant little. He had the spear in his grip as he was knocked flying, rolling over and over.

But like the true near-beast he was, he came up on a knee with the spear raking up before him, his face now showing that rictus of anger and vicious temper that marked the savage he truly was.

"You have been warned, Hekeu. I have told you. If you will not let me be, then the shamans can see I can do no other than—this!"

The spear flew.

It sped with an explosive surge of super-powerful muscles.

The flint head cuts its way through the tawny flank. The flint pierced the heart. The heart burst asunder in a great sundering of blood vessels. The lion roared, a deep mountain-shaking roar. It rolled over. It attempted to bite at the spear-haft. But its heart was burst and it was dead even as its claws retracted and thrust out razor-sharp. For a few moments a long rippling shudder passed over the tawny body. Then the head lolled, the great mane in the dust, and the massive form lay still.

As was proper, a ritual he had been shown and told, Odan placed his foot upon the lion's neck. For only a dagger-tooth lion might the victory cry of the Hekeu be sounded.

He lifted his head and screamed the ritual word—a long

rolling succession of sound that bounced and reverberated among the hills.

Then, and not without a small feeling of awe, for this was his first hekeu kill, Odan set to work.

The dagger-tooth lion lived by its own prowess, its skill in hunting, its savagery and strength. It was a fit totem for the people of the tribe, who lived in like manner.

Now, when Isthi saw this! When she saw the lion skin and heard that Odan, the stranger, had done this deed! Well, then might he not hope?

No man, not even a shaman, could condemn him for saving his life at the expense of the totem animal. Survival was the creed by which they lived, self-reliance, and if any animal or man sought to slay one of the Zumen of the mountains, then he was fully entitled to defend and slay in his turn. Not entitled. It was his duty as a member of the tribe for the good of the whole tribe.

Every single person in the whole of Zumer—in the whole of the savage lands north of the mountains—understood that as a simple part of life.

With the two trophies slung over his shoulder, the tawny skin of the lion and the grey pelt of the wolf, Odan loped in his long tireless stride back to the secret camp.

He had completed a part of the tests.

Now he would face the rest with a heart lighter by far than when he had begun.

Blood dripped down his back from the pelts and from his wound. They mingled before they fell, drop by drop, to the dusty ground beneath his padding feet.

Chapter Seven

Of the initiation of a warrior of the Hekeu

The initiation tests went on.

The wise elders had conferred, the bones had been cast, the dust had been sieved, the winds consulted. Odan the stranger had not broken any taboos in his killing of the totem animal, the hekeu, and so Hekeu himself would not be offended and bring blight upon the tribe.

All the same, it was judged expedient to make sacrifice, and to inflict a ceremonial degree of pain upon Odan in mitigation and in propitiation.

Odan bore the pain without flinching. It was severe; but a Zuman learned to live with pain and to use it. The rites used were thoroughly painful but they left no permanent damage. That would be counter-productive and contrary to the spirit of the tribe, in which self-reliance depended upon perfect physical fitness which in its turn gave to the whole tribe the survival it sought.

The secret camp where no women were permitted within a mile broke up and the men moved northwards towards the lakes. Skins wrapped the sacred masks and symbols, the spears and swords of bronze. Bronze was come by only in raiding the barbarians to the south. The yellow-haired women were of little value among the hills and might be kept as pleasure objects by the greater warriors of Zumer; it was unusual.

As for the yellow-haired barbarian warriors with their barbaric clothes and ornaments, their mighty longswords of bronze, their moustaches and horned helmets, they were regarded with the same deep suspicion the Zumen accorded a wolfpack or a dragon-horde or a prowling yeti. They were wary of them but had no fear of them. Any Zuman could take on two or three barbarians with their bronze swords and see them off before the barbarians had finished bellowing their battle cries.

Primeval savagery had a knack of killing first and then of saying little afterwards.

As for the barbarians, they and the men of the cities called the Zumen of the tribes of Zumer Khuzuks and both detested them and were somewhat shy of them, deep in the innermost recesses of their hearts. No greater glory, it seemed, could accrue to some shaven-polled priest of the northern reaches of The River than when he placed a Khuzuk across his sacrificial stone and swung his harpesh and so sent another barbarian and pagan soul to perdition, to the greater glory of the god of the city in which he worshipped.

This did not prevent the young men of the tribes repeating stories about famous Khuzuks who had travelled The River, seeing the sights, selling their martial skills, and returning with a doubtful title to honor among their own. Outcasts they had chosen to be, and spiritual outcasts they would remain. And this despite the profusion of gifts they brought back. The primeval minds of the men of the mountains sought for survival of the tribe; all else was frippery.

Thick-boned were the Zumen. Thick-skulled. Not over-tall and with a strong dark pelt of hairy hair, quite unlike the flowing golden locks of the barbarians. Soon Odan would stand out among them, unmistakable. If he successfully passed the tortures of the initiation, completed the tests, learned the secret knowledge, then he would be a member of the tribe, and none to say him nay.

This was all that Odan desired—this and unimaginable delights of some mysterious future with Ishti.

The days passed as the year drew on filled with the strenuous pitting of courage and cunning against real and artificial foes. Odan could feel the strength in him. He gained in confidence with each test, each agony of endurance, each scarlet split-second of bloody action. He had learned well as a naked savage. Now he proved he was fit to become a warrior of the Hekeu.

Much magic took its place in the rites. The boys were deliberately hazed, scared, made to withstand the most horrendous situations. Wraiths were conjured, gibbering spirits of the departed. Skulls painted and befeathered descended unexpectedly upon them. They were confined beneath skins and left for dead. They were left for hours of the sun without being told what was happening, left for dread anticipation to eat away their courage like gnawing worms.

Only four boys of the group with Odan broke.

He sustained the others not only by his example which they sought to emulate; but chiefly because he was a stranger, not one of themselves, and one therefore to be shown up and beaten.

The tests went far beyond the simple technical skills of hurling a spear, shooting an arrow, throwing a knife, stalking a kill, concealing every action from intolerantly-watching eyes. These skills were ingrained in the boys, their company from the time they could walk. These tests sought deep down into the spirit of a boy, sought to draw out all that was in him to be seen and inspected and judged.

Odan passed all that he was asked to attempt.

Came the night when the final ceremonies would be performed.

The tiny curved knives of flaked flint were red painted and streaked with black, the bowls were painted in zig-zags of red and black, the fresh skin loincloths were on hand to hide the manhood of the new men. The girls, primed and ready, were waiting in the darkness in withy cages to play their parts.

Solemnity held everyone. The stars blazed above, fat and bright in the clear night air. The Moon would rise at the full. The air smelled sweetly of the end of summer. When the rites were over the tribe, united and swollen, would wend their way back to the foot of the mountains. Life would go on.

Eagerly Odan looked for Ishti as the girls passed. They all wore long plaited coverings that concealed their bodies, and their faces were covered not by masks, for masks were reserved for the secret societies of men, but by bands of leaves threaded with flowers. In all those pairs of bright eyes, could Odan think he could single out Ishti?

He thought he could. His heart thumped as it never would when on the trail stalking wolves.

Women held a secret power vaster than all the mammoths ever could when those huge beasts were hunted far to the north.

Each boy would be taken away from the fires, away from the camps, taken out into the wildness and there receive the final instructions and secrets. There much magic would at last make sense to him. There he would become a man.

Stooped over as was his custom, Odan listened intently to the masked figure vaguely lit by starlight. They sat in a small space cut from bushes, surrounded by the deep-breathing night.

"And Ke is the Great One, the Old One, the One who created all things in heaven and earth and in the hells beneath. His sons gave forth the goodness and their sons brought forth men and women for men's pleasure. Ke is the Great One, and he ordained that Hekeu the greatest of the totems should be our totem. The dagger teeth of the hekeu are our greatest protection. There are new gods in Ea and these work wonders for the sons of men; but we of Zumer know the Old Ones, and the totems, and we are a people united yet apart, decried and dedicated . . ."

Odan listened, drinking in the wisdom, storing it away, and as the masked figure intoned on in words long-since learned by rote, he understood much of what magic was and why sometimes it worked and sometimes it did not.

Odan's lot had fallen to be last in these final revelations. When he returned to camp all his friends would be men. As would he. He had absolutely no idea of what form the final revelation would take. The masked figure before him was standing up, and so Odan rose, also, stooped over. He looked about him with every sense alert, quite instinctively, without thought, as would any primeval savage.

"She will show you—" began the masked figure.

Almost, because the shaman had said 'she' Odan almost missed the tiny insignificant sound from the darkness.

But, because he was a primordial savage, a man hypersensitive to the sounds of nature, adding and weighing all that went on about hin, he heard that tiny noise, knew at once what it was, and so dived flat onto his stomach.

The shaman had grown old in the service of his tribe.

His ears had perhaps dulled, his perceptions grown less quick. Odan rolling over, felt shock that the shaman still stood up, was only just beginning to react. The old man was slow.

With a meaty thwunk a spear stood out in the shaman's chest.

He staggered back, clutching the spear to him, staggering and falling in the starlight. His huge ornate mask of hair and skin and bone and wood fell off. Odan saw with a fresh surprise that the fearsome shaman who held the secrets of life and death was an oldster of the tribe who had often cuffed him about the ear and yelled at him to give him some peace from his eternal racket.

That was the thing Odan saw when he finished his first sprawling roll. His second took him into a bristly bush where he held for a moment, abruptly stock-still, listening.

The spear had a little knot of snake-skin just aft of the flint head. The dragon totem, then. Hated enemies of the Hekeu, the Dragon-totem boasted of the power of their dinosaurian totem, and derided the long sharp teeth of the hekeu.

Looking up against the stars Odan saw a figure pass against the three bright stars over the indistinct outlines of the bush. He reached out and grasped an ankle, and pulled.

Before the Dragon man hit the dirt Odan's fists clamped around his neck, choking any cry. The man was powerful—he would never have survived in Zumer had he not been incredibly powerful—but the fall had surprised him for just long enough for Odan to choke in and then break. The depth of Odan's chest was deceptive by reason of his stoop. His arms bunched once, his hands moved, grindingly, and the Dragon man's head lolled.

Instantly, moving soundlessly, Odan snatched the man's fallen spear and knife. He slid effortlessly from the bush, keeping low, in a single snake-like glide reached the next bush.

His hand touched something wet.

In the starlight he saw the naked body of a girl. She was lying sprawled, her throat slit, and her dark hair dabbled about her body and glittered with the starlight.

'She—' the shaman had said.

Odan looked at her.

She was not Ishti.

A great and unreasoning agony began in his head.

The Dragon men were raiding the camp, catching the Hekeu at their least prepared, and Ishti must be there—and Ishti might end like this poor girl here . . .

He tested the air about him with exquisite care, sieving out the stink of this girl's spilled blood, the blood from the shaman, the alien odor of the Dragon man. Upwind of him there was nothing, as he had expected nothing. The Dragons had come in from downwind as would any sensible hunter. He did not lift himself more than a hand's breadth above the ground as he wriggled and sinuously glided back towards the camp. The knife and spear made no sound. Odan the painted savage was on the warpath.

He reached within some two hundred paces of the camp when all secrecy was swept away in the screaming bedlam that broke out.

Odan covered the two hundred paces flat out, and burst into the fight, degutting a Dragon with his first slash, ducking the thrust of a second, seeing fragmentary glimpses of insane combats raging all about him. The Hekeu were not caught entirely unprepared, for their sentries had picked up the attack the moment it came within range. They had perforce given up all hope for the three Hekeu outside the camp—the shaman, the girl, and Odan.

Now Odan, like a spectre from the graves beyond Alpaslan, leaped into the fray.

The fight was just beginning to become interesting to him, for he found he could outplay these bastards of the Dragon with quick little chirrups of his spear he had developed himself in hours of mock combat with the rowdies of the tribe. He was just beginning to think instead of everything being a red haze to him, just beginning to realize that no girls could be seen, when the fight stopped.

The Dragons were only a smallish raiding party of twenty men, out to catch the Hekeu off guard and steal women and weapons.

Now they had been forced into the bad position of having to fight they had fought, and right joyously, for that was a natural thing to a man of the hills, until their leader yelled them back to sense. So they disengaged and ran off without any women and with only an old flint spear as a trophy. They left six of their men dead behind them, and three prisoners.

These might be killed at once, tortured to death or used as a medium of exchange. Slaves were uneconomical in the harsh life of the mountains, and the Hekeu had no use for them.

Later on when complete order had been restored, the chief called Odan before him.

If Odan had no fear of wolves or dagger-tooth lions or other Zumen of the mountains, he had a healthy respect for the chief of the Hekeu. He did expect, and he admitted as much to himself, that he should be praised for not being killed and for slaying his men. Although that was a mere part of being a man, the deeds smacked of extra coup in the circumstances.

The chief sat upon a lion-skin and held the single object fashioned from gold the tribe possessed, a small gold cup engraved with a deplorable scene of satyrs and fauns and various sprightly goings on. Over his shoulders and reaching well past his head he wore the symbol of the Hekeu, two dagger-teeth reaching up almost like horns. But any Zuman would instantly recognize them and know them for what they were.

Because of the gold cup and the teeth, Odan knew the affair was of great moment.

The elders sat at either side, with the tribe clustered in at the back, so that Odan stood in the center of a three-sided square. He tried to hold his back up; but years of stooping over merely made his head snap up, like that of a turtle, with his monstrously thick body and swinging arms remaining bent over.

"Odan the stranger! We have taken counsel and we see we were misguided. You slew the hekeu and we condoned the deed. But now Hekeu has sent this punishment upon us. Four of our fighting men are dead and two lie close to the slopes of Alpaslan."

Odan felt all his eagerness drain away. He gripped the Dragon spear—carefully so as not to touch the snakeskin strips—and he waited for his doom to be pronounced.

Chapter Eight

Nadjul the Quick

"But, Odan, I could never marry you even if I loved you."

The concept of the word love remained obscure to Odan.

But the rest—

"Why not, Ishti!"

They stood by the beck that ran between stony banks to disappear over the lip of the waterfall where the nymph lived in her arbor. The tribe was moving out. The warriors took up their gear and spread to take the lead and flanks and rear. The women and children marched in the center, carrying the tribe's worldly possessions. Savage, painted, primeval beings, they would find a fresh ground for the autumn and stock their larders full for the winter.

"You are not a man, Odan. That is your own fault for you slew the hekeu. But—" Her youthful voice lifted over Odan's scowling interruption. "You are a stranger. You are one of us, yes, but your initiation ritual was never completed. I am a woman and should not talk of these things. But I know much, for am I not the chief's daughter?"

"Then I am outcast from the tribe."

"Only if you so choose. You may remain among us, so my father says. You may not style yourself warrior and you may never take a woman. Even if you could, I—" And then Ishti gazed on Odan with a look far different from the impression her words conveyed. "Oh, Odan!" she moaned, leaning forward. "Why did you slay the hekeu!"

He wanted to touch her, to hold her, to feel the warmth of her in his arms. But he held back. The idea of holding her smooth body close to his filled him with a weird trembling he could not control. He did not understand.

"Love," he said. "Is love so important?"

"I would have shown you, Odan—Odan the stranger. But now I cannot, for you are not a warrior—you are not a man!"

She turned away, her naked body so slender, so firm, so smooth, turned and ran and as she ran to the other women so Odan heard her sobs, muffled, constrained, forced away as all such weak sentiments must be forced down by a Zuwoman and the daughter of the chief.

In all of Zumer were there two more miserable beings?

The facts had been explained to Odan. Hekeu had spoken in the savage raid of the Dragons. This boy who sought to become a warrior and a man was not fit. His rituals had been cut short. He did not know the final secrets. Now he would never know. He might fight for the tribe, act as a porter, stand guard, hunt for food—but he would never be accorded the status of a warrior and he might never have a woman.

Such a fate was more than Odan could bear.

Not scowling, for his feelings ran too deep for mere facial grimaces, Odan strode to take up his appointed position on the line of march. He did not march with the warriors as did his boyhood companions of yesterday. Nor yet was he obliged to walk with the women and oldsters. Together with half a dozen youths who had failed the rituals and the tests he walked sullenly along at the rear of the central body, before the rear-guard, ready to take up the best position in the ring if the tribe was attacked. He was not a front-line fighter.

Many tribes would have slain him at once, as they killed all who failed to pass the tests. But the Hekeu were wiser than most in Zumer and took all the value they could from every skin able to pay its way. The instant a failure proved incapable of his own sustenance, the instant he was a burden upon the tribe, he would be put down.

Game proved plentiful in the lush Alpine valleys and the tribe was busy about its tasks. The hunting was so good, the stores laid in for winter so abundant, that the inevitable outcome was a raid. The chief of the north wind lodge of the Hekeu would lead a raid against the yellow-haired barbarians. There would be much bronze, and perhaps some of the liquid fire that turned a man's belly to a furnace and his bones to jelly.

Some of the warriors, the younger ones, of the golden sunrise lodge clamored to go. A few representatives of each of the other eight lodges of the Hekeu went along, and with them went Odan the stranger. He would go as a porter to bring back the booty. Holding down the shame and indignation, Odan went.

He would never be a member of a lodge, never a warrior or a man of the Dagger-Tooth Lion.

The journey through the mountains was one that would have shattered the toughest of barbarians, and been impossible in four times the period for a civilized man of the cities of The River. Perhaps, had a dagger-tooth lion, or a wolf, or some other feral beast, determined to perform the feat it might have matched the men. But even this is doubtful.

The snow-capped peaks passed to the rear. The savages poured down from the high passes and stormed into the first barbarian town they came to. The wooden walls and watchtowers proved of no avail. There was considerable slaughter. The yellow-haired women screamed and ran. But they were of no real account to the Zumen. The barbarians, proud in their strength, swinging their longswords and their battle axes roared their battle cries and joined combat; but the savage cunning and beast-like strength of the men of the mountains overbore them.

When the town was one sheet of golden fire, the primitives withdrew. Many were already drunk on the liquid fire. Odan hefted three times his body weight of bronze, and the chief of the north wind lodge was a man most content.

That night Odan took a decision.

Without any false pride, for pride in self meant only pride in tribe and totem, he knew he was a better warrior than any other of the Hekeu here present. Already he had proved that to his own satisfaction, and if any man sought a quarrel he was fully prepared to prove it on their hide. But he would never be a man. The wound had bitten so deeply he was hardly aware of his own reactions, vague, and mistily conscious only of a blight on his life that, not of his own doing, destroyed him.

But—perhaps Ishti was right. Perhaps he should not have slain the dagger-tooth lion. But—had he held his hand he would be dead. Was that, then, the real doom upon him? .

He would not sneak away in the night. The rigorous demands of the Hekeu constrained him in that. Savages they were; they held their own codes, magical and mystical. He sought out the chief of the north wind lodge and saluted him and said:

"I, Odan the stranger, will take my leave of the Hekeu for a space."

The warrior gaped at him, unclamping his teeth from around a joint of lamb, poor stuff compared with the antelopes hunted on the far slopes. "Take your leave, boy?"

That 'boy' jarred.

"We are called Khuzuks. I shall go down through the barbarians, to The River of which I have heard. Perhaps I shall come back one day as a great Khuzuk, and give you a skinfull of bronze and a bellyfull of liquid fire."

"And mayhap your head will be spitted over a city gate."

Savages and primeval, the Zumen; but they had heard of these things.

"I believe Hekeu to be with me still. I know that Ke watches over me. I shall go in their protection."

The warrior grunted, and took a sliver of meat, and chewed. Then he glanced up and said: "If you go, boy, you do not take a weapon from the tribe."

Silently, Odan handed over his spear and knife. He unslung his bow with its score of arrows and handed them across. Parting with them caused a sudden quick ache; but he kept his harsh face rigid, downbent, lowering from his stooping body.

Abruptly the warrior laughed.

Laughter was a rare and almost insane phenomenon in Zumer.

"You will soon take new weapons, boy. May Ke go with you."

Odan turned away. He would be leaving all he knew. He would be leaving Ishti. The thought of the world beyond the mountains, past the barbarians, filled him with a quick and convulsive loathing, and a sickly yearning he could not explain.

The warrior, the chief of the north wind lodge, said: "I have heard the mountains curve down to The Salt Sea. The barbarians of the west raid across the water. You might go that way and avoid them—"

"I shall avoid no man from now on," said Odan, the Khuzuk.

He went away, then, from all he knew in Zumer. He carried nothing. He wore nothing. He walked steadily into the darkness. All he took from the primordial savages of the mountains was a superb body, a cunning warrior's brain, and the memory of the mystery of magic and of a woman he had never known.

Nadjul the Quick groaned in anguish as he lumbered along the muddy trail beside the narrow irrigation ditch. He panted as he ran, panted much more than he cared for. He cast a look back. The damned barbarians were gaining on him, their cursed yellow hair floating from under their bronze and bone helmets, their faces bright with exertion, their weapons brilliant and glittering under the sun.

The anguish Nadjul felt was not connected with fear. Oh, yes, he was frightened. By Anki! Who would not be after the caravan had been destroyed, the onagers slain or dispersed, the guards killed? And now Nadjul the Quick ran for the city walls ahead and hoped he could get in before they slammed and bolted the gates. They wouldn't rush out to save him, that was as certain as Zamaz rose and set each day.

Yet had he not earned his salt as a guard on the caravan? He had thrown down his big oval shield so as to run faster. But he still clutched his bronze leaf-shaped sword. It was fouled with blood to the hilt. Yes, he had dispatched four of the hulking barbarians with their damned yellow hair and their bronze-studded leather jerkins before he had seen the caravan was doomed. Then he had thought to see about his own life. He was not called Nadjul the Quick for nothing.

His bronze corselet strained against his chest as he gasped with the effort of running. He lost one sandal and hopped and skipped and jumped before he got the other off and could run slapping along the muddy path in bare feet. His pteruges banged about his thighs. Everything else had been dropped. Give Nadjul a sword and he would face any man alive.

But these Anki-forsaken barbarians and their monstrous longswords and axes! They made a man's arm ache. And Nadjul the Quick was no longer a young man. Twenty years ago—ah, then he would have turned and dealt a few shrewd blows to the barbarians so fleetly pursuing him.

There were six of them in a bunch, and three more following on to see the fun.

He opened his mouth, panting, and sweat ran down his face, and he cursed all the decadent gods of the yellow-haired barbarians to the deepest hells beyond the ken of man.

A figure rose from the mud before him.

Nadjul skidded on the mud. He staggered to a halt, glaring, his chest heaving, dragging warm air in through his gaping mouth.

The figure had appeared so suddenly he had acted purely instinctively. Now his sword snaked up, the blood thick and red and glistening.

"Out of my way, friend," growled Nadjul the Quick.

A glance at the figure told him the man—the boy?—wore no bright yellow hair. He had a thick tousled brown mop which fell across the face, casting it into shadow, so that the swordsman could not make out the features. The figure puzzled him. It was held stooped over, the arms dangling, and the size of the body made him realise that if this was a boy—or could it be a man—it was almost deformed.

"If you do not mean me harm, my friend," said Nadjul, "then let me run on. For these damned barbarians are at my heels. And they will slay you, too, if you do not move."

The figure before Nadjul was quite naked save for a clumsy scrap of skin about the loins. But the man carried a knife in a sheath, and a spear, and a bow with its arrows snugged in its case at his side.

"If these barbarians displease you," said the naked, mud-spattered figure, in a voice that betrayed him as a boy and not a man, "then, as you call me friend, I will scatter them for you."

Nadjul heard the slap of feet on the muddy trail at his back. He could never run to the city gates in time now. With the quick resignation of the fighting man he twitched himself about and threw himself into the on guard position. He would have to fight without a shield; but he had done that before.

He felt the youth push past. Now, close at hand, he saw the incredible depth of the chest, the way muscles ridged and roped along the arms. The bow was out of the case and an arrow nocked, the string drawn back, and the arrow on its way in the time it took for Nadjul to blink his amazement. Before the arrow struck another followed.

Nadjul the Quick looked at the oncoming barbarians. They had been whooping in their wild barbaric fashion, chasing a lone man for sport. Now the first two staggered. The first had an arrow through his throat. The second an arrow through his right eye. These two fell. The next two arrows dispatched the following two. The remaining pair skidded to a halt. They stopped yelling for a moment. They could not understand what had happened.

"If you let them go," began Nadjul.

"They are barbarians, fit to feed dogs."

With that the last two arrows sped true.

"Their friends will not rest until they are avenged."

Nadjul felt the beating of his heart slowing. He could breathe more easily. The young giant at his side, stooped, glowering upon the barbarians, was a man to have there in a fight, that was clear. "I am Nadjul. I am a swordsman. Men call me Nadjul the Quick."

"I am Odan."

"Well, Odan, you have seen off six of them, a sight I am glad I have lived long enough to see. Now, I think, it is my turn."

"I do not have a sword. But I will fight at your side."

Nadjul grunted and hefted his sword. The three barbarians stared under their hands, their heads on one side and then the other. They appeared confused.

"Why do we stand?" asked Odan, in some puzzlement. "There they are."

Without another word Odan leaped forward. When he was well within a comfortable distance he hurled the spear. The heavy shaft with its bronze head flew. It struck the first of the remaining three barbarians in the chest, and smashed through his ribcage and silenced his heart. It also knocked him bodily backward into the next man.

Before this wight could disentangle himself from the body Odan, in a silent feral rush, was on him.

The bronze knife licked out.

The barbarian screamed and staggered back with his face slashed.

Odan wasted no time on cursing.

He bore on, his arm lifting and the knife swirling, and the barbarian, unable to shriek, collapsed. His throat was cut clean through.

At that instant a long leaf-shaped bronze sword, smothered in blood, lanced past Odan's side and drove deeply into the laced side of the last barbarian as he sought to strike Odan. He fell. As he fell so Nadjul withdrew and smashed his face in.

"You have to be careful with these tigers," he said, quite

matter-of-factly. He bent and began to wipe his blade on the barbarians flung-back cloak.

He spoke like this because he did not really believe what he had just witnessed.

He was sure, now, that this savage was a young lad. But the ferocity of him! The incredible power!

"We had best get into the city before any more barbarians come along, Odan." He squinted along the path. "They have done for the caravan. Well, I served for my hire and did what I could."

Nadjul hawked up a great gob of spit, and almost hit a fat brown lizard on the ditch bank. He felt pleased he had some spit left. The whole fight had been a damned near thing. This peculiar younker was going about from body to body and for a moment Nadjul had the vision that he might ceremonially disfigure them in some barbaric and obscene way. But no—the boy was collecting the weapons and equipment, rolling a wolf-tooth helmet into the ditch with a grunt of contempt, pulling a scrip from a corpse's belt, hefting it, looking up at Nadjul.

The swordsman was having notions about this strange savage young fellow.

"Aye, Odan. Money. The curse of us all. You maybe haven't run across it before?"

"I have heard of money."

"Ah!" Now Nadjul was sure. He helped in collecting weapons, for that was a part of the mercenary trade, and he kept looking along the back trail in between glancing at Odan.

At last, as they stood up, their arms full, and began to walk towards the city walls, Nadjul swallowed, and said: "Odan. That is a name to conjure with. But you, Odan—I'd say you are a Khuzuk."

As he spoke, Nadjul's right fist felt the hilt of his sword, beneath the lumber of gear. He could, if this boy reacted in the wrong way, have the sword into his naked guts in a trice.

Odan nodded calmly. "That is so. That is the name we bear in these outlandish parts."

That made Nadjul smile.

"Outlandish parts! Why, friend, this is The River! This is the heart of civilization." He paused. "Well—not perhaps so far north. They are a pretty uncouth lot up here, I vow. This is the city of Timgat. It is strange how with wide pastureland

and forests to sustain them up here, the people are as uncouth as they are. Down in the lower reaches of The River where all is desert save for the narrow strip of irrigation, why, friend, that is where true civilization is!"

Odan drank up information and clamored for more.

"And you come from the lower parts?"

"Me, Odan! No—I am from Shanadul, the most perfect city on the coast of The Sweet Sea."

"Ah," said Odan, as though comprehending perfectly.

So the man from the north and the man from the south came before the closely bolted gates of Timgat. A row of heads surveyed them from the battlements. A surly voice below a conical bronze helmet called down: "Who are you? Where are the barbarians?"

"I am Nadjul and this is Odan. Our caravan was destroyed. And the barbarians will be about your ears before you have time to wet yourself! Let us in!"

The head disappeared and then returned with another head, this time with a conical helmet topped with a tuft of bright feathers. The head below this helmet bellowed.

"Let them in! Let in Nadjul the guard and Odan Crookback."

As they walked into the blue shadow under the gateway Odan felt around the name the guard had called him. Odan Crookback. This was the first time the name had been applied to him. Odan Crookback. This was the first time a civilized man had called him that name which was to twine about his life from now on, stinging, apt, clinging to him like a burr.

Just inside the gate he stopped.

"I am not Odan Crookback," he said. His boy's voice caught at a lower octave, ludicrously. "If anything, here, I am Odan the Khuzuk."

"Hush, Odan!" Nadjul hurried him along. "You had best not be a Khuzuk so far north. Lower down the river no one will mind—they will even give you a strange kind of kudos. But here—better Odan Crookback than Odan the Headless!"

So it was that Odan returned to civilization, clad in the skins and linen of a barbarian, carrying what was to him a fortune in bronze, a few gold and silver coins that were new and strange, and with a new friend in Nadjul the Quick.

In the event the barbarians did not press their attack on Timgat and with a careful day left with the gates shut, the city once more returned to its usual occupations and the farmers went out and the vessels shoved off from the jetties. Raids of this kind usually followed a pattern. Once the barbarians from the northern hills had gained a sufficiency of booty they would withdraw, boasting and singing, half-drunk, ready to prance and sing and boast to their fellows in their own land. The caravan of which Nadjul was the sole survivor had provided booty enough.

Now, as the swordsman told Odan with some lugubriousness, he must perforce find another employment.

"This is to obtain money?"

"Too right. Without money a man may die, or sell himself as a slave."

"Yet there are beasts in the field for food."

"Not my beasts. If you slay one for your dinner the lord or the king or whoever owns the beast will hang you by your heels from the city walls."

"Yet are not all beasts made by Ke and free to all men?"

"Not in a civilized land."

A younger Odan might have replied: "Then perhaps I was not wise to leave Zumer for this civilization."

Instead, Odan pulled his lower lip, and said: "Then I must acquire money so that I may have my own beasts."

He had made the decision to leave Zumer and come to the land of Ea and so he would do what was necessary in Ea to live. This was the survival the Hekeu taught with so much blood and pain.

Odan had to remember that he could take nothing from a city if he did not pay for it with money. And if he took money without giving something in return for that he would have his hand cut off.

"Your warrior skill, my friend. By Anki! If I was a caravan master I'd be mad not to hire you as a guard."

Then Nadjul screwed up his shrewd old eyes. He was no longer young. He had travelled the world selling his swordsmanship and where had it got him? He wanted now but one thing in life. He wanted to return home to Shanadul by the blue grotto of The Sweet Sea and there pass the rest of his life with a flagon of wine and a cosy corner and cronies to listen to his stories of travel and adventure—stories to which the chief interest was added now in the strange and powerful form of Odan the Khuzuk. He would not take employment any longer with the caravans going to the east and west across the grass lands to the forests and mountains from which came the stone and wood craved by all the cities of The River.

"All traffic of any distance goes by vessel along The River. Guards are needed. The dangers are various and often surprising. I am travelling south, and will eventually reach my Shanadul—by Anki, yes! Will you come with me, Odan?"

But Odan was entranced by the city. Timgat held him enthralled. He was used to the wide spaces of the plateaus, the steep mountains and the lush valleys, the hurtling rush of a beck down the stony slopes. Now this confusion of white walls, of roofs at all crazy different levels, of ladders here and steps there, of paved streets and streets of mud, of bright carpets at windows, of flowers drooping from parapet and balcony—all held him as though some long-buried memories stirred.

"But Timgat is a flea-bitten little place! Miles from anywhere! Just a stopping place. Odan—come with me and see the great cities of The River! There are Eradex and Karkaniz, Sennapur and Dilpur, Eresh and Endal—although we leave The River at Eresh and take the Golden Road for Shanadul. And," he added with a look that stopped short of a leer, "there are girls in every city and all of 'em finer than the flea-bitten lot here. Come with me, Odan."

But this first shock of the city had hooked Odan deeply, the barbs sunk into his imagination. Money, beasts, girls, bronze—all these were here and he meant to have his share.

"No, Nadjul the Quick. I cannot tear myself away—but I will come to the jetty tomorrow to see you off."

"You're headstong enough now, young Odan—Anki knows what you'll be like when you're grown up. D'you think you are able to manage in a city all by yourself?"

"Ke and Hekeu are with me. I will manage."

"Then let us find a tavern so that I can drown my loss of faith and my sorrow in you, Odan the Khuzuk."

Chapter Nine

In which Odan learns city ways

The water of The River this far north still ran blue and clear between the wooded banks. Irrigation ditches had been cut and were kept clear and used; but they bore little resemblance to the complex interlocking systems of waterways flanking The River as it wound lazily through the deserts of the south.

The grasslands here supported vast herds of onagers and horses as well as sheep and cattle. Here was the source of the motive-power of the chariotry of the armies of The River. Yet the strength, the wealth, the culture and the power of cities lay all to the south, in those series of wide curvings of The River in the land of Ea between the two seas. Much of the reason for that, of course, lay in the trade between the two seas, east and west which ran along the broad central arm of The River from Karkaniz in the west to Eresh in the east. The Salt Sea provided much that The Sweet Sea peoples desired, and vice versa, and trade was brisk and continuous.

Nadjul the Quick and Odan the Khuzuk stood on the jetty with a skittling little breeze ruffling their cloaks. The day would probably be fine, although the scurry of high cloud might later on bring rain. Odan was as used to rain as he was to sunshine, to snow and to the parched lands.

"No," said Nadjul. "No, they don't know what rain is, down south."

"Then how—"

"I'll tell you this. There may be a lot of grass up here; but the cattle and horses of the land of Ea are nowhere better than in the cultivated lands of the central cities. Mark my words. You'll do better down there."

Odan shook his head, and then wished he had not. The

tavern sold a fierce beer that had filled his head with wild phantasms. He had decided out of principles the shamans of the Hekeu would recognize, not to indulge so freely again.

"Is that your boat?"

"Aye. A great broad-beamed crawler. But we're going down-stream and that makes life easy for all aboard. We're carrying rough-hewn stone for some temple or other, and we're trailing baulks of timber floating astern. Old Jaipur the master seems a fair man, and the guards are all professionals."

Odan looked at the vessel which seemed to him like a monstrous house of the barbarians afloat on the blue water.

"And will you bring all that back upstream?"

Nadjul laughed and slapped his scabbard. "Nay, friend. She'll be broken up for her timber. Jaipur and the others will sail back upriver in a light nimble craft and when the next consignment is due they'll slap together another broad-beamed crawler. Only a fool makes work for himself."

Odan rubbed his nose. "And you will guard this stone and this timber all the way down The River to Perar?"

"Perar or Persar, in the Persaran Bend." Nadjul looked about with that swift lift of his head that had heralded many a death in swordfight. They stood alone. "But I shall jump ship at Eresh. Then it is the Golden Road to Shanadul for me!"

"Suppose someone from one of these cities you talk about—Dilpur or Endal, say—take a fancy to the stone before you reach Perar—"

"That's when I earn my salt." Nadjul clicked his sword in and out of the scabbard. "I would welcome a strong young arm with me them—"

"I have not finished seeing Timgat."

"By Anki!" burst out Nadjul. He was exceeding wroth. He did not notice the rivermen filing along the jetty towards the boat, broad, squat men with seamed brown faces and the agile walk of men accustomed to hauling oars and ropes and of setting and handing sail. "Timgat! A flea-pit! A cesspool! You come with me, Odan, and I'll show you cities that shine like gems!"

The leading riverman grunted. He had heard. Standing aside, Odan watched as the riverman took Nadjul by surprise, seized him up, whilst two of the rivermen's mates began to punch Nadjul in the belly. The swordsman could not free his sword. His arms were pinioned. He kicked out, bellowing, promising the rivermen what he would do to them, and a squat man smashed him across the mouth, with: "We men of Timgat will show you, you dog, how we treat those who blaspheme our fair city."

Nadjul the Quick had not been quick enough. He coughed and spat a tooth and blood. He yelled. He kicked out. Again the rivermen smashed him across the face, and all the time his mates smashed Nadjul in the guts.

Odan had been trained to be self-reliant. He felt puzzlement that Nadjul had first put himself in a situation where this might happen, and second that the swordsman had not been ready to cut these dogs down.

Then he remembered the dagger-tooth lion that had nearly got him, that he had been forced to slay. Was this a repetition of that awful situation? Would disaster befall him once more if he did as his quick instincts suggested?

He moved forward with his silent tread and took up the man beating Nadjul across the face. He lifted him with every intention of snapping the fellow's backbone.

Nadjul saw that intent.

"No, Odan! Do not kill him!"

Odan said: "Why not?" and kicked the fellow grasping Nadjul so that he screamed and toppled away, green-faced.

"Do not kill them. This is just a brawl—I shall not draw my sword—"

So Odan, sorely puzzled by civilized behavior, did not kill the rivermen. He picked them up and threw them into the water as being the quickest way of disposing of them. Like half-drowned rats, sleek and shining, they swam to the bank, well away from the swordsman and the young maniac with him.

"Follow me, Odan!"

Nadjul leaped for the boat. Odan followed. The master, old Jaipur, laughed showing broken blackened teeth. He wore a gold ring in his ear.

"You have stirred up a hornet's nest now, Nadjul the Quick. They will surely beat you with canes if they catch you."

"Aye—so if you are quite ready let us, for the sake of Anki the All Powerful, push off at once."

Jaipur bellowed orders. The warps were cast off and the sweeps dug in and brawny backs heaved. The broad vessel hauled out to the center of the current.

Other boats passed, going up and down, and further along two more broad-beamed crawlers pulled out to take up station astern. The three would form a little convoy and thus give some protection from marauders and reivers along the winding course of The River.

As the smooth sliding waters took the three vessels along Odan stood, black-browed, stooped over and his head jutting arrogantly, staring back at the disappearing walls of Timgat.

Perhaps the next city would prove that much better, as Nadjul had promised.

The waters of The River ran brown, rich with the silt that brought life to the lower reaches and the Delta to the south.

The crawler swung along with the current. Foaming up against the flood came a long slender craft, decked in, with her square sail slanted around on the drooping yards to catch a quartering wind. Nadjul, sharpening up his sword, looked across and sniffed.

Odan put a hand to the hilt of the bronze sword he wore at his waist.

"No, Odan. Not enemies. But rascally slavers. Taking a parcel of poor devils upriver to slave their guts out in the mines, like as not. Slavers. Pray Anki you are not taken up as a slave, Odan the Khuzuk."

Looking at the lean lines of the other ship as she passed, hearing the long wailing keening of the slaves penned below her deck, Odan wrinkled up his nose. A memory, something ghosting in, vague, misty, less than half-remembered—no. No he could not bring the elusive thought into his head. He pulled his new sword out and turned it over and picked up one of Nadjul's polishing rags and gave the bronze blade a wipe.

Nadjul sucked a gap in his teeth, to make a whistling noise he found amazingly soothing, a reminder of the brawl on the waterfront of Timgat.

"You want to polish your blade, right enough, Odan. But you'll have to let me knock you about for some time yet before you're likely to need to clean blood off it. Ha! I'll beat you black and blue!"

Odan did not make a face, as a man of the cities might. He said: "I will learn how to handle a sword, Nadjul, for it seems to be necessary among the Cities of the Plain. But if I need to kill a man I shall shoot him clean with an arrow, or—"

"Aye! Or tear him inside out with that monstrous spear of yours. I've never seen a man throw a spear like you, and that's Anki's solemn truth."

"Yet you throw a good javelin, Nadjul."

"Javelins were meant to the thrown. They do not compare with your great spear."

"Will you show me that pass by which you caused this bruise upon my chest yesterday?"

"I'll show it to you—and I'll show you the counter. The counter you should have used, and so given me the bruise to wear." Nadjul half-closed his eyes. "Although, young Odan, if you do learn the counter and do try to give me the bruise, I shall use the counter-counter on you—so watch out."

"I do not wish to bruise you."

"Nor I, you. But you must learn how to handle a sword."

And, to himself, Nadjul confessed that never in his whole life as a swordsman had he ever run across a young fellow who took to the bronzen blade so quickly and deftly. In only a few weeks as they floated down The River Odan had picked up so much proficiency that Nadjul was forced to exercise all his skill to stay ahead and beat the younker. Such skill, Nadjul considered, was near magical or near-divine in its inspiration.

Placing the bronze swords carefully in their scabbards on the deck and thonged up safely, Nadjul and Odan picked up the wooden swords and so fell into the onguard position. As Nadjul had said: "You must learn to fight without a shield as well. Shields get lost, as I have no need to tell you."

So they set to, and the wood cracked and banged as they swirled and struck and leaped on the broad space over the piled massy blocks beneath.

Looking up from where he stood by the helmsman at the starboard tiller, Old Jaipur bared his broken teeth. Let the guards practice. They would have to fight and fight well when the reivers attacked. Let them practice. That was what he paid them for.

Karkaniz overwhelmed Odan. They had passed fine cities strung out along The River. But Karkaniz situated in the bold curve of The River as it swung a hundred and eighty degrees from west to east and so passed The Salt Sea at a distance of some fifty or sixty miles, shattered him with its magnificence.

He plunged into the life of the city without thought. Separated from Nadjul as he wandered about, entranced, he thought only once that old Jaipur would be down at the docks anxious to push on south. Going south down The River from Karkaniz all the way to Eresh meant travelling in an almost due easterly direction. Odan the Khuzuk thought of the vessel and then he banished work from his mind and went haunting the pleasure spots of fabled Karkaniz.

Rich was the city, terraced and bowered in flowers, alive to the sound of running water. Her irrigated fields stretched for miles. The traffic from The Salt Sea must pass through her wharves and warehouses. Odan found much that a lad would delight in. When he woke up on the following morning, naked, without clothes, weapons, or money, and with a head that ached from some noxious poison more than simple drink, he cursed and realized that he was a true Zuman, who knew nothing of city ways.

How they had gulled him, those happy acquaintances of the previous evening! He was, in all sober truth, lucky to be still live.

He staggered up and found a piece of filthy cloth in the corner of the barn they'd thrown him into, cackling no doubt at their own cleverness and his own stupidity, and so tottered off to the docks. The crawlers were gone. Old Jaipur, Nadjul, all of them, all were gone, sailing away downriver.

Odan whom some called Crookback and others the Khuzuk, paused to think. Self-reliance. Survival. Look to Ke and Hekeu. He found a man walking in an alley with a loaf of bread and the man sank senseless to the mud and the bread went down Odan's gullet. He found another man and was the richer by a cloak, a pair of sandals and a scrip with three copper coins. Each coin bore the finely cast rendering of the head of the King of Karkaniz. Kings meant nothing to Odan the Khuzuk. The only thing they were good for was to give a picture to one side of a coin.

Munching the last of the bread, for he had been sharp set and in a city packed with good things he felt he had no need to practice the habits of the hills of Zumer, where the loaf would have lasted a week or so, he was pounced on by four plug-uglies. They wore leather jerkins with a little bronze here and there and they wielded short hard billies. The first blow was taken by Odan on his left-forearm—a shaky beginning to the fight and proof to him that he was sinking into slothful city ways.

He kicked one of the fellows, ducked and twisted, broke the neck of the third. The last one—for the first one who had struck lay with a smashed face against the wall—hesitated. About to smash him, Odan saw a small body launch itself from the shadows of the alley and grip thin arms about the plug-ugly's legs. The man went down with a smash. Two more urchins leaped on the fellow's head and chest and silenced him.

They jumped up, panting, and stared first at Odan and then at the two corpses.

"Jiggedy!" said the first urchin. "You've killed 'em!"

"That's big stuff," said the little one who had trapped the man's legs. "They's slavers, right enough. They'd a taken you orf to slave like an animal, right enough. But—you've kilt 'em!"

The three boys were joined by three more. They were thin, furtive, brighteyed, with shocks of filthy hair in which the fleas jumped. They wore patches and scraps of clothes. They reminded Odan of the wolves of the hills, but scrawny, underfed, pathetic wolves.

"We're running," said the tallest. "You coming?"

Odan ran with them. They appeared to know what they were doing and where they were going. Also, they treated him like someone they could relate to. They were riotous children, and he fancied the tallest was older than himself. The gang of street urchins vanished into the shadows of the networks of foul alleys in the back areas of fabled Karkaniz, warrens of poverty and filth and vice—haven for a boy who did not wish to be taken up as a slave.

Odan the Khuzuk joined the gang of boys, these street urchins, realizing they gave him fresh opportunities.

The predominant sensation of this new experience was the smell. Effluvium coated everything in a tarnish of stinks. But Odan the Khuzuk, sometimes called Odan Crookback, persisted with the life given him, and learned, and grew quick and cunning in city ways.

So Odan entered upon another phase of his life in the land of Ea, the Land Between the Two Seas.

Chapter Ten

Of the Terror of the Souks

The leader of the gang of street urchins was Pepe. Odan made no offer to challenge him for the leadership. It was perfectly clear to Odan that he could whip Pepe—or any of them—with ridiculous ease. His habitual stoop brought his brown shock of hair down to a respectable level among his peers. But he knew well enough the wolfpack mentality. If Pepe felt himself pushed or challenged he would fight. Odan had no wish to make himself the leader. What did he know of the intricacies of this half-animal half-civilized life in a great city?

He was of inestimable worth in the forays the boys made against authority, when they overturned markets stalls, ran screeching with chickens and fruit and meat. They were real bazaar pirates. The Terror of the Souks. The soldiers sent to catch these small bazaar pirates knew before they started that they had no hope in the mazy tangle of alleys and courts with the uneven rooftops and the rickety ladders giving myriads of boltholes and hideaways.

The children themselves were the cast-offs of society. None knew of any parents. They were the refuse left after the slavers came. They were the illegitimates, the children pushed out when families grew too large to feed every small mouth, the runaways, the scum of the city. There were girls there, too, running with the boys. Wild-eyed sprites with long tangled hair and brown naked legs flashing. Odan looked at these girls, and thought of the girl with her throat slit in the bush—and sometimes he thought of Ishti who had been denied him—and he dreamed.

The days went by. The sun burned down. Karkaniz grew richer and more powerful as the merchants in their fine houses concluded fresh deals and ever their coffers swelled. The infantry of the king paraded and marched, and the boys darted and dodged among the crowds, and many a paunchy citizen and many a plump dowager found their scrips cut away from their leather thongs, many a fine piece of cloth or a jewelled brooch missing.

Older thieves there were, and fences to take in what the boys could procure and pay them. But sheer gain did not motivate the bazaar pirates. In them Odan the Khuzuk found the same self-reliant spirit of survival he knew from the Hekeu. How different the surroundings might be and the drgrees of skill required meant little. For, as Pepe once said: "I heard tell of a fellow who fought lions for a living. Barehanded. He was a fellow either too brave or too stupid. Jiggedy, yes!" He sucked in his breath, and then said: "But little Push, here, was just as brave when he knocked over the market stall and we all snatched the eggs before the bust."

And, silently, Odan agreed.

Many of the market-stall people paid the local wizards for protection. The more they could afford the better the grifting. In the nature of things, such being the chicanerous way of man's life in cities, the fences who secretly supported the boys' gangs as well as the more adult robbers would provide counter-spells at nominal cost, so that their agents could circumvent the market people. Odan saw a boy with a nose so large it dangled on the ground and tangled in his feet.

"Nosey," said Pepe. "Dunno his real name. Stole a crate of oranges and the spell got him just as he was running off. The idiot dropped the oranges—nothing to show for it."

"I would guess," said Odan, "his nose caught in the box."

There were various areas of the city in which the gangs operated, and territories severely marked out. Pepe's gang, as Odan found, was a light-hearted bunch. Some of the boys carried initiation and secrecy to extreme lengths. Some were out and out murderers, a thing that Pepe frowned on.

The bazaar pirates lived in no set house or rooms but moved on from hiding place to hiding place as whim or necessity drove. Anyway, the houses were always falling down. This was the natural result of hasty building in sun-dried brick, and the action of only a few years would tumble down a wall. Then the family would look and ponder and decide either to rebuild or to tear down and start afresh on the rubble. The creeping arms of The River also tumbled down the houses by the bank at frequent intervals. Sometimes a house would be built high in the air overlooking its neighbors, a proud multi-storied place on first inspection. But the house would only be one story tall, all the lower depths were rubble-filled and solid.

One day Odan came running cheerfully down an alleyway aiming for the house in which the gang had settled the previous night. He saw Push and the expression on the boy's face. Odan swung a live pig by its hind feet. The porker was squealing and grunting away and Odan was laughing and life, indeed, was good.

In the house perched against a blank wall with a wooden ladder as an escape over the next roof, Pepe said, sharply: "Where'd you get the porker, Odan?"

"Master Worlton's porkery—look, you must see his brand."

"Yes. I saw the brand. I didn't believe it, thought you must have picked it up summeres else."

"No. Worlton's."

"Didn't you know, you idiot! There's a new spell on Master Worlton's. We heard last night—you got wax in your ears?"

"A spell? Well, it couldn't have worked, could it."

One of the girls cackled. "You just wait!"

"Aye," said Pepe. "You donno what's gonna happen now."

"Nothing," said Odan, stoutly. He had felt an odd little tingle as he snatched up the pig. But then he had been so busy running and ducking and weaving that he put it away as of no consequence. But—suppose he had been spelled? What kind of grifting would Master Worlton choose for a pig stealer?

"Yore gonna git pig's trotters," said one boy, sniggering.

"Naw—he'll get a pig's snout," offered another.

"Maybe it'll fall orf of him. What a shame!"

The girls shrieked at this, and one or two, with bold flashing glances, chorussed out: "Oh, no, don't say that!"

Odan left the girls strictly alone. They smelled. Their hair writhed like—like—and here the image escaped him. There was something there, in his infant mind, about writhing hair. He threw the pig at Pepe. "Here he is! If you're too scared to take him there's those that aren't."

Nothing did happen to Odan on the spell's account. Later that day they heard news that caused them to roll over and double up with mirth. The paymasters who bought their hard wares and bribed the local petty officials also passed word of any new spells the wizards had sold. Corruption was not absent from the ranks of the small local wizards eking out a living with small magics.

A member of another boy's gang of bazaar pirates had raided Master Worlton's. Evidently he, too, had missed the warning.

Now he was the proud possessor of a pig's snout, pig's ears and pig's trotters. He looked strange and frightening, and, to Odan at least, pathetic. The emotion surprised Odan the Khuzuk. If one was unlucky one might as well pack up shop, close the quiver, sheath the sword, break the spear. But the boy looked so woebegone—for he had been thrown out of his own gang. Odan said to Pepe: "Take the poor bastard in, Pepe. He will serve to remind us of our own luck."

So that was settled.

But Pepe, for one, pondered the enigma of this big round-shouldered boy called Odan.

Because of his stoop Odan's hair would fall across his face. He took to wearing a headband which confined his mop to a reasonably respectable bunch at the sides of his face. He used a plain unbleached linen band. He did not want leather and he resolutely refused to have anything to do with snakeskin.

Some of the bazar pirates stuck feathers in their headbands. This seemed somewhat vugar to Odan, and also stupid, inasmuch that the hunter strived always to keep as low a profile as possible. The idea of breaking up the hunter's hard outlines was well understood by the Hekeu; one or two feathers, or even a whole tailfull, stuck up and quivering from the top of the head would scarcely accomplish that.

During this period which occupied a relatively short time Odan learned much. He came to see the workings of the markets and understood the chicanery and corruption that went on. He found that those establishments catering for the temples were particularly prone to temptation. There were many temples to a variety of gods in Karkaniz. The vast and swollen ziggurat near the royal palace at the northern central apex of the city dominated the skyline. From its summit, incredibly high in the air, always a thin plume of smoke floated heavenwards.

This ziggurat, among the most famous of all the riverine cities of Ea, was dedicated to Tia, goddess of love. So much wealth was stored within these cyclopean walls that men whispered it would pay for a night of love for all men through all the cycle of the heavens. Whatever the truth of that might be, Odan often felt an itchy hunger to go up against that ziggurat and quell the shaven priests and break down the bronzen doors and so enter and take for himself all the treasures therein.

Of course, he breathed no word of this fantastic notion to any other living soul. But the idea persisted.

The next decisive step in this life was caused by a simple misunderstanding on the part of a guard hired to protect a consignment of barley. A single qa of barley might not satisfy a worried mother trying to feed a hungry brood. A qa of barley weighed roughly a little over a pound. Wheat weighed more. Odan and Pepe and the gang had decided to relieve a certain fat and grasping merchant of ten baskets of barley. Each basket held between forty-five and fifty pounds of barley, around a bushel, and the gang knew that they could sell it the instant it appeared on the streets in the poverty-stricken quarters. They would sell the barley for something like a hundredth of its value.

The guard, a blue-chinned, heavy-set man with a bronze spear and a wood and leather shield and a very bad temper, attempted to halt the lads.

Push went sailing back with a nasty cut on his arm.

Pepe was thrown to the floor and the spear would have parted his stomach from his backbone had not Odan flung a brick.

The brick was only fist-sized. There was a deal of noise coming from the curtained entrance, and the cavernous storage chamber echoed with the shouts of boys stirring trouble so the leaders could remove the barley baskets. The racket spread through the bazaar. Perhaps that distracted Odan. Perhaps he disliked what he instantly saw in the guard. Perhaps he did not like the thought of the spear degutting Pepe. The brick flew with tremendous force. It shattered against the guard's blue chin.

The man went down poleaxed.

"Grab the baskets, Norli, and you, Setsi, jump to it, girl!"

Pepe gathered himself together in time to see the last of the baskets being whisked out and away.

Odan hauled him up.

"Come on, Pepe! Shake!"

"The guard is dead, Odan."

"Him or you. Come on."

"This is big stuff. Not like before." The curtains shivered as bodies blundered against them. Stalls were crashing over out there, and donkeys were braying and kicking, and pots and eggs were smashing, and chickens were escaping to brave adventures under the feet of prancing horses.

The two boys ran out.

The hullabaloo started at once; but as soon as the lads were out of the souk and into the alleyways no one would find them. They had had warning of an enchantment, and the vial Pepe had brought had countered whatever grifting would have harmed them.

In the lair Pepe and the others looked on Odan, wide-eyed.

"We kill if we have to, Odan. But generally we do not. Now the king's soldiers will come through here with spear and sword—and with fire. They will burn the quarter out."

Everyone knew what would happen then. Contractors would buy up the desolate land cheaply and build rickety tenements and so the whole vile business would begin again, with the exception that the people who had lived here would have to squat and shiver miserably wherever they could find some ruins in which to shelter. Odan had not served them well this day.

"The guard should not have tried to kill you, Pepe."

"He made a mistake—and he paid for it with his life. Jiggedy!" Pepe burst out, all his careful phrasing vanishing. "You've gone and dropped the leavings of Setto on us, Odan!"

"It is not as bad as all that, Pepe," put in Setsi. She was a lithe half-naked sprite, all hair and legs. She had a fondness for Odan he resented, because he did not know what to do about it. "We can move on. The people will find homes."

Various calls came, for and against. But Odan recognized the symptoms. He was by way of being something of an expert in the ways and means of being kicked out of a society.

He said, and now he did scowl, so that some of the boys blanched and turned away: "Very well. I will leave. Then you can say truthfully that the murderer is no longer one of you."

"Oh, Odan!" said Setsi. And stopped, unable to go on.

"Goodbye," said Odan the Khuzuk.

He took up his scrip, saw to his weapons, favored them all with one last dark look, and departed.

"Farewell, Odan Crookback!" they shouted after him.

Odan experienced some adventures on his journey down-river to the next small city of Kheru, some interesting, some comical, the most salutary. He found he could not obtain employment as a guard, for as a boy he was considered a laughable candidate, and he no longer had the protection of Nadjul the Quick to aid him. He prayed to Ke and to Hekeu that he might once more find Nadjul; but his prayers were more in doubt than hope.

Almost every man owned a master along The River, and a man was proud of his own city. Even the bazaar pirates owned their city. But there were masterless men, mainly employed along The River in odd jobs, and Odan was able to gain employment as a porter, a humble laborer loading vessels. He slipped quietly aboard at night and so was discovered the following morning, and, perforce, allowed to remain aboard.

The master would have thrown him overboard for the crocodiles; but Odan, for all he was a stooped-over boy, looked abruptly fierce. The master laughed nervously, and patted the green sash over his stomach.

"Let the boy stay. Why should we feed the crocs. But see he is put ashore at Kheru and not allowed back."

So they pushed Odan ashore, and he stood on the jetty, looking with some disfavour upon Kheru, which was a small city and in fief to Karkaniz, its king frail and easily overawed.

His plan—for he believed whenever possible in thinking ahead, although that was often impossible—was to go and find the bazaar pirates here and join them. He'd show them his fist if they opposed him. He was in a foul temper.

"Look at the boy," came words from the loafers, waiting for the next vessel to load or unload. "Like an ape! Bent over and with dangling arms—by Kanikan, what a monstrosity."

Odan lifted his head so that it jutted from between his shoulder blades. He glared on them. If he had to chastise them he would. They could not know he was a Khuzuk. Had they known they would have fled, shrieking, rather than face his wrath, boy or no boy.

He started towards them, arms swinging, ready to use

whatever weapons they chose. A voice, blasting the morning air, brought him up short.

"Odan! By Anki! Odan the Khuzuk! I have found you at last!"

He turned, bemused, and there was Nadjul the Quick, striding down the jetty towards, him, his face one great beam, his bronze sword slapping his thigh as he broke into a run.

Chapter Eleven

"Odan the Khuzuk! Run!"

"Eresh!" said Odan the Khuzuk. "So this is Eresh."

"Aye, lad, a finer city you'll have to travel many miles to find—although, of course, Shanadul is the finest city in the whole wide world."

"Of course."

Nadjul fleered him a look; but there was no telling what Odan might be thinking.

"Mind you, they do say Karkaniz is richer. That may be so. They stand one at each end of the great river highway between the Two Seas. But Karkaniz—"

"I know about Karkaniz."

"So I gather."

Odan had told Nadjul most of his adventures. The swordsman had been four times up and down the central arm of The River, specifically in search of the wild Khuzuk. Odan felt a wonder in this.

"Well, never married, d'ye see, lad. In my profession—well, the sword has always been my mistress. Liked a son of my own, though."

Here Odan had looked at him, lifting that great head of his with the straight firm nose beaking out, the hair falling away past his cheeks.

"Although," said Nadjul, judiciously, "if he'd been like you, Odan the Khuzuk, I'd have tanned his backside for him."

"I belive you would, Nadjul the Quick."

"By Anki, believe it!"

Nowadays Odan made no mocking references to Nadjul's calls upon Anki. Once he had made a jocularly slighting reference; not really minding, and had winced back with the bronze point of Nadjul's sword pricking his throat. So quick, it had been, that even the primeval savage of the far northern hills had been forced to pause, breathing lightly, as Nadjul's eyes glared into his, and the sword trembled between them.

Then: "By Anki, young Odan! Learn this well. Never make mock of the god of a man's city unless you wish to fight to the death."

And Odan had learned something more.

So now he said: "And the god of Eresh is Zadan."

"Aye. You'll be at home. They have a temple to Odan here. There was a great vogue a while back for naming boy children Odan. Seems that Odan En-Ke put in a personal appearance. I don't know the full story—no one does, I dare say—but you'll find Odan an accepted name in Eresh these days."

Together, they walked up to the riverine gate. This was the Tik-bird Gate. Odan marvelled at the height and strength of the walls. Eresh stood upon an island in the flood. The bend of The River here had been used by the architects of Eresh in the long ago. From the inner upriver side they had cut many channels running down to join again with the inner downriver side. These channels encompassed many square miles of fertile soil, well-irrigated. Small farms and communities dotted the level plain. The city lorded it over a great and populous region. But the wide course of The River itself was thus artificially narrowed near Eresh, and this meant that a wonder of The River could be built here.

Spanning the outer arm of The River towards the east a great bridge leaped from bank to bank, supported on many sturdy piles of brick and stone. Broad the bridge, wide enough for two wains abreast. At the center, over the deepest channel, a cunning arrangement of levers and rollers enabled a portion of the bridge to be swung aside to allow vessels to pass up and down.

In this fashion the king of Eresh made sure no craft passed his city without paying their proper tolls.

Tier on tier rose the city above its flat island. At the center, dominant, towering, stepping up to the very gates of heaven rose the Ziggurat of Zadan. The royal palace with its many towers lofted close by. Other temples lifted within the walls. Nadjul pointed out the tower of the temple of Odan to the boy who bore the name of the god.

"I shall go there, and shall steal a pig to sacrifice."

"There speaks the true Khuzuk!"

"I revere only Ke and Hekeu!"

"Oh, aye. Here in Eresh be seemly when you mention Zadan—that is my advice."

"Zadan, Tia, the others, they are but the new gods. Ke and the old gods are the only true realities. I know." But, even as he spoke so Odan wondered. What would the shaman have said to him touching the gods of Ea if the Dragon totem men had not slain him? He saw Nadjul's quick scowl.

"Anki is a new god, Odan. Must I keep warning you?"

"I shall not step aside for any man, Nadjul. But, perhaps, for a god . . ."

The River exerted a powerful fascination on Odan. He could watch the sliding water for hours, revelling in the subtle changes of color, the passing yellow sandbanks, the rich earth of the banks, seeing the surface filled with the long shapes of boats and the lumbering crawlers like myriad beetles upon the water. Flocks of wildfowl circled endlessly, crying, eternally crying. The heavy log-like crocodiles invoked an uneasy feeling, a sense of disgust he made no attempt to master. The shadufs on the banks intrigued him, the oxen hauling plows, the white clad men and women busy about the always demanding tasks of cultivation. The great herds of animals of all kinds aroused his primitive hunting instincts; yet he would relax, with a little inward grimace, for these were domesticated beasts and therefore not fit as quarry for a hunter of the Hekeu.

The smell of The River! How it got into the guts of a man and tore at his memory when he was away from that ever-sliding sheet of water! Long odorous reeds, bulrushes, the floating islands of green plants, the fish leaping—what a fantastic world it really was!

And when the sun sank and threw everything into molten gold and bronze! The purple shadows against the light, the streak and gleam of the water, running, ever running, sliding between the banks down in its lazy curves to the Delta and The Sweet Sea . . .

Nadjul had a piece of gold—a real piece with only one edge clipped and the face of King Narziphernes plainly visible—and he was minded to seek out a tavern of some repute. They avoided the tumbledown hovels by the waterfront, for they were endemic, it seemed to Odan, to every city, and wended their way up over the rooftops and along the bridges between houses and so down the last steps into Corn Street. Here lamps were beginning to throw their yellow and orange patterns onto the dusky streets. The sun sank more and more quickly as Odan travelled further south, a fact he noticed with amazement.

They found a warmly lit house with an amphora hanging outside as a sign and went in, to be met by the rowdy noise of men enjoying themselves after a day's work.

"The Lamb and Sword," sad Nadjul. "That does not fit us, my lad, even though many will think it."

They were served beer by a slave wench in a clean but worn linen kirtle, her hair bound up and with a few yellow flowers gracing the black locks. Odan looked at her with interest; then he carefully sipped the beer. Two flagons only, he had told himself, sternly.

Nadjul drank deep, wiped his hand over his sudsy lips, leaned back on the stool and looked about.

"Tomorrow," he said. "Tomorrow first thing as ever was, we find a merchant taking the Desert Road to Shanadul."

"Shanadul?" said the sharp-faced man at the next bench. "Aye, One-Eyed Lorto is taking a caravan in the morning. If you can pay, you will be welcome."

"Pay?" said Nadjul, lowering the flagon he had just lifted. He blinked owlishly. "Pay? Since when does Nadjul the Quick pay to travel with a caravan?"

"Oh," said the man winking. "A guard, are you?"

"Only the best there is," said Odan, drinking again and then belching.

"A real fire-eater, this one," said the man, picking his thin nose. "Can he stand up, and if he does, will his knuckles brush the floor?"

He started to laugh at this. The sally afforded him great amusement. His cronies at the same bench rocked back on their stools, joining in the merriment. Nadjul reached out with that quickness that had earned him his name and put a hand on Odan's arm. He shook his head. "Let it lie."

"If this is Eresh," said Odan, "I think we do well to go to Shanadul."

Nadjul had travelled The River and between the Two Seas for nearly all his life. He leaned back, assured that Odan would keep his temper. "Men will always tease the stranger. They are no worse here than anywhere else—more civilized than many. You will even be prodded in Shanadul, by Anki."

"Maybe I will become tired of being prodded."

"You will. Be sure of that. But think, my lad. Think of the consequences before you draw your blade."

This was sage counsel. Odan drank again and found the flagon empty and so, as he had seen others do, he banged it on the bench. The slave wench came across, tossing her head, looking charming in a tired and worn way.

"Some people are not all arms," she said.

The sharp-faced fellow convulsed at this, and Odan half-rose, but Nadjul hauled him in. "Sit, lad. Sit and prove you are a civilized man who fights words with words and not a Khuzuk or a barbarian—"

"I am no barbarian!"

"I would not dream of so calling you. They are milksops compared with you, Odan the Khuzuk."

The sharp-faced fellow stood up with his flagon and went to refill it personally. He did not look back and when his jar was full he found a seat in the very opposite corner of the tavern.

Nadjul smiled.

In the city of Eresh one hundred and one silver pieces, new minted, were equal in value to one new-minted gold piece. There was a degree of haggling and hurly-burly when Nadjul paid the reckoning. The clipped coin of King Narziphernes was weighed and tested and found to be worth but eighty-three silver pieces, to Nadjul's annoyance and to Odan's quickly stifled displeasure.

"A bed for the night, and a bath and clean linen, and a dawn meal—yes, we can provide these," said the landlord. He squinted a little but did not look overly vicious as landlords went. The price was settled and Nadjul and Odan, yawning, ascended the outside stairs to sleep on the roof. Nadjul was soon ready and lay down with his sword hilt to hand. Odan stayed for a space by the parapet, looking at the sleeping city.

What a great and grand place it was! And yet how strange that he, a wild primeval savage from the lands beyond the mountains, should feel this affinity for the city. It was beyond him. The smells attenuated here and the night air struck cool. The stars provided a luminous coverlet and he lay down to sleep, at last, deeply content and yet quite unable to explain himself.

Nadul mumbled and turned over. Odan heard him say:

"Old King Narzi was worth more than eighty-three silvers. That scoundrel had his finger on the balance, by Anki!" He snored and snuffled then, and drifted off to sleep.

In the event they had received ninety-two pieces of silver, for many of the coins were clipped. Odan had very quickly come to understand the value of money and how it was calculated, and Pepe had shown him the mysteries of numbers. Such things were requisite if a man and a Khuzuk was to make his way in the cities.

How would he fare in Shanadul? With a comrade like Nadjul at his side he had no apprehensions for the future. Anyway, what was to happen on the morrow and the morrow after that were hazy, seldom discussed, insubstantial dream things. He had prayed to Ke and Hekeu, and they had answered his prayer. He had found Nadjul again, and he was content.

In the morning as they ate the dawn meal the slave wench had her hair unbound and loose about her face. She looked even more tired and worn than she had the night before. Odan looked at her and something in his face made her wipe her own smudged cheeks and say: "Be careful on the streets in the Caravan Quarter. The lord has his men out slaving today."

"Thank you," said Nadjul, and he left two copper coins for the girl. She might save them for her manumission. She might spend them on a bright ribbon, for she was a reasonably privileged slave. Nadjul did not mind; he felt the warning valuable, and well worth two coppers, to a slave. So many there were who would have gleed at the thought of free men sharing their miseries.

"Are we always to be plagued by these slavers?"

"Not always. The market fluctuates. We are not of this city and therefore susceptible." Nadjul spoke with Odan in this way to ease him into city fashions. Like the sword practice, Odan picked up turns of speech rapidly, with that near-magical or near-divine facility so impressive to Nadjul the Quick.

"If a slaver tries to bind me—"

"You will run, Odan the Khuzuk. You will run like any sensible man. You will not stay to fight. You will run. Is that understood?"

"I? Why should I run when I wear a sword and carry a spear?"

"Because the slavers are man-managers. There will be many of them. They will use nets and weighted balls. They will take you, Odan, if you do not run, and they will see it goes hard for you for giving them the trouble."

"Well, if you, Nadjul the Quick, run, then I will run, also."

"Oh, I shall run. By Anki, yes! I shall run."

The notion of running away from a danger, from an enemy, set a prickling itch between Odan's stooped shoulder blades. But he trusted Nadjul. He did not think he would trust anyone else.

The bustle and clamor of the early morning streets filled Odan with the same thrilling wonder he had experienced in Karkaniz. There was a subtle difference about Eresh. But there were the same strings of donkeys, the same onager-drawn wagons, the ox-drawn wains, the same hell-for-leather belting of a young blood in his chariot, scattering chickens. The day-long ceaseless turmoil of a great city boiled about them as they picked their way towards the East Gate, the Golden Gate, the gate that led out onto the Desert Road to Shanadul.

Many a faithful traveller called that road the Golden Road to Shanadul. Thus Nadjul the Quick apostrophized it as they sought Master One-Eyed Lorto. He filled Odan with the liveliest of anticipations of the grandeurs ahead. The Sweet Sea and the blue grotto of Anki and Spired Shanadul itself aroused a dream-like swelling of emotions.

The caravans formed up in long lines. Many traders sought positions with their goods. All the way from The Salt Sea, from the pastures of the north, from the very lands of the barbarians themselves, produce of a world flowed through the Golden East Gate of Eresh. The noise and the dust and the bellowings of irate animals filled the wide collection square with uproar and animation. Chained in long pathetic lines crowds of slaves waited to begin their agonizing march. Odan eyed them, and then looked away. These things were beyond him.

The very first intimation Odan had that things were not as they seemed came when he saw Nadjul the Quick whip out his sword and throw his long oval shield forward onto the point of his left shoulder.

Men and women were screaming.

A swirl began in the crowd. Men were running. Shrieks filled the bright morning air.

"The damned slavers!" growled Nadjul, and he swung the shield forward in a short savage punch that dropped a fellow dead in his tracks. The man wore the leather bronze-studded jerkin of the warrior, with a conical helmet adorned with crocodile hide. Two men dressed as he was followed on, yelling.

Odan said: "You said run, Nadjul."

"Aye! Run!"

"When you run, I run."

"I'll run presently. When I'm good and ready." Nadjul swirled his sword, took a blow from a cudgel on the shield and flat-bladed the slaver across the guts. The fellow's cheeks puffed, his eyes stood out like chariot knobs, he whooshed and fell away. "Now run, you stubborn donkey!"

And then—and then Odan saw it all.

A man ran in from the side. He held a spear. Someone in the background was yelling, fierce high words.

"Don't bother with him! He is more trouble than he is worth! Kill him and move on! Hurry!"

Nadjul fended off a hairy man to his left, his shield the same inflexible barrier as of old, and he let the flat blade of his sword swing across. The man from the side hurled his spear. It thudded into Nadjul's right side. The bronze head buried itself deep. Odan saw the man who had thrown. He saw the left hand uplifted, back to him, saw the huge black haired and wrinkled brown wart upon that left hand. He hurled his own spear with an inarticulate cry of rage. The spear smashed into the body of another slaver who ran full-tilt upon Odan and upon his death.

Nadjul was down.

Blood seeped around the spear head in his side.

He stretched out a hand.

"Odan the Khuzuk! Run, my lad! I am Nadjul the Quick and very soon I will be Nadjul the Dead! *Run*!"

Odan stood firm, swinging his sword up.

There were very many slavers. He remembered what Nadjul had said. But Nadjul was dead, limp and flat in the dust, bloody, finished. And Odan the Khuzuk obeyed Nadjul the Quick.

Turning like a great dagger-tooth lion, Odan ran fleetly away from the slavers, ran sobbing into proud Eresh.

Chapter Twelve

Lych-life

Odan Crookback put his lean brown foot into the soft rump of Mitsi and pushed her out of the wide bed. She landed on all fours and sprang up, her breasts shaking, her hair swirling about her face, her fists clenched.

"Fetch me beer, Mitsi. And prepare the morning porridge. We have much to do this day."

"Yes, Odan," said Mitsi, and she lowered her eyelids submissively. Odan Crookback was a man not to be argued with—ever.

The tumbledown ruin in which the gang were holed up grew loud with the noises of the early morning. Odan ran a tight organization. For nearly two years he had bossed this gang of bazaar pirates, selecting new recruits with care and vicious ritual tests. Of them all he was sure, all save for Sarian, a hulking lad of nineteen, a man, low-browed and sullen, yet fast and deadly and a useful member. When Odan had at last discovered why Ke had made girls as well as boys he had taken Mitsi from Sarian, with a quick and abrupt fight. He held her in no special esteem, taking what girls he wanted when he fancied. But Sarian—yes, that fellow had to be watched.

Today they raided a warehouse down in a quiet corner of the docks away from the bustle of the royal wharves. A merchant greedy like all the breed Odan had so far encountered and a man they had gulled before had received a consignment of mother of pearl. The shipment, all twenty bales of it, had travelled from the shores of the Salt Sea, passing through many hands, for the deal had not been a through transaction, under the well-known seal of a single merchant all the way. Now this Photapharnes had bought it. Odan's information, as so often in these matters came from the receiver of purloined property, a man of standing in the district, a fat jolly rubicund fellow called Manastastes.

He had provided a grifting to take care of the spell on the goods free of charge. He had a certain sale for the mother of pearl—the cabinet-makers clamored for the material for inlays. The Salt Sea provided oysters. The wealthy of The River demanded first class furniture. Demand created supply, and the presence of that supply bred bazaar pirates like Odan and his gang. His Terrors of the Souks had a name.

Sarian had wanted to call themselves hekeu, saying that of all the beasts the dagger-tooth lion was the bravest. Odan had simply said: "No." Then, without raising his voice, he had said: "We will call ourselves the Tigers."

He did not explain. But he did this to honor Nadjul the Quick who had often spoke of the tigers of The Sweet Sea regions with a similar mixture of affection and fury as people not privy to the mysteries spoke of the dagger-tooth lions.

And, quite clearly, Odan could never allow this raggle-taggle bobtail of bazaar pirates to take the name of Hekeu in vain, although his feelings for the Hekeu as his people and for Nadjul as his friend twined and were mixed up and, even to him, did not make proper sense. He remembered what Nadjul used to say concerning the sayings of the people of the land of Ea: "The fool layeth his hands together and eats of his own substance."

Today they would be up and about and laying their hands on other people's substance.

Under Odan's ruthless direction the Tigers had prospered from a mere gang of street urchins thieving the odd basket of fruit, or string of fish or basket of eggs. Now they raided storehouses and barns and were a sore trial to the merchants of proud Eresh. Odan Crookback kept his own counsel on his motives. Truth to tell, he had no motives that he could identify apart from those of his earliest youth—self-reliance and survival.

Something about the way Nadjul the Quick had died. Yes, that most certainly had something to do with it. In all the hurly-burly as the slavers chased the screaming people, pilgrims, travellers, free porters, Nadjul had stopped to fight so that Odan might escape in safety. But for the bustle he would have held the slavers up long enough to have joined Odan. As it was, the abrupt change of mood when the captain had shouted for Nadjul to be killed, the sudden appearance of the man with the wart, the frenzied scurrying all about, the dust and confusion, yes, all these things had resulted in that damnable spear piercing through Nadjul's side.

Sullenness, viciousness, a surly contempt for those in authority in Eresh marked Odan in these days. If ever he found the man with the wart on his left hand, he would—yes, by Anki! He would!

The day was spent in careful reconnaissance of the warehouse and the surrounding wharves, the lanes leading back and of the best bolt-holes and runs. Eresh in most areas was a mere hodge-podge of white-walled brick houses jammed closely together, so that streets led crazily up and down ladders and across roofs, and where a man's front door was a skylight in his roof. But across the city in huge sweeping slashes the great streets had been laid out. The more important temples stood in their own precincts. Many wealthy lords had villas surrounded by gardens. And there was the infamous ebon tower of the necromancer Chaimbal. As for the ziggurat and the royal palace, these stood aloof and dominating at the center of vast enclosures, pleasure gardens, rides, miniature lakes and canals, lesser buildings, the whole creating as it were two separate cities within the city. Only on the southern side of the ziggurat where the spaces lay open and bare could the common populace have free access to their principle temple, the Ziggurat of Zadan.

The hours passed marked by sacrifices, processions, the chants of prayers. The Tigers were fond of practical jokes, and Odan himself had rushed madly from room to room of the house they had been in searching for a mirror, a pool of water, anything to show him his face. Sarian had said Odan had been spelled and although he could not feel for himself, he had a viper's snout and forked tongue instead of his own face. He had believed, too, despite that he could feel his own familiar features harsh under his fingers. He had not beaten Sarian; everyone had rolled about and held their guts, and so it was a great jest.

But Odan the Khuzuk remembered.

When the lamps were lit they began their expedition, a challenge hurled in the face of authority.

The Salt Sea provided the best mussels as well as their oysters, and the mussels of the Sweet Sea and parts of The River cculd provide no mother of pearl with the rich iridescence so craved by the cabinet makers. Real pearls, of course, came up from those mysterious regions to the south east, beyond the deserts, brought by long slow-moving caravans heavily guarded by the hawks of the desert. The sages said the waters of the Salt Sea were not quite hot enough for top quality pearls.

The raid itself went off well. With the smooth economy of effort so harshly drilled into him by the Zumen of the uplands Odan organized every last detail. They touched nothing but the mother of pearl bales, they destroyed or wrecked nothing else. One did not kill the cow that yielded milk until the last. With the bales safely delivered into one of Manastastes' secret caches, they spent the rest of the night sleeping and early on the following morning Odan and Sarian prepared to return to collect their reward.

Before they reached his house they saw the crowds.

The word spread swiftly.

"Manastastes has been killed. Spelled, more than likely. He lies there dead and not a mark on him."

Sarian swore.

"There goes our profit! By Zadan! We have been gulled."

"If Ke wills it," said Odan. There would be other times.

They withdrew quickly so as not to arouse suspicion. They heard that Manastastes had been ceremonially laid out awaiting the ritual burning he had prescribed for his funeral. Sarian fumed and swore, in a vile temper.

They sat around, drinking and playing knucklebones. The atmosphere grew thick with barely-controlled anger.

There had been a special kind of relationship between the receiver Manastastes and Sarian. All day Sarian brooded, saying over and over again: "If only I could see him again!"

Manastastes' death had been a shock to Sarian.

That night, remembering the jest of the viper's face, Odan slid quietly into the nighted alleys of Eresh. He worked with speed and skill. He broke into the vault where Manastastes lay and took up the body in his arms. The white linen wrappings were tucked in securely. He carried Manastastes on his back through the alleys and over the roofs, and kept out of sight and was not observed. He dropped down through the hole in the roof of their house and carefully propped Manastastes' body in a withy chair. He arranged the grave wrappings. He found some of Mitsi's cosmetics and painted the face to the life.

Then he went out and summoned the gang and said to the assembled Tigers: "There is a man come to see Sarian. Do you go in, Sarian, and speak with him and learn the reason of his visit."

Everyone looked through the open door as Sarian, bearing a small clay lamp, entered.

With his finger to his lips and his head thrust forward, the unholy light of deviltry in his eyes, Odan warned the other Tigers. They looked and understood and began to clasp their fists about their mouths, to clamp their jaws shut, to hold their bellies. Odan stared like a hekeu stares upon his prey.

Sarian, entering, holding up the lamp, said: "Yes?"

He saw his friend Manastastes. The lamp quivered and eerie runnels of light and shadow fled across the cobwebby walls.

"Who are you?" And, then: "Manastastes?"

The body slid a little in the chair. Odan bent the full glare of his merciless eyes upon it. If it fell and sprawled Sarian would know he was tricked. So Odan glared with awful fury upon the dead Manastastes, willing the body not to fall any further.

"Manastastes!" yelled Sarian. "But you are dead!"

Again the body slipped. The eyes were closed. Odan bore down with his will. Curse the fool corpse! It would spoil everything. Sarian was coming nicely to the boil. In the next second he would believe—if the corpse did not topple from the chair. The corpse slid again. "No!" Odan was barely conscious of the words forming in his head. "No, Manastastes! Stand upright you old fool! Stand upright!"

The gang watching, ready to burst into roars and shrieks of malicious laughter, goggled, and gaped.

The eyes of the corpse snapped open.

With a long sighing groan the body rose, standing, tottering, rose to tower over Sarian.

He gave one horrified look, dropped the lamp and bolted.

Everyone else shrieked with the terror of hell and fled.

Odan was left in the gloom with the moving form of the corpse.

By the time Odan had brought another lamp the body lay limply in the center of the floor. But, the lych had moved, it had! The corpse had stood up, its eyes had opened, it had tried to speak from beyond the grave.

The jest was explained to Sarian, and his dark face went

mean and his eyes narrowed, all perfectly normal reactions. Odan returned Manastastes to his vault, as was proper. But the Tigers decided to find a new hideout, from that very moment.

The jest was upon Sarian. Yes, the corpse had moved; but that must have been merely his sinews contracting, his eyelids decaying. Perhaps some residual spell still lay on him. But the fence was dead. There was no arguing with that. Even Odan accepted that as true. For, indeed, it was.

"You are a great man, Odan Crookback!" Sarian taunted him, trying to recapture his standing in the gang. "You carry dead bodies—"

"And your hair went up, Sarian. We saw it! Your jaw nearly hit your ankles! We saw!"

"Corpses mean nothing to me." In that, of course, he lied and everyone knew he lied. "You are a brave fellow, Odan. But against a sorcerer you are as a new-born babe."

"Well, of course!" snapped Mitsi. "Anyone is."

"But the so-brave Odan could steal anything, has he not said so? He could steal from a wizard and the wizard would not know."

Incautiously, Odan, still buoyed by the jest with the corpse, blurted out: "Steal anything, Sarian? From a wizard? Of course!"

The others mocked Sarian and supported Odan in the heat of the moment. Sarian looked narrowly at Odan. "You could not steal so much as a wooden pin from a wizard, Odan. Asshurnax has caused us trouble—"

"Aye, that he has!" exclaimed Nadu, famed for his light-fingered living. "He will protect the souk's stalls with a spell and will not sell the counter to us."

This Asshurnax, who lived in a cluttered eyrie in Yellow Lotus Street, believed in integrity. If he sold a spell to a customer he would not betray the trust. The gangs disliked this trait.

"You steal a cat from Asshurnax, Odan! Then we will believe you!" So Sarian taunted, and so Sarian trapped Odan in his own boastfulness.

Abruptly sobered, Odan said, stupidly: "A cat? From Asshurnax the Wizard?"

"Aye!" chorussed the gang. "Aye, Odan the Khuzuk! A cat, from Asshurnax the sorcerer!"

"No!" screamed Mitsi. Her face flushed and her hair

swirled wildly. "No—wizards are a sure curse! No man can do it!"

"But Odan can!" mocked Sarian.

Odan breathed deeply. He had only himself to blame. If he refused, despite the known horrors of tangling with wizards, he would lose his authority and Sarian would be leader. He glared around on them all, stooped over, his head jutting, his brow very black and down-drawn, his face scowling.

"Very well," said Odan the Khuzuk. "I will."

"You, Asshurnax, old friend, are a fool to yourself."

The chamber atop the eyrie was lit by two small clay lamps and the shadows, very comforting to the two wizards, would have sent a common citizen screeching with fear. Dorhutinax had come to Yellow Lotus Street to borrow certain ingredients he did not often need in his work with The River. Now he leaned back, sipping the wine Asshurnax had provided, ready to lecture.

Asshurnax would have none of it. "Your work is different. I sell protection to merchants. When the vermin of the city seek to buy the counters—should I betray my customers?"

"It is common. This new fellow lately come to the city, this Master Ubonidas. He is a villain, yes, I know. But he prospers, and he takes much of your business."

"He is vermin, too. I spoke to Master Kidu about him only yesterday. The palace is sorely troubled by the corruption."

Dorhutinax wrinkled up his nose. "The king should have appointed me court wizard. Then we should have seen."

"Aye, by Zadan. But that is a long time ago now, just before Odan En-Ke appeared. The tragedies began, then."

"Time will cleanse all." Dorhutinax was fond of aphorisms, and his work with the folk of The River stretched remorselessly. His pomposity could not dislodge the favor he found with Asshurnax. When the mage of The River rose to go Asshurnax sighed again and wished him Health and Wealth with Zadan, and saw him off. He went back to his eyrie, climbing the rickety stairs, in search of his ginger cat, the last of many.

In his murky chamber he paused. Instantly, he knew without doubt that another presence stood in the room with him.

If this was Master Ubonidas, the wizard was a sore fool to challenge another wizard on his own ground. But no—by the shuttered window stood a strange hunched figure. The dim rays of the lamp picked out a man—a boy?—clad only in a breechclout. His long brown hair was caught up in a linen band. His depth of chest and length of arms astonished Asshurnax. He saw at once the incredible strength and ferocity of this younker and knew that only a swiftly flung spell would save him.

The Paralysis of the body and the lower limbs should do, for Asshurnax wished to talk to the boy. And the arms, as well, to be on the safe side, for the boy's spear looked formidable.

As quickly as he was able the wizard hurled the spell.

Odan, about to snatch up the cat from its clay box, heard the wizard enter and remained still. His savage training would allow him this absolutely motionless stillness. Even his breast barely rose and fell as he breathed. He had climbed in through the window, prizing the shutters apart, and he would take the cat and depart the same way, climbing back up to the roof. If he made no sound, no movement, the weak eyes and dull ears of the mage would never suspect he was here . . .

The wizard spoke.

"By Abimalaikal and by the liver of Herguineas, by the spawn of the lion-lizards and the blood of the Scaled One, I draw down upon the inner ka the blight of paralysis, so that your body will not obey your heart and your legs likewise." He went straight on without pausing to lick his lips as he desired. "And your arms in due order—"

Odan felt the tingle all over his body. He shook his head, and found his head did not move. By Hekeu! He must return—he could not fail before the assembled mocking Tigers! He did not know what he did; but he felt the tingle fade away, and he stood, motionless, alert and ready for instant action as though he hunted among the bitter uplands.

"Now, my lad," said Asshurnax. "Let us have some light and see what we have here. By Zadan! What a monster! I have never seen your like in all my years in Eresh. From whence come you, thief who steals in the night?"

"I am Odan the Khuzuk."

"Ah! That explains much. But not all." Asshurnax moved forward, tiredly, letting his scrawny body down into a deep withy chair plaited with rushes from the banks of The River. The intricacies of the plaiting formed cabalistic symbols. He stretched, feeling his weariness. He was no longer a young man. "I shall hand you over to the guards of the king so that he may deal with you as is proper. But I do not understand why you sought to rob a wizard. Did you not know the perils, even in your far country? Do they not know of the power of sorcerers in far Zumer?"

"We respect only Ke and Hekeu and our shamans."

The weariness overcoming old Asshurnax was a purely physical thing. There was no magic about it. Every time he used a grifting to strengthen himself he felt ten times worse afterwards. Now he would have to rouse himself and summon the night guards and see this wild savage off his hands. By all the Names! He was tired!

He stared with his old eyes as bright as ever at the young man. What an enormous rib cage! What tremendous, frightening power there was! And that hunching over, that concealed the lad's true height. He was a monster, right enough.

Had the boy moved? No, of course not. How could he? He was securely held in the Paralysis—was he not? Yes—of course!

Odan stepped forward.

"I mean you no harm, Master Wizard. I shall not take your cat, as I purposed, for I think you value the creature and I intended to steal him for a gang of malicious fools. But if you will give me something to prove I have been here—"

Asshurnax could only sit and gape. The boy had thrown off a sure grifting. He had not been Paralysed—incredible.

"You—" croaked Asshurnax. "You are a priest of a god?"

"I am no priest. My gods are Ke and Odan and my totem is Hekeu." Then, because Nadjul the Quick had warned him and the swordsman was proving after death still to be a true friend and mentor, Odan added: "And Zadan."

"No priest? And no wizard? No—then how—?"

Asshurnax perceived what he considered to be the true reason. His own powers were deserting him. He was growing too old for the work demanded. Oh, woe, woe, he cried in a desolation of spirit. And he said, groaning: "What is to become of a wizard who has lost his powers? Where will he find shelter and food when every man's hand is turned against him in remembrance of past mischief?"

And so, in that moment of despair, bleak and humiliating, all Asshurnax's protections were stripped away from him.

Starting up with the suddenness of a revelation, the wizard Master Ubonidas saw and understood. He commanded and those men he had aforetime commanded and primed responded instantly. In a close knot of hard-faced murder the paid assassins, assured that the wizard Asshurnax could do them no harm, passed rapidly along Yellow Lotus Street. They came to the wizard's eyrie and they burst in and began to mount the stairs.

Odan heard them.

"Men come, Master Asshurnax. I hear the clink of weapons. They mean you ill."

Asshurnax started up. He swung his arms. "I am doomed! If I cannot spell a younker how can I spell armed men, mighty in their wrath, armed with sharp bronze?"

As the door broke in with the sundering of bronze and the shattering of brick, the once-powerful spells all torn away by the despair of their creator, Odan drew his sword in his left hand. The right hand hefted his spear.

"Do you throw a spell at them, Master, while I throw a spear and then get my bronze into their bellies."

But Asshurnax could only stand, trembling, one thin hand to his mouth, as the hired assassins trampled in, feral and murderous.

With a shout they advanced.

Silently, like a monstrous dagger-tooth lion of the hills, Odan charged.

Chapter Thirteen

In the eyrie in Yellow Lotus Street

Master Ubonidas had heard much of the demon skills of old Asshurnax. Determined as he was to oust the older wizard, his spells had all proved fruitless. He had waited for just such a chance as this, his band of hired assassins primed. Ubonidas intended to make an end to the thing. He sent ten men.

Fronting them as they broke through the door, Odan gave no real thought to the odds. His every instinct, hot, passionate, feral, and yet cool and cunning with a nimble brain, fixed individually on each man as a target. One by one they would die. He would not think of them as a mass but as a body of mortal individuals.

His flung spear burst through the first man, tearing his heart to pieces, flinging him sprawling to the clay-tiled floor.

Before the shouting men could realize what manner of doom it was that broke upon them, Odan had spitted two and had slashed the throat from a third.

The rearmost men carried torches, held high and smoking against the low ceiling. In that wavering light it was difficult for them to distinguish what was happening. They heard their comrades scream. They saw exaggerated, elongated, jagged shadows flung upon the far wall, where skulls and alembics appeared to writhe and shimmer upon undulating shelves. They saw the briefest glimpse of a shock of brown hair held in a linen band. They saw a bloodied brand darting, always moving, never still, slashing and thrusting.

They were brave men, even if their profession called them into contempt. They shouted to hearten themselves and pressed on. To slay a feeble old wizard with brittle bones when his spells were all done was child's play.

But, bemusedly, the last four found themselves suddenly in the front rank. Their comrades littered the floor, one man writhing to himself as he sought to thrust his red and purple intestines back into the jagged slit in his stomach.

"Step forward," said Odan. He spoke lightly. He had learned much with Nadjul of the art of swordplay; he knew very well he needed three or four years yet to make him a master swordsman. What had destroyed these men were the quickness, the savagery and the very bestiality of his onslaught.

The men hesitated. Odan stuck his head up, scuttling forward like a monstrous spider.

He took the first blows on his blade and, as Nadjul had taught him, flicked and so licked his own bronze in. He felled one. A second, with a sweating curse and a full-muscled blow, cut down at his head. Odan ducked like a dancing butterfly and thrust his sword up under the bronze-studded jerkin. Even as the man staggered away grappling with dangling intestines, Odan saw the remaining two turn and attempt to flee.

"Dogs!" roared Odan Crookback. "You cannot escape your fate!"

He ran and slashed down on the naked neck of the nearest wight, under his close-fitting leather helmet. He did not take the head off, for Nadjul had warned him against extravagance in fighting. The last man ran out of the doorway, jumping the shattered wood and bricks, started to clatter down the stairs.

Odan leaned over, at the top, lifting his arm. He threw the sword.

The leaf-shaped bronze blade jutted from the center of the fleeing man's back, punching through his leather jerkin with all the awful momentum of Odan's throwing arm.

Asshurnax, dazed, stood by Odan and said: "By all the Names, Odan the Khuzuk. You are, indeed, a barbarian-killer!"

"If barbarians fought like these dogs, they would starve."

"Come," said Asshurnax. "Let me bind up your wounds."

"Wounds?" said Odan. He looked at his arms, at his body, at his legs. It was known for men to be wounded in a fight and not know until it was all over. "I am wounded?"

But when they looked neither could find a single spot on

that stooped but enormous body of Odan's where a sword or spear had touched him.

"It is a miracle," said Asshurnax.

"It is survival," said Odan.

"I think," said Asshurnax as he set about re-establishing the spells to create an inviolable net about his eyrie. "I think, Odan the Khuzuk, that you and I have a lot to talk about."

"Leaving," said Tansi, she who had followed Mitsi in Odan's bed. "But you can't leave the Tigers!"

"I am leaving, and Sarian can be your new leader." Odan could not forego a last dig. "And I wish you well of him."

Sarian bristled; but Mitsi held him back. Tansi darted a vicious look at her rival, and clung to Odan, begging him to stay, running her hands over his body, kissing him, moaning, pleading.

"I shall keep an eye on you all," said Odan. "If aught of harm befalls Tansi—or anyone else who has a kind word for me—be sure I shall know and wreak a just vengeance."

He fancied they believed that. Certainly they had been mightily impressed when he had returned all those weeks ago from the sorcerer Asshurnax. He had not brought what they expected. He had put down a ginger cat on the table. They had crowded around. Sarian had been dumb-founded. Odan had smiled his thin cruel smile—for he laughed seldom—joying in the bargain Asshurnax had made with him. "Strike your knife through the cat, Sarian," he had commanded. Sullenly, suspiciously, Sarian had done so. The cat squawked and died. Suddenly, with a pass shown him by Asshurnax, a cunning folding of the fingers over the body, Odan reanimated the corpse. It sprang up, its fur on end, squawking. Everyone fell back, astonished. The cat sprang to the lintel, squawked again, and then slowly faded into a fine blue powder which drifted on the air, sifting onto the floor.

So, now, the Tigers believed Odan when he promised them he would watch over them. He did not lie. That had been a part of the bargain. Asshurnax would send a grifting, and Odan would know if Tansi was being ill-treated for her love for Odan Crookback.

Odan tumbled Tansi one last time, for the sake of friendship, and then he packed up his gear and took himself off to Yellow Lotus Street and the eyrie of Master Asshurnax the Wizard.

Asshurnax had probed him and tested him and pronounced himself not exactly baffled as astonished. "You, young Odan," he said, pulling his second-best gown of potency about his scrawny body. "You, I can make into a first class wizard."

The idea tickled Odan's fancy.

There was in these early days no close and intimate comradeship as there had been between Odan and Nadjul. Instead of roving the bends of The River together, these two roved the mysterious and shadow realms of the occult. But Odan learned. He proved an apt pupil, quick and eager, and yet always just a little cynical. Oh, yes, magic was a most powerful force; but, all the same, it did not seem to touch Odan personally.

As for reading and writing, these mysteries were shown him from a sorcerous point of view. Many people could puzzle out the meanings of the picture writing on the monuments set up by the king and the priests, for that was a part of their function. But the hieratic and the rudimentary cuneiform—these portended great and grave matters of secrecy and arcane knowledge. To know how to fill a clay tablet with the rapid squiggles that made sense at a distance, this was the mystery.

"You have a facility, Odan. By all the Names, do not ask me how or why. I might fancy your name-god took a hand. Odan En-Ke although dropping a little out of fashion now, was once, sixteen or so years ago, a great and awesomely projected force in Eresh."

"So I have heard. Many times I have stolen a chicken or a pig and sacrificed in the Temple of Odan En-Ke."

"I think you are wise. If the deal we have with that rascal of a caravan master goes through, I shall buy you a bullock."

"Thank you, Master."

One side-chamber of the eyrie contained rolls of papyrus and baskets of tablets. Among these Asshurnax rummaged off and on when in need of some particular enchantment. One day Odan, sent to discover the grifting that laid a fish-head on a thief, for Master Dorhutinax lay abed with a flux and Asshurnax had agreed to take on his contracts for the time being, saw a rat chewing away at the papyrus. Even as he started forward there was a long amber streak and the ginger cat, whose name was Best, pounced after the scuttling rat.

All Odan's primitive hunting instincts were aroused. He had not hunted for so long. His eyes grew brighter, he leaned forward in the pose of the mighty hunter quite unselfconsciously, his breathing quickened.

"Go, Best, go!" he said, excited, aroused. "Get him!"

And then, with a weird sensation as of falling from a height into a sheet of water, and breaking the surface of reality into millions of shards of illusion, Odan saw with the eyes of the cat, felt the surge of blood within the cat's body, smelled the infuriating stink of the rat, leaped after him as though he, Odan, was Best, and Best no longer existed.

The rat squeaked and ran and Odan's claws extended and ripped, his paws cupped, he batted the rat backwards, this way and that. He felt the surge of blood through his body, through Best's body. He, Odan existed and had his being in the body of a cat.

In the next instant he found himself leaning against a rack of papyri with a basket of tablets strewn across the floor where his staggering fall had knocked them. Asshurnax came running in with an alchemical powder floating about his head. Before he sneezed the wizard roared: "And what mischief now?"

Odan told him. He finished soberly: "And I swear by Odan I was the cat! Best was me and I was Best."

Asshurnax nodded sagely as he finished sneezing. "This is a well-known grifting, my lad. A useful art. Practice it. You will find you will be able to enter the bodies of small animals, and then larger." Asshurnax spoke without any of the pompous pride so many sorcerers fostered to the credulous. "I, myself, am able to soar with an eagle, charge with a bullock, and, also, crawl on the ceiling with a fly."

All these things Odan stored away in his heart.

The deal with the caravan master was duly completed and the fellow, he was a spry oldster from Shanadul who knew how many eggs made a trader's dozen, went off well-satisfied with the vials in their straw wrappings. If the desert nomads tried to waylay his caravan they would have a most uncomfortable month thereafter.

So the bullock was purchased—as always at an usurious price from the temple merchandisers, for only specific bullocks might be sacrificed to the gods. Asshurnax and Odan, inconspicuously dressed, for they wished to attract no attention, went up to the Temple of Odan. They wore white linen, and carried green branches, and the bullock, freshly gilded and garlanded, was led out for the ceremony.

Odan prayed to his namesake Odan En-Ke, for he had developed an affinity with this god that had nothing to do with his devotion to Ke, the Great Old One, or to Hekeu, his totem. When the bullock had been offered up and the priests had departed and the smoke wafted heavenward, they walked slowly back. The way lay past a cross-street before they could take to the roofs. This street was The Way of the Silver Elephants. Odan walked along lost in his dreams, wondering what life held for him, hoping he might become a successful sorcerer. He had told Asshurnax of the jest with Manastastes, and Asshurnax had pursed up his lips and said that, by the Names, necromancy was a serious business and one he had never really dabbled in, although he had once brought a poor man to life so that his wife, who had been visiting relatives, could have her generation for her old age assured. But, as a general rule, Asshurnax did not take on necromantic contracts.

A hubbub in the crowd ahead brought Odan to instant awareness. Never again would he forget the sage advice of Nadjul the Quick.

But this was only a procession wending down the center of the street preceded by hardy heavy-set servants using flails to clear a passage. Everyone was swept against the walls. Odan pressed back in the dust and confusion, hearing the yells and cries, watching for the thieves who were everywhere like the plague.

A body of spearmen passed, and a body of archers. Chariotry trundled past, the chariots very powerful and glittering in the sunshine. Plumes nodded from the horses and their harness burned in the sun. The charioteers wore red and yellow feathers over their brown and yellow helmets and robes. Following them came a four-wheeled chariot drawn by six milk-white mares. Odan gaped. This was magnificence.

The purple curtains of the chariot's body were drawn back to allow a fresh circulation of air from the ever-waving peacock fans of the wafters standing fore and aft. A chariot drew level at the side to protect the important occupant of the great chariot from molestation.

But Odan, his eyes wide, the blood flushing painfully all through his body, had seen.

In that gorgeous chariot sat a girl who turned all that magnificence to dross.

He saw her face, for her veil was drawn back. He saw a

pale and perfectly formed face, eyes of a deep lustrous brown beneath perfect eyebrows. He saw the small finely-straight nose, the rich curve of the lips, moist, soft, half-parted, laughing. And, half-free half-caught beneath the gold-tissue headdress the girl's hair blew in a gauzy confusion of beauty. A light brown, that hair, lighter by far than the usual black of the people of Eresh, fresh and springlike, summoning an ache to Odan's heart.

He saw the girl and he saw her spirit. He felt deep and unsuspected depths within him move and turn and, lo!, he was not the same man. He grew deathly pale, and he sweated, and his hands gripped and bit one into the other.

He would be a great wizard, with power and pride and wealth. He would wed this girl. It was a decision taken before thought, natural, inevitable, a thing ordained.

"What ails you, lad?"

"That girl, Asshurnax. That creature from the gods! I shall marry her. I swear it on the honor of the Hekeu! I shall!"

Asshurnax did not laugh. Such a thing was known. It would be a thing exceedingly difficult; but, then, this Odan the Khuzuk was no ordinary man. He could do this difficult thing.

"Who is she, Master?"

"She is the Princess Zenara, the daughter of the King, Neb-ayin-Ke and the Queen, Momi."

Chapter Fourteen

Princess Zenara

From that day of the sacrifice of the bullock to Odan En-Ke, Odan the Khuzuk dreamed of one thing and one thing only in life. He considered Odan En-Ke had directly answered his unspoken prayers. Surely the god would not have shown him this glorious girl, this Princess Zenara, without good reason? And what other reason could there be but that Odan was destined to marry this divine creature, to make her his own?

"I will marry her, Asshurnax. I will. There is a way and I shall surely find it. If I have to lay waste and sack a city of The River and make myself its lord, this I will do so that I may return with wealth and power and offer myself to the Princess Zenara. Was ever there ever a girl so wonderful in the whole wide world of Ea?"

"I think, my wild Khuzuk, I really think you would. And if you did, why, I fancy the princess would take you."

So Odan's fervent imaginings were fed potent fuel. His desire burned like a palpable flame within his spirit. Now, he knew what he was doing in life.

The dangers were understood. There would be other princes, time would be needed, there were a hundred and one disasters and horrors. But, Ke and Hekeu and Odan willing—and Zadan, too, to be on the safe side—this thing he would do.

So he studied with Master Asshurnax.

Also, from time to time when a choice piece of information came his way, he would return to the Tigers and lead them on a raid. He would never go up against any merchant who had bought protection for his wares from Asshurnax. By these means Odan amassed a small brass-bound chest of ingots and specie. Jewels, also, he stored away. Asshurnax sighed and took no notice, but he did, privately, place a small protection spell on Odan, for one could not have too many protections from the multifarious dangers of life in Ea.

A week or so before Odan's day, which was by way of being Zadan's day, also, hunting around in the library Odan ran across a tablet of a kind different from those in general use. To his annoyance he could not read the writing which squiggled maddeningly across the baked clay surface. He took it, puzzled, to his master.

"I am not surprised." Asshurnax put down the intestines of a rat which, mixed with sundry other savory ingredients, should help relieve the internal pains of goodwife Makansi who lived over the sandal makers. "No, my lad. I can only read a word here, a line there and hope I have ferreted out the general sense."

"But whose writing is it? Gerdas west of the Salt Sea? The far southeast where the men wear veils and the women have three breasts?"

"No, no. This is a tablet from the olden time. You know the land of Ea between the Two Seas along The River is the first great civilization of men—men like you and me, that is, although, to be sure, I'm not all that certain about you, Khuzuk."

"Yes, yes." Odan usually welcomed such raillery. Now he felt a strange tingling as new horizons opened before him. "Go on."

"The worm-people. They built a mighty civilization, and they were proud in their strength. They banded together into what they called an empire. The worm-men were strong. But we poor men grew up and ousted them, and they hide now in far away places and practice their black religions and occult arts where the light of our civilization does not reach."

Odan listened enthralled as the old story came out, of how the worm-people grew into awareness and intelligence and so dominated the land. And then men stood up and lifted flints and were crushed by the worm-people. And then the new gods came in glory, their dream chariots flashing with supernal fires, and gave into the hands of mankind the bow and bronze and the plough and heavy-eared wheat, and the horse and chariot. And so puny mankind raised itself from the dirt once again and drove the worm-people away and made of Ea and the bends of The River their home.

"It is a brave old story, Odan. And no man will agree just how many years ago it all happened. Thousands, hundreds; it was a very long time ago and there have been kings in Eresh whose names adorn the steles and the monuments for near a thousand years, and before that there were others whose monuments are vanished and lost."

"And there are no worm-men left at all?"

"Oh, yes. Hidden. There are stories that there were dragon-men even earlier; but that may be mere myth. But—" And here Master Asshurnax scowled. "Some foolish men there are who still traffic with these degenerate worm-men. I have no proof, but Master Kidu, the king's wizard, shares my opinion. And we think that the necromancer Chaimbal traffics with the worm-men."

"From what you say," observed Odan, "he is a fool."

"But very clever in his foolishness. Before he is struck down he will wreak much mischief."

"And the dragon-people? I," said Odan with great force, "I do not like dragons."

"Maybe they are merely phantoms, bad dreams, evil visions."

"I pray so."

Asshurnax took up the tablet and tilted it so that the sunlight through the opened window cast sharp shadows from the writing. He frowned. The tablet was a deal thinner than the normal run. Usually a man along The River had merely to bend down and pick up a gob of clay, wet with river water, and work it in his hands and smooth it and so, cutting a reed, have a writing tablet. But this tablet was thin. It was fragile. Asshurnax scowled at it, and held it out almost at arm's length, and turned it this way and that. Finally he laid it down and said:

"Something here to do with turning a man inside out—I think. We have no real understanding of the worm-men's writing. It bears very little relation to ours."

"You will show me what you know, can read?"

"I am not sure I should. It is bad. They were an unhealthy lot and their magics were dark and poisonous."

"But they held knowledge."

"Oh, aye, Odan, my eager apprentice. They held knowledge. But that knowledge helped in their destruction. The gods knew how to handle the worm-men. We practice in the light of the gods and our sorceries are not an offence in their nostrils. Well, by the Names, not all. I will not seek to question the wisdom of the gods in allowing Masters such as Chaimbal to practice their evil designs. The gods have their reasons, strange and mysterious. But the knowledge of the occult drawn out by the worm-men, this is dark and evil and to be shunned."

"Yet, master, it is all knowledge."

"Yes, it is all knowledge," sighed Asshurnax. "Under the sun."

The next day the nomads came to the city for the fortnight's junketings each year in which they attended the temples and joined in the worship of some of the gods, and held their incredible dhiljazls on a specially cleared space outside the walls. No citizen was fool enough to let them in, even in these holy days. The custom was usually for the people to flock out to see the dancing and the chariotry and generally have a whing-ding time—and maybe do a little business on the side.

For once foregoing his usual daily walk around the outside of the palace walls, from a vain hope he might catch sight of the Princess Zenara, Odan with Asshurnax went to see the sights afforded by the nomads.

All was laughter and boisterousness; only a few quick fights and these usually with hands and feet and billies, seldom with knives or swords. The air rang with the noise of the multitudes. There was much bartering and great gambling in the races and feats of strength, and huge quantities of beer consumed with barley bread and other delicacies reserved against this time. A man and his family might live on a few handfuls of parched corn; but in the weeks of the dhiljazl and the days of Zadan they threw caution to the winds and ate and drank hugely.

Coming into the outskirts of the cleared area where many chariots from the city were parked, with asses with downdrooping heads, Odan paused. Like all the men he carried his weapons. Nomads were nomads, never mind that this was a time of truce and jollity. He looked at a chariot on four wheels, with plain white curtains, drawn by four onagers. But—surely that was the self-same chariot as the one in which the divine princess had ridden. Yes—he felt sure. It was! She was here!

He would find her. In all this swarming mass of humanity, he would find her. She was here incognito, that was sure, come to see the fun. Odan put all his trust into the god whose name he bore, for he had come muchly to trust Odan En-Ke in these latter days when the god had so clearly marked him for fortune.

With the sure power and portent of Odan En-Ke to sustain him he would find her this evening. It was ordained.

Separated from her handmaids and the guard from her personal bodyguard common sense told her she should bring, Zenara stood confused in all the babel. The sun was sinking and torches and lamps flared. The nomads were wonderful, wild and free and racing their chariots in extravagant displays of reckless driving. She had seen the strong men, and the dancing snakes, the dragons tied with bronze chains eliciting gasps of awe from the onlookers. She had seen everything so much more than ever before, for this was the first real time she had been able to slip away alone—and now she was alone, adrift amid a sea of aimlessly surging people.

She would not allow herself to become frightened. She was the Princess of Eresh. But she was sensible that she should not ever allow anyone here to know that. So she drew her white veil, grey now with dust, about her face. She thought the chariot lay in that direction, towards the city; but in all the pushing surging throngs between the lines of tents and booths where magicians and defters and tricksters plied their trades she could not make her way through. She fought down the panic clawing at her.

"And here is a ripe beauty, lads!" called a rough-looking fellow. He guffawed, his strip of black beard very dark and glittering in the torchlights.

Zenara turned away and tried to push along, but the throngs impeded her and the group of laughing rowdies followed, teasing her, working their own courage up, joshing, but, all the time the ugly undercurrent of what they intended to a lone and defenseless girl ran like the dark understreaks of the treacherous portions of The River. She was what she was because she was alone. She knew what to expect, didn't she? Well, then, lads, this was the time for some fun.

They laughed as they jostled her into a dark gap between tents, almost falling over guy-ropes, giggling, already putting out their hands to touch her body and to pull away the veil.

"By Tanitra, lads! What a beauty!"

For a spell they halted, awed, the distant torchlights throwing a golden sheen over the pale, set face of Zenara.

"Never mind her price, lads—I'm first!" And a swarthy fellow, the dust of the desert still upon him, started to throw off his heavy riding cloak. His linen was not as clean as it should have been. Zenara felt his hands upon her. She could not cry out—and yet she must, she must. What would her father say? And her mother, sweet Momi?

"Zadan!" she prayed. Her eyes moved desperately seeking a place to flee. "Zadan! Aid me now!"

"I'll give you all the aid and comfort you need, my dove! Hold still and we'll soon be in paradise—"

Over his shoulder as he bore her down Zenara saw his comrades laughing and urging him on. She would have to tell them who she truly was—and then they would whisk her away for ransom. But, then, they would not harm her. No, Zadan would aid her . . .

"Zadan!"

She felt his hands on her body, tearing away the tissue vest, probing. She felt her limbs, on a sudden, turn to milk. She gasped, her ripe mouth suddenly dry and devastated. She saw past this fellow, saw his friends suddenly falling about, saw them staggering, saw a monstrous hunched shape moving through as the reapers moved through a ripe field of wheat.

She saw the hand placed on the shoulder of the man attempting her. She saw the strength in the hand, the power of the fingers with their trimmed nails devoid of all dirt. She saw the man's shoulder jerk back and then as he twisted his face around, saw that face explode into a red flower.

A hand, an arm, was about her. She was lifted up. She was carried. She did not swoon; but moments later she came to herself away in the light-streaked shadows with a great form supporting her, a face close to her own, a face that smiled.

"Princess Zenara," said Odan. "You are safe. There is nothing to fear."

"Fear? Oh, no, I do not fear." She could not explain her words. Then: "Who are you?"

"I am called Odan the Khuzuk. I am at present apprenticed to a great wizard. But I am going to make myself a king. A king of a great city of The River. Then I shall say to your father the king, Neb-ayin-Ke, I shall say, I, Odan, King of—of wherever it happens to be—I, Odan the Khuzuk, demand the hand of your daughter Zenara in marriage, for she is the fairest and most perfect of damsels in the whole wide world and I love her to distraction and will never give her up."

Shattered by this stream of words, shaking with a tremble forced on her by the violence with which this strange boy spoke, Zenara essayed a laugh. But she could not laugh. She shuddered. She believed him. Something about him as she looked more closely, some spirit burning in him—She felt her heart melt. Yet how could it, so quick, so quick?

"No!" she said, and struggled up, putting a hand to her hair.

"Never say no, Zenara, my princess. I know my place at the moment. But that place will not always be so. I have seen you and I love you and you will love me. One day—and soon—I will come for you. Your father will never say me nay. It is a thing Odan En-Ke has written, and I am sure."

"Odan—The name is painful to me. Painful."

"Because of your half-brother? He is dead and gone these many years. I have heard the stories. My master knows Master Kidu, and I have been told. Will you not for the sake of my name, at the least, look on me kindly and remember what I have said?"

"I am a princess . . . That I do not forget. If you are found talking thus to me they will hang you by your heels from the battlements, they will do terrible things."

"Do I fear anything for one glance from your eyes?" Then Odan stopped, and grimaced, and said: "No, such story-tellers' devices are not for me, not for you, not for us. I say, simply, that I do not wish to hang from my heels from the battlement; but that terror would not deter me from you. Not ever."

She believed him. His face stirred something she could not understand within her. It was as though the great Ziggurat of Zadan of the Sword had turned in the air and stood upside down, balanced on its topmost turret, that now bored into the ground.

"Odan the Khuzuk," he whispered. "You make my heart—"

She could not go on. It was ridiculous. He bent closer, and she felt his arms tighten about her.

"You are my only love, Zenara, my princess."

[illegible]he swallowed down. She pulled her linen robe straight. [illegible]ld tissue vest was all torn and ruined and she must hide that from her slaves. She stood up and Odan assisted her, rising like a monstrous ghost at her side.

She gasped.

"My princess?"

"You—you are so—" Instead of completing the words she turned away, indicating that she wished to return to her chariot.

Odan did not grasp the cause of her sudden astonishment. He was Odan, a Khuzuk, one of the Hekeu—or, well, nearly one of the Hekeu—from Zumer. He had aped city ways and he knew his way around the corruptions of city life. Was he so very different from ordinary men?

Bending down, as he seemed always to have to do to be on a level with other men and women, Odan walked at her side across the wide space where the torchlights fleered their hair in the background and the shouts and roars rose from spectators at one or another of the sports going on. A little wind raised a few phantoms of dust. The city glowed ahead, like a jewel. Stars sparkled in the calm dark waters of The River. The night breathed a sense of universal peace shot through with the boisterous activity of men.

Walking thus at the side of this enormous man whose hunched-over shoulders brought that superb head close to her own, Zenara experienced a profound mood of warmth and safety. Of coolness and safety. Of a delicious danger and of safety. She looked up at his face, and marked the features, the frowning brows, the straight hard nose, the lips that, she felt sure, could firm into a sword-blade of purpose and that now smiled and seduced her with their curves.

"Odan," she whispered. "I think you will—you may—"

"I will, my princess. And there is your chariot and those rogues who let you wander off. I've a mind to whip them all for it and teach them the error of their ways."

"No, Odan." She laid her small pink-nailed hand on his arm. She felt the bronze-hardness of the muscles. "I must keep this silliness a secret, for the king does not know—must not know—and my mother—"

"Your mother must be near-divine, I know. But I honor her for you, Zenara, my princess. I will wait here and see you safely away." He turned his arm and caught her hand. She trembled at his touch. "Remember, Zenara, remember what has been said and what has passed between us. It is the will of Odan En-Ke. I know."

"My poor half-brother—the will of Odan En-Ke then did not—"

"Hush, hush. That is long done and forgotten. I am Odan the Khuzuk. You are promised to me by the gods. And I shall claim you . . . Remember and wait, my Zenara."

"Odan the Khuzuk—" She was almost sobbing, and laughing, and her heart would burst from her breast. "I think—I think I shall wait, my Odan!"

Chapter Fifteen

Of three prison lamps

Odan the Khuzuk had no time to waste.

There was a suitable city to find, men to enroll, weapons to be bought. There was a king's throne somewhere along the hazy bends of The River on which he would sit. By Ke and Odan! There was much to do!

Still, he must make a great fuss on Odan En-Ke's day. He would make a great sacrifice and pray for guidance, and trusting in the god, his namesake, would go forth refreshed and strong.

Most of the populace of Eresh would celebrate the day of Zadan. But Odan now felt absolutely certain the god whose name he bore looked with loving kindness upon him. There were four other gods whose day this also was; but only two possessed a temple in Eresh, and one, Sis, a goddess who shared a complicated family relationship among the Old gods, owned only a small edifice built of mud brick. Her priestesses were represented by a handful of old women well past the time when they might pleasure the devotees of Sis.

So Odan decked himself in his finest raiment, white linen and bronze armlets, and he donned a pair of stout sandals with brass fittings which, for all they were made by the sandal-maker beneath the goodwife Makansi's house in gratitude for the relief of her internal pains, sat uncomfortably on his feet. He was more accustomed to go padding on naked feet across the mountains and plateaus of Zumer; but he had early observed that civilized men went about wearing sandals or slippers. He carried his sword; but he left the great oval shield and his bow case and his spear in the eyrie in Yellow Lotus Street.

With beads of glass and semi-precious stones about his

neck, with a flower decking his linen headband—this at the suggestion of Asshurnax who still understood more of the ways of the city—rejoicing exceedingly, Odan Crookback went up to the Temple of Odan with the blood price of a bullock for sacrifice.

The whole city boiled with the ferment of religious zeal. Enormous processions wound through the streets. Everyone poured out from the jam-packed houses, running over the roofs, casting down flower petals. The images of the gods would be brought out in stately procession and conveyed in their arks from their temples to be carried to The River where their feet would be washed. Then they would pass the palace and receive offerings from the king. After that, in a blare of trumpets and cymbals, with the decorated chariots rolling amid the dust and thunder and the devotees dancing before, they would return in all state to their temples.

The high priest of Zadan, the chief minister of the city, had organized affairs so that the different processions did not clash. As for Sis, her aged handmaidens would seek for young damsels to induct into her service, and mothers kept their daughters close. Odan En-Ke, glorious in his chariot, glowed with fresh paint and new gems, gold and silver, and with the offerings of the faithful. Odan, exalted, followed in the procession, proud that he bore the name he did.

The priest of Odan En-Ke, old Nabozinadas, seemed to have been miraculously rejuvenated since the day his god had come personally to Eresh. His great olive stave was now a divine symbol once more and not merely a prop to support his trembling limbs. He raised his hands high from the podium as the procession halted. The devotees shuffled their feet, the dust rose, men and women drew corners of their scarves across their mouths, the trumpets pealed a last commanding blast.

Nabozinadas opened his mouth to speak.

Straight as Loti's arrow a twinge shot through Odan. He understood at once. Asshurnax was sending a grifting—not to warn but to scream for assistance.

Instead of the solemn words of the ritual from Nabozinadas' mouth, Odan heard Asshurnax speaking over the multitude.

"Odan the Khuzuk! Odan Crookback! Aid me now, aid me now. Ubonidas strikes! His spells are powerful, they break down my protections one by one, and his men armed with bronze clamor at my door! As you love and serve your master, Odan, aid me now!"

Instantly Odan was pushing and elbowing his way through the throng. Men shouted after him. He ran. As a warrior of the Hekeu runs when the tribe chases the fleet antelopes along the high slopes ran Odan the Khuzuk. As the dagger-tooth lion charges upon his prey in the land of Zumer, so charged Odan towards Yellow Lotus Street.

Apart from the bronze and leather-armored men at Asshurnax's door the street was deserted. The king's soldiers kept up good patrols during these days, for impious thieves were known to break in and steal when the pious citizens attended their religious devotions. But no spearmen in their brown and yellow were in sight. Odan drew his sword and roared towards the assassins. They had not heard what had befallen their predecessors.

They turned at Odan's shout. Their dark faces were mean with the danger of their work, the difficulty of earning their hire. But they had been warned that Asshurnax had a new young apprentice and they would chop him with a will before carving his master. Odan knew that, even as he flung himself forward with his sword thirsting for combat and for blood, on the occult plane Asshurnax grappled no less desperately with Ubonidas.

"Cut the puppy down!" bellowed the leader, a burly ruffian with a mass of cock's feathers in his leather and bone helmet.

"He is mortal big!" said a little fellow at his side.

"Then shaft him, you pigeon-dirt imbecile. Shaft him!"

The little fellow lifted his bow, an honest horn and wood and sinew bow of The River lands, reflex, cunning, powerful and deadly in skilled hands. Odan could send a shaft from a bow of that nature clean through sheet bronze. He saw the shaft wing towards him. He dodged with the perfect reflex actions to be expected of the Hekeu. His sword looked sharp and bright and menacing to the hired killers.

"Again, dolt!" roared the leader. "He'll be on us next. Break down the door, vermin! Put your shoulders to it!"

Again Odan dodged the deadly arrow.

He was almost up to them, now. He saw the door break down and two men stagger back, shrieking. Their arms were withered to charred black twigs.

"Ha!" roared Odan. "That for meddling with a master wizard!"

"Ignore it!" screeched the leader. "Master Ubonidas will spell you right!"

Confusion boiled, with men going one way colliding with men going the other. The leader raised a curved sword—doubtless it was a sacred harpesh stolen from priests and put to profane use—and swung at Odan. Odan put the breadth of his bronze into him, stepped sideways and back, clearing to strike again. He saw the familiar brown and yellow robes wink into sight at the end of the street and he bellowed, ferociously.

"Well, you take your time! Help me see these carrion off!"

Arrows were singing. He lifted his sword, determined to slay every last one who attempted to molest Asshurnax. He felt the blow only as an afterthought, after the blackness.

The blackness took him like Nirghal's wings.

"By Kurd, old comrade. You invite the droppings of Setto upon us if we are betrayed."

"I will run the risk, Kidu. But I will ask of you nothing more than the averted eye, the temporarily suspended enchantment, so that I may rescue this young hooligan Odan from the prison."

"But he is a known criminal! A bazaar pirate! He has never been apprehended before. What will the king say?"

"I say, Kidu, that Odan is a reformed boy. He is apprenticed to me and, by Zadan, he is a wonder!" Here Asshurnax began to talk of the remarkably rapid achievements of Odan and Kidu, attempting to interrupt, fell silent and listened. He nodded wisely once or twice. "I tell you, Kidu, the boy is a marvel."

"I have heard tell of these boys touched with the gift early in life. You are fortunate and to be congratulated he is apprenticed to you. Yes, Asshurnax, for the sake of our friendship I will avert my eyes, both physical and occult. But, for the sweet sake of Kurd, be quick!"

"Thank you, Master Kidu. The king, may his name be praised, is fortunate in a court wizard like you."

"Enough of that, you old thaumaturge! And, this new fellow, Ubonidas. I hear he may well league with Chaimbal—"

"Zadan! No!"

"Aye. If he does, then we must put our heads and our wits and our arts together for the good of the city and the king."

"We will all say ahmeen to that."

The prison stank.

Sunk deeply into the soft alluvial soil of the island, faced with baked brick with a few pillars of stone to underpin the edifices above, the place ran with slimy moisture, was noisome, and frogs and snakes and scuttling things had their abode therein and resented the humans who hung from bronze chains on the walls. Many of the humans turned into mere collections of bones after a time, and rotted and fell.

Odan gazed about and saw nothing, for the darkness was complete.

The fools of soldiers had shot their arrows and one had nicked him across the head and then, the imbeciles, they had taken him up for an affray. And he had been recognized, at last, as, inevitably, he must one day have been, and so they took him below and chained him like a wild animal to the wall.

How long he waited, sweating in the stifling darkness, he did not know. A think trickle of radiance seeped in past the warped bars sealing the opening. The light strengthened. It glowed now outside the bars. Odan screwed up his eyes and stared, sparks in his eyes, water running on his cheeks.

A common clay lamp, with a twisted wick floating in oil, hung in mid air.

No human hand held that lamp.

A voice, ghostlike, whispering, said: "Come forth, Odan the Khuzuk. Leave your chains, in the name of Aboipheraz and of the lion-lizards. Step ye forth, Odan Crookback!"

And the bronze links fell away and Odan half fell, and began to crawl towards the bronzen bars. They parted like reeds of the banks of The River. He passed through. He stood up. He staggered and then all the harsh training of his youth asserted itself and he was alive again, a savage primeval, able to endure.

He followed the apparition of the lamp. Up slopes of packed dirt, running with water, along narrow corridors, past piles of bones, through low archways. Up stairways of baked brick and stairways of sun-dried brick that rotted and crumbled away. Once he passed a place where a man screamed insanely, and could not stop. The sound of rushing water faded away below. He walked lithely through a room where four guards, stout strapping fellows in their bronze and their brown and yellow, slept. He picked up a spear as he went.

Through a stone-supported arch of brick he padded, following that eerie lamp. A long corridor opened ahead. Along this corridor came a female slave, a lamp in her hand, her face covered with a cloth, and, following her, another wrapped all in a huge black cloak and carrying a basket and a bundle. The spear in Odan's hand pointed suddenly at the throat of the girl with the lamp.

"Silent, girl, or you die."

The second girl gave a gasp. "Odan!"

He looked.

Yes. Yes, this figure swathed all in black, this figure prowling in secret with but a single slave, yes, this was Zenara.

"My princess!"

"Oh—Odan! I heard. They have caught you. Father says—he said horrible things. I am a princess and these things should mean nothing to me. But you, my Odan, have done wicked things."

"I have, my princess. But those days are over."

"I believe you. But they will not. They will kill you!"

He did not laugh; but the light from the two lamps caught in his eyes. "Kill me? With you to succor me? Never!"

"No—that is right. But you must hurry. Here are clothes and food and a rope. Take them, take them. I see you have a spear."

So he had picked up a spear and not a sword. Interesting.

Gently, Odan said: "I thank you, Zenara, light of my life. I must escape. But I will come for you. This I promise by the strength in me, in the name of Odan En-Ke and of Ke and Hekeu."

Suddenly, all unexpectedly, she threw her arms about him. She hugged him close. In the dolorous stinks of the cells he smelled the pure sweet perfume of her. Her body pressed against him, firm and soft.

"I do not understand myself, Odan. So soon, so quick—and yet I know you. We two are one. This I know. I am a fool, a silly credulous girl, even if I am a princess. What mother would say—" She laughed, then, a laugh like a sob. "Put me from you, Odan, my heart. You must go—you must go—"

He put her from him. He stared down into her face.

"Do not think I shall ever forget you, Zenara my beloved. From beyond the grave I will return to you."

She shivered. He bent, swiftly, and kissed her. The lamp in

the hand of the girl slave fell to smash onto the floor. For the other lamp had risen from the floor, had risen of itself, had floated into the air. And a voice said: "Hurry, yourself, Odan, my lad! Guards come and the time runs short! Kiss the princess and have done—and then run, Odan Crookback, run!"

Master Kidu, the king's wizard, was now a man very assured in these days of his strength and power. He could remember very well those early days, and how he had been plagued by the high priest of Zadan, Mnenon-Ket. And of how the king's uncle, Gabal-ayin, had sought always to have him put down, plotting against wizard and against king.

Well, now poor Mnenon-Ket was dead, slain trying to save the young prince whose disappearance remained a mystery. Many men had been tortured to death. No answers had been found. And Gabal-ayin sat with crippled legs and back, still scheming, still plotting; but a cripple, a man doomed, a man forbidden the throne. He plotted now to place his son, the miserable weakling Galad-ayin, upon the throne. Kidu had thwarted more than one plot, more than one palace revolution.

So, although he had promised his old friend Asshurnax, still, wise in the worldly wisdom of his age, Kidu kept a watchful eye on what went on. His grifting followed, observing, seeing the figure of Odan following the projected lamp along the foul dungeon passageways. He saw the meeting with Zenara. Kidu sat back and pulled his long moustache. This was something new.

This could topple thrones, take heads, cause the ranks of impaled soldiers outside devastated cities to call down their gods for just vengeance. This was high politics. He had become more versed in this tiresome business of politics, although still hating chicanery. Give him a good honest enchantment any day.

So now he pondered. Asshurnax had said the boy was a marvel.

There must be something unusual about him—apart from his monstrous size and shape and that hunched stoop of his—to make the princess act like a soft-witted kitchen maid flattered by a randy guardsman. She was promising all kinds of things. She was actually—no, impossible! But she was. The princess Zenara was actually kissing this monstrous lump of savagery.

Kidu had a duty to the king and his family. He could not allow this. The princess, the greatest pearl in the kingdom, throwing herself away on gutter-bred scum! It did not make sense. It was past reason. Unless—A grim and ugly frown settled on Master Kidu's face. Unless an enchantment was in use. By Kurd! That must be it. His duty was now plain.

He would test this young barbarian. He would sound him out, probe him, turn his own inner soul out into the bright sunlight for inspection. No promise to an old friend, even to Asshurnax, could stand before his duty to the king and the city. Didn't old Asshurnax understand *anything*?

Delicately and yet with ruthless power Master Kidu extended a probe of detection. The grifting was a strong and sure source of knowledge. Abruptly, Kidu leaped from the chair, staggering.

The grifting had been caught, turned, hurled back!

The blood thumped in his head. Again he forced the grifting out, furious, compelling. He could sense strange shapes, monstrous forms. He felt the grazing blast of divinity. He felt whirling sensations, unknown experiences—he collapsed over the chair, gasping for breath. But, in those last few moments as the Khuzuk left the princess and ran fleetly along the foul passageway, Kidu had touched infinity and understood.

He was shaking. His face was grey.

But he understood.

He did not know how or why. He only knew this was.

The king!

Queen Momi!

Would they bless him for the news? Or would they blast him with insane oaths? No—this must be done carefully. It would be risking an impalement or a dangle from the battlements should he simply rush in, yelling his news. Softly, softly . . .

The marvel of the revelation came to Kidu and left him. As a practicing thaumaturge his world consisted of marvels; this was a happenstance he must put to the right use, or his head would adorn a spike, for sure, after he had dangled or wriggled.

But, all the same, what had taken place all those years ago, what had intervened, must be marvellous and wonderful and altogether superb!

The little common clay lamp went out.

Through the pitchy darkness Odan heard Asshurnax's voice, coming as though from miles away, echoing and re-echoing like distant thunder among the mountains of Zumer. "Odan, my lad! Brace up—find your way if you can!" And then, the voice grew sharper and spiteful as it waned and vanished. "And is this how you value a promise, Kidu, a friendship? What has Odan done that you—?"

The silence lasted only for three heartbeats. Then a fresh light glowed into life, an orange lambent flame from a golden lamp hung with gems. The light blazed and Odan whirled and the cunning bronze links of the net settled about him. The dark brown jerkins of men closed in. He was thumped—not hard but hard enough. He went limp. The warders picked up the net and slung Odan across a pole. Then they took him up to Master Kidu, the court wizard, a man for whom they entertained the liveliest respect and fear.

"You poor witless loon, Master Asshurnax. Don't you know who he *is*?"

"He is Odan the Khuzuk, Odan Crookback, who is my apprentice and who has been betrayed to the king's mercy by a brother I called friend."

Kidu breathed deeply. His eyrie atop the Tower of Relicts had been freshly spelled to keep out the slightest attempt on privacy. Everything had been painstakingly gone over anew. Now Kidu sat in his great carven chair and brooded on Master Asshurnax, who fretted and fumed and prated about promises.

"So you do not know. Have you probed him?"

"I tried to spell him—the Paralysis from the Book of Abimalaikal the Abhorred, you know the one—and it had no effect. He has always been good to me, and I have not needed to try—"

Kidu punched his fist into the air, opened his fingers wide, as though he sought to grip the vitals of the Oojandhard bird, and let a great sigh burst from him.

"And if I tell you I probed him—as best I could. Mark me that well, my brother. *As best I could*! And me, the king's wizard! He was with the Princess Zenara. That helped, that helped."

"You make a mystery where there is no mystery. Why did

you go back on your word? Can we get Odan out again, now, please."

"No, we can not. He must go before the king and Queen Momi. And, before that, I must tell them. That, I cannot riddle if I should welcome or dread."

"Why?"

"By Kurd, Asshurnax, you must swear by Kurd and Zadan and by Bel-Eresh-Ke, that you will not speak of what I tell you until I release you from your oath."

The lamps flickered. Two corpses in a side room lifted under their shrouds, sitting up stiffly. Lightning broke crimson beyond the window in that rainless land.

"Go back to sleep, lyches," said Kidu, testily.

"Very well," said Asshurnax, with equal acerbity. "I so swear. Now, for the sweet sake of Kurd, tell me!"

"This Odan the Khuzuk, this Odan Crookback, this savage primeval, this is Odan the Half-god, son of Odan En-Ke and the Queen, Momi!"

After a space, Asshurnax whispered: "Poor devil!"

"What? What do you say?"

"Can you not see, brother Kidu?"

"I see many things. Children's loves mean a great deal to them and nothing in the destinies of cities and of kings. I see bleakness ahead unless we plan aright."

"We?"

"Aye, brother Asshurnax. We. Now let us put our heads together."

So they began to plan. Master Asshurnax, for a moment, let his thoughts drift. Odan the Half-god! Incredible. What had happened, then, all those years ago? And, as he had said about the Odan he knew—poor devil. The truth explained much. And Master Kidu was a good man. But he had the destiny of the city and of the king and all his families resting on his shoulders. Asshurnax reflected somberly that he had come to cherish and to rely on Odan. He would do all he could to help him. There was that bastard Gabal and his vicious son Galad to consider. There was the Queen Fretti. There was the high priest, Kephru-Ket. Odan's young feet would be strewn with thorns and traps and devil's tricks. Asshurnax would help—then he realized bitterly—there was no help for Odan the Doomed now.

Chapter Sixteen

In the crocodile pool

The crocodiles bunched hungrily in the pool below him. Their ugly knobbly backs glided this way and that, eagerly. Their enormous foul jaws rose and snapped; their knobbed eyes regarded Odan with great relishing favor. Naked, bound, he stood on the topmost step. At his back the brown-clad executioners waited for the signal from the court chamberlain, old Narpul the Staff.

Narpul had no stomach for these ceremonies any longer. It was time he retired to a little quiet cubby of the palace where he had spent his life and was waited on and doted over by his grandchildren, as was proper. In the meantime, whilst Kephru-Ket the high priest of Zadan intoned prayers and cast incense and besought Zadan of the Sword of his justice, Narpul must fidget and wait until Kephru-Ket finished, the king nodded just the once, and Narpul the Staff could signal to the executioners.

Then this weird being with the monstrous body, stooped-over, with the long arms and the shock of brown hair and muscles more fit for a dagger-tooth lion could be shot over the edge into the pool of sacrifice.

Narpul the Staff could no longer lean over, like everyone else, and draw greedy satisfaction from what went on in the crocodile pool.

Kephru-Ket intoned. The incense smoked into the still hot air. The populace jeered from the far banks of the pool. Most of them were of the merchant class, the rich traders who had suffered at the hands of Odan the Khuzuk and his bazaar pirates. Strong contingents of soldiers stood ready in case a gang attempted a last minute rescue. It was known.

The importance of the bazaar pirates was not over-rated by

the presence of the king. The criminals had waxed powerful of late. This example should cool their ardor. And, as the chief source of justice of his city, the king's duty lay here, and with a heavy hand.

Kephru-Ket ceased. A last handful of incense was cast upon the sacrificial flame. The blue smoke wafted high into the air, puffing past the lofting tiers of the inner wall where the Gate of Sacrifice allowed the waters of The River to enter. The noise subsided. Narpul squinted up at the king.

Neb-ayin-Ke stood with a regal dignity. He had gained weight; his enormous official beard jutted, black and stiff with gold wire and gems. His robes glittered like the sun.

He nodded.

Narpul turned and signalled the executioners.

The executioners took up the bound body of Odan. One slashed through his bonds. Another thrust a knife into his fist.

Then, in a swirling tangle of arms and legs, Odan the Khuzuk, bazaar bandit, hurtled head over heels into the pool of the crocodiles.

"This is a grifting from Sebek-ghal. Fight, Asshurnax! Resist! The fate of all Eresh lies in our hands!"

The walls of Kidu's eyrie wavered eerily. Black smoke puffed, thick and choking, within his chambers. A shrill and nerve-thrilling and yet consciously unheard vibration tingled all about the two master wizards as they fought the enchantment sent by Master Sebek-ghal from far Endal. They fought.

From the wraiths of black smoke gruesome forms flashed. Giant crocodiles, hissing snakes, panting dragons, horde after horde of eerie demons belched from the smoke.

Open on his knees Kidu held the scroll of Daimonidas.

Grasping the Staff of Light, Asshurnax pressed close to his friend. Together they chanted the requisite spell to counter each apparition. Each time a grifting appeared they countered. Their bodies ached. Sweat ran down in streams. Their eyes grew dim and their ears dull. They trembled. And all the time the eyrie shook and shimmered like a mirage of the desert.

"It would have to come now!" swore Kidu. "By Kurd—" And here he sent the vicious form of a phantom eagle to snatch up a clutch of serpents wriggling from the black cloud. "Those devils in Endal—they wait and plan and then they strike—"

"Aye!" Asshurnax held himself up; but his will was failing. He was old and frail. He could not last out much longer. "They strike just as the king is sending Odan to the crocodile pool!"

"Hold on, Asshurnax. It is for the city we fight now, not just for one man!"

"But that one man—could this attack from the devils of Endal be caused by the revelation about Odan? Could it?"

"How? My eyrie is sealed well, as you know."

A griffin appeared and was whiffed away. A loathesome stench began, making the wizards choke; a spell cleansed the air although the black smoke remained, powerful, belching phantom horrors that could kill.

"Others could have been watching, as you were, Kidu. Another grifting could have witnessed my attempt to free Odan. And, witnessing"—here Asshurnax broke off to join in a chant that drove back a ghastly milk-white specter that advanced with clawing arms and leering, diseased face, blazing scarlet eyes hungry for their destruction. "And, witnessing, understood also."

"It is possible. And, if so—"

At once both wizards saw the answer and the solution.

Together, they bent all the strength of which they were capable into a powerful, horrific grifting. The mages combined and hurled their force. Clear across Eresh hurtled that supernal cloud of wrath. Around the ebon tower of Chaimbal it settled, clawing, screeching, breaking down sealing spells with the soundless noise of thunder.

Within his chamber Chaimbal cowered, aghast at the demons conjured. He resisted. But as he resisted so the link he had established with Sebek-ghal in Endal attenuated and faded.

At once the black cloud of smoke in Kidu's eyrie thinned. It whirled, a last cloud of frogs descended and were consumed by fire, and the eyrie was once more still, once more its old self.

In his eyrie atop his ebon tower Chaimbal sagged back, sweating, swearing, gasping with effort, cursing the wizards in the palace, and already thinking up excuses for Sebek-ghal.

"There is no time to tell the king," cried Asshurnax. "We must act now, Kidu, now!"

"As you have faith in that young man, Asshurnax, so I have faith, also. We will act together, in concert, and—at once!"

Tumbling head over heels Odan sprawled down towards the pool of the crocodiles. As he span he looked down, and then at the crowds, and then up, and then at the king, and so down again.

As he glared madly upwards he saw a brilliant fire burn across the heavens. Glowing like a second sun, brilliant, that supernal fire drew near and then, abruptly, as though withdrawn behind a black sheet, the heavenly fire vanished.

Odan struck the surface of the water and plunged instantly for the bottom.

The thought obsessing him all the time he had been cooped up awaiting his execution had been that of profound gratitude and relief that Zenara had been sent out of the city on a visit, that she did not know of his second arrest and condemnation.

He might die, now; but he would fight as a Hekeu fought before they chopped him up.

Vast reptilian shapes moved above him. There were at least five of the monsters. They swung down, jostling. He could hold his breath for a long time; but even all his vicious training as a Hekeu in the lakes of Zumer could not make him breathe under water. That was reserved for gods and madmen, craving death.

A dirty grey belly swung above him. From the side he saw the foreshortened head, snouting, the long narrow jaws gaping. He drove for the belly above him, hooked on, drove the knife savagely where he had been taught. In the sudden smother of blood roiling the water he dived away, slanting down, almost running over the nose of another crocodile. He kicked off. He hit the beast's snout with both feet and sprang up through the water. As he went so he span, avoiding a rush from yet another reptile. The harsh skin scraped past. He slid the knife in; but a hacking blow from a clawed foot drove his arm away. He did not drop the knife.

The monster who was dying had taken the attention of two of the others. There must be a few more heartbeats of air left in his lungs. His head felt as though it would burst in the close confinement of the water; but he must try, he must try . . .

He went after the croc who had rolled past, dived beneath it, saw the vicious tail flick and only just avoided the full force of the blow. He was sent flailing through the water with an enormous smashing pain in his side. He did not drop the knife.

As savage and as vicious as the crocodiles, Odan the Hekeu forced himself back, He got within range and plunged the knife in deeply under the foreleg. The croc span like a mad thing. This time as the blood poured out the knife was wrenched bodily from Odan's hand.

Spots jumped crazily before his eyes. His lungs were on fire, giant bands constricting about his chest. He kicked and soared to the surface. Before he broke surface he doubled, fighting the wracking pains, looked.

The last crocodile was arrowing up for him. It would take his legs as he breathed.

Why couldn't the fool thing go after the wounded croc as its two brothers had done after theirs?

Odan forced himself to skim along just below the surface, parallel. He stuck his head out of the surface. He was barely aware of the sun and the noise. He sucked air and went around and down, doubling, reversing, without looking.

He felt the enormous rush past his body, the sensation of a great serrated bulk whooshing past. He saw. He saw the croc's side going past, the tail would be coming around to smash him—now—

He went down and came up again in a long semi-circular curve, twisting his body. He came up alongside the croc. He put one leg over the scaly back just abaft the head and he got his arms around those cruel and jagged jaws.

He compressed all that vicious power.

A crocodile could chop through flesh and bone, through bronze, through anything, if it closed those massive jaws. But to open them—even a small lad could hold a crocodile's jaws shut. Odan clamped the jaws shut and hung on as the beast went berserk.

How long this could go on for he did not know. All he knew was that a Zuman of the Hekeu totem would not give in before a stupid brainless crocodile.

The water boiled white. Enormous splashings broke the surface and died away again in a long descending trail of green bubbles. The crowds were insane with excitement. The king came forward three regal steps to gain a better view.

Old Narpul the Staff looked down, and marvelled, and then looked away. There could only be one end to this, no matter how savage and strong this wild man of the north might be.

Swirling over and over, attempting to drag the crocodile to the edge of the pool, Odan saw the other two monsters leaving the body of the first to be killed. Now they would come for him. Now, indeed, it was over.

This was the end.

Abruptly, so that his arms clashed together, he was grasping a frog. As it leaped away his first shocked thought was to attempt to enter the body of the frog. But then, if his ka did get into the frog, his real body would drift down and if it was not drowned the two crocs below would chew him up. He looked down again, and was just in time to see two frogs desperately flailing their way upwards through the water.

Crocodiles! Frogs!

Master Asshurnax!

Odan swam to the surface and curiously surveyed the king and his ministers and the populace. He paddled cautiously to the lowest step. He climbed out. He stretched that magnificent body, fighting the permanent stoop in his back, the hunching of his shoulders. Water dripped from him. He looked a superb, gigantic pagan from the bleak wastes of the north, savage, primordial, indestructible.

The crowd fell silent.

Odan looked at them, and his head went up as his shoulders hunched forward. He glared balefully upon them. Already he marked the way to run, the weapon to seize, the wall to scale . . .

Here came two figures running—one running and helping the other along, who tottered and staggered as he fought for breath to run.

The king turned, displeased, his regal face severe.

"And is this your work, Master Kidu?"

Kidu made the requisite obeisance.

"It is my work, oh, king live for ever!" They were in public. Protocol, discipline, the divine and the kingly and the sorcerous must work in strict and demanding codes of conduct in public, exposed to the vulgar gaze. "My handiwork, O great king, whose name be praised."

Then, stepping closer, so that the guards and the priests bristled, Kidu said in that voice reserved for their private moments together: "King, there is a matter that must be told to you." Lifting his voice, he shouted: "We have been attacked by the devils of Endal. They have sent a grifting." As a stir began and people began to scream Kidu lifted his arms. "Fear not! The danger is past. But the devils of Endal, may their livers rot in eternity, have attempted to destroy this Odan the Khuzuk. See how we requite the devils of Endal—"

The king was no man to brook delay. He shouted in his brazen voice: "Kephru-Ket, high priest of Zadan the All Glorious! Attend me. Narpul the Staff. Close down the ceremony. Have this Odan sent to me. Send the people away—with my blessing, with my blessing. As you value your tripes."

Odan was seized up. Asshurnax had hurried to him.

"Do not resist, Odan! There is news—I cannot tell you. Come with us and all will be explained. Although," and here Asshurnax shook his old head. "Although explanations will not help in the slightest."

For the next fortnight Odan the Half-god lay in a feverish stupor. He could only be fed by force. He sweated and grew thin. He moaned and tore his coverlets to pieces. He attacked the guards. He groaned and writhed and blood poured from his nostrils and mouth. He wasted away.

"What ails my son?" demanded Momi. Always, she visited him and sat by his pallet for hours on end. She could scarcely believe, and yet she knew, in her heart, that this great and beautiful young man was her true son, little Odan, grown, her own boy. Yet, piteously, she said: "What ails him? He is back with his mother and with the king who is his father, as Odan En-Ke commanded."

The king rejoiced that his son was returned from the dead.

As for Queen Fretti and her boy; that problem would be faced knowing that problems lay ahead like a thorny thicket. But, for now, rejoice! Rejoice! For Odan the Half-god is alive and with his family—

And Odan lay and sickened and would not eat. He wasted away, and none there were who could—or would—say the reason.

Asshurnax sought out Master Kidu.

"No, Asshurnax. My counsel is to keep our counsel. I am relieved that the king whose name be praised welcomes back his son. Queen Fretti's boy will cause trouble, never you fear; but I know things about that boy the king had best not learn.

Until," added Kidu, reflectively, versed in politics. "Until such time as I choose."

"I do not wish to know. But if Momi the Queen, the most gracious lady in all the land of Ea, could be told she would understand and would help—"

"No one can help, now. Although," said Master Kidu, scratching his chin, "men said an enormous star was observed in the sky as Odan was about to be sacrificed in the pool of crocodiles. Mayhap, Odan En-Ke can help."

"I will to his temple at once. A bullock. Two bullocks. Gold and silver—I will pray—spell for me, Kidu, my friend. Send an enchantment to aid me in this."

"Oh," said Master Kidu. "It is not wise to mix sorcery with religion. The two are too strong medicine, one for the other. But I will pray for you to Zadan of the Sword."

"Pray for Odan. Pray to Kurd."

"Very well. I will pray for Odan the Half-god to Kurd."

Chapter Seventeen

"Farewell, my own lord."

Two days after Master Asshurnax sacrificed to Odan En-Ke and Master Kidu sacrificed—not with bullocks but in the sorcerer's fashion—to Kurd, the Unnameable, and the king and his ministers and all the priests and people sacrificed to Zadan the All Glorious, Zadan of the Sword, the god of Eresh, Odan the Half-god who had been Odan the Khuzuk and who remained Odan Crookback, rose from his sickbed and washed and dressed and ate a meal and said: "I will go up to Dilpur and see my sister."

Overjoyed at her newly-found son's recovery, Momi clapped her hands together.

"Yes, my son. Your sister will rejoice that her brother that was dead is alive! And I shall go with you, for I love you so, and cannot bear to let you from the sight of my eyes."

And Odan, who found he loved this regal and still incredibly lovely woman, said: "I want you near me—mother. Mother. It is strange—And the king?"

"You may call him father, as you used to do, in the old days."

"But he is not my father."

"Your father commanded it. King Neb-ayin-Ke has been a father to you, until—until—"

"Yes. I must learn what happened."

"Well, my dear, now you are home again it has all turned out for the best."

Odan swung away, knocking over a priceless jar from the pottery cities of the south. He could barely see. "Yes. It is all for the best. I must see my sister."

"You shall, my dear, you shall as fast as our barge can row."

Why he felt as he did, Odan could not explain. He had wanted to die. He had simply wished not to live in a world in which Zenara was denied him. But he felt detached, as though some force had removed a part of his will that was dark with horror. The horror remained; but now it was directed outward. He no longer wished to die. Now he wished to see Zenara and tell her, explain—try to explain—and help her in her own agony.

The barge proved to be sumptuous, magnificent, furnished with all the things required by a king. Odan barely noticed. The oarsmen pulled up against the current. The River looked marvelous, as always; Odan sat hunched, brooding.

"Can you not sit up, my dear?" said Momi. "All crouched over like that. It is not good for your lungs."

The king had not accompanied them. He was concerned over the onslaught from Endal to the south and was concocting plans. Chaimbal had fled from his ebon tower and no doubt was closeted with the devils from Endal, plotting fresh mischief.

So it was left to Asshurnax, who was asked to go with the party, to say to the queen: "Your pardon, my queen whose beauty shames the dawn. With a chest of the size and nature of the one possessed by Prince Odan, he has room enough to store away two sets of normal men's lungs."

Momi favored Asshurnax with a glance, and folded her hands in her lap, and accepted a date stuffed with honey proffered by one of her handmaids.

"Yes," she said when she had swallowed. "But he should still sit with his back straight. I wish I had been able to train him. I'm sure they must have neglected him dreadfully."

"Oh," said Odan. "The Hekeu have a way of training."

Privately, the vicar of Zadan, released by the high priest to go with the queen, said to his confidant: "Had the prince stayed in Eresh he'd have been the worst disaster to hit the city since the Great Floods. Now, at the least, he is a man."

Through it all, Odan remained eerily aloof, as though he still roamed the far hills of Zumer, or swaggered in the riverside taverns with Nadjul, or ran with the bazaar bandits in Karkaniz or Eresh. He had prayed so much to his father, Odan En-Ke, that he felt sure this uncanny calm must be the answer. At least, he was not mad. Or, not more mad than ever he had been. Yes, his father, the god Odan En-Ke, had reached out a finger and cleansed the horrors and left him empty, hollow, a mere man of the city with nothing in life.

King Norgash of Dilpur made the correct and polite form of parting, his hands together, as the lord Andan and his son, Ankidu, left the audience. It was proper that a visiting lord should bring his son, the young lord to be, to pay his respects to the king of a city in alliance with that lord's city. But Norgash of Dilpur turned away as soon as the chamberlains bowed themselves out. He was shaking with anger.

"Fretti!" he called, and the tone of his voice made his daughter run in, swiftly, meekly, as was proper. Fretti had aged in the years since she had married Neb-ayin-Ke, King of Eresh. She still loved the king, of course; and, she felt sure, he loved her still in return. But, now, this news, ghastly, undreamed of, horrible!

"If you do not plan with great care, Fretti my daughter, Queen of Eresh, you will be cast off. Now this god's bastard has returned—" Norgash dripped spittle. Everything had been perfect—and now, this!

"I have invested too much in this son of yours, my Fretti. Numutef is a poltroon, a ne'er-do-well, a disgrace—and yet he is your son and my grandson—"

"Blame his vices upon his father!" flared Fretti, goaded. "Whoever he was!"

"Daughter! Silence! That is a subject never to be discussed. Never."

"I hear, my father," said Queen Fretti, abruptly cowed. She felt a chill of fear. If Neb-Ke ever found out! The nightly procession of men, creeping secretly to her chamber, her father's grim guards slaughtering each one as he consummated his orders—and which one was the father only Ke himself could say. But out of the hideous experience of degradation and shame a son had been born to Fretti—and King Neb-ayin-Ke had rejoiced exceedingly, seeing that his eldest son, the god's son, was gone.

And now the bastard had returned!

Norgash stood with wrinkled brow, his hand to his lips, plotting. He spoke as the gravel shifts in a badly-loaded barge of The River.

"I have many years left to me, in the hands of Redul and of Lufali. Those years will be spent as king of Dilpur and grandfather to the king of Eresh. Nothing must stand in the way. Nothing."

He did not say aloud that once Neb-ayin-Ke was dead Numutef, the fruit of an unknown father, would quickly follow him, and Norgash would be king of Eresh and Dilpur. That was ordained in the stars. Shadophernes, his favorite astrologer, had promised him. There could be no mistake. He savored the names in his heart. Norgash, King of Eresh and Dilpur . . .

"And you are my brother," said Zenara.

"And you are my sister," said Odan.

"Truly," said Zenara, and she swayed and sank down upon a cushion-strewn bench in her private chambers in King Norgash's palace in Dilpur. "Truly, the gods mock us!"

"Aye! The gods make sport of us. I would tear them down from their airy palaces, drive them deeply underground to the seven hells. I have no more truck with gods. And yet—and yet I think the finger of Odan En-Ke has reached out and touched me. For I thought I would go mad, and die, for love of you, my Zenara. And yet I am whole, and live and breathe, and can walk and talk as any mortal man. And yet my heart is dead within my breast."

"I have no heart, for it is all melted away." Zenara had not touched Odan and he had kept well away from her. "Perhaps Ke or Zadan has touched me, for I feel the same as you do. I am numb, dead, paralysed. There is nothing left to say."

"Nothing save I shall always love you, Zenara, my sister. My rage against the gods, against fate, against whatever dark and malign forces have made a mockery of my life—that rage burns me, dead though I am."

"Do not struggle hopelessly, my love."

"And you are my sister and I may not call you my love."

"No, Odan. You are right. I am thoughtless."

The agony knifed Odan. He stared at her, at her downdrooping head, the curve of her cheek, her eyelashes, the tears wet and warm upon her pale cheek. "You are my love and I hurl the words proudly in the face of our destiny. Yet must we part. There will be no peace for us. Not ever again in this whole wide world."

"Never."

"My heart, which is dead, burns for you, Zenara. I cringe at your sorrow, at your agony. Your sufferings cause my suffering ten-times over." He was shaking, and he clasped his hands together, twisting and gripping—uselessly. "I can offer you no hope, no cheer, no false words of comfort. All I can say to you, Zenara, my princess, my love, my only heart, my true beloved is—farewell."

"Farewell, my brother—farewell, my own lord."

In the secret passage within the thickness of the walls Norgash the king of Dilpur listened and stroked his beard. So that was the way of it! The dirty little perverts! This was a great and wonderful secret. There was much to be made of this.

Yes, decided Norgash, yes. This secret knowledge gave him power. This was a giant stride on the road to his own glory. Yes, by Lufali! Here was the key to open the throne to his own vaulting ambition . . .

There was a rottenness in the stench of The River in Odan's nostrils in those days. He did not know what he should do. He was lost, adrift like the wights in the stories, alone and forsaken upon the Salt Sea. He drifted.

Perhaps in all that evil time he drew most enjoyment atavistically in bashing with his wooden sword at young Ankidu, son of the lord Andan of Eresh. The two spent hours together in a small sandy space within the walled enclosure of the palace. There was never a hope for Ankidu that he would best Odan; but he tried nobly, prancing and swishing and sweating and panting.

He was a lithe, limber young fellow, this Ankidu, with a round cheerful face and keen bright eyes, his shock of jetty hair confined in a band like Odan's. His father was a rich man, wealthy in the phenomenal fashion of the lords of Eresh, and yet Ankidu remained untouched by the vices common to his station.

Denied Zenara and therefore, for the moment, finished with all women, Odan turned to male companionship and the sweating muscular exertion of bodies forced in exercises and swordplay to strive until they flagged, until the blessed oblivion of sleep drugged all his tortured senses.

He found Ankidu to be a good companion, and on the day they had a scrape with a desert lion, their chariot horses bounding terrified, Odan pitching from the bucking car and lying winded on the sand, the lion snarling and getting set to spring, Odan discovered a little more of what friendship meant.

For Ankidu swirled the chariot in a wide swathe of wheel-spinning dust. He drove back like a maniac, his whip flashing. Straight for the lion he forced the horses, lashing them unmercifully. They reared and then stampeded. Chariot and lion collided in a spitting smother of sand and timber, of dismembered wheels and of terrified horses bolting. Odan sprang. He snatched up Ankidu and then, seizing a heavy spear from the wreck of the car he hurled it true. The lion shrieked and span about, clawing at the deadly barb, spat and died.

Ankidu breathed in a shaky breath.

"By Anki!" said Odan. "You are a man, my friend."

He did not say that he could have no real problem with a mere desert lion. He still had his knife. One of the Hekeu would scarcely bother over a great cat with a keen bronze blade in his fist. But Odan, for all his primeval savagery, recognized the gallantry in what Ankidu had done. The young lord had attempted to save the life of the prince at the cost of his own.

"You are well named, Ankidu. I knew a swordsman—once—whose god was Anki. You would have liked him—as he you."

"I am overjoyed that my prince is still alive."

"Ump. And so am I—" And, with that, thinking he lied, Odan the Khuzuk saw he spoke the truth. Survival. That was the test. Despite Zenara, he must survive. Doomed, yes, he was doomed in life. But he felt sure there was a work set to his hand before he went to the seven hells.

With the majority of the other young lords of Eresh he found a hidden mockery, a sense of contempt, a rude refusal to recognize in his boorish form the true prince of Eresh. Yet he was the son of Odan En-Ke. He was no changeling. The wizards and the high priest had confirmed the truth. So Odan was grudgingly accepted, and snubbed whenever it was safe, and after he had near broken the backs of a couple of the chief mockers, a chilling silence greeted his entrances.

He was not welcomed in Eresh by the young bloods.

His savagery put their own city-bred qualities to shame. And, yet, his own city cunning, learned as a bazaar bandit, gave him the equality anywhere in the city apart from the palace. Only with Ankidu could he feel at ease.

The day came when the high priest, Kephru-Ket, went up to the Ziggurat of Zadan the All Glorious to give thanks. A great plague had broken out in Endal. No one doubted—Odan, who understood a little of the supernal power of Zadan, did not doubt—that Zadan had inflicted a punishment on the hated rival city for their presumption in attacking the wizards of Eresh and of attempting to prevent them saving the young prince.

Zadan, it was known, it was proven, was a great and puissant god. He was a new god, his chariot of fire was seen in the heavens, his hands were made manifest in deeds throughout the city state of Eresh. Zadan was immanent in all things.

Downstream the cities would be closing their water gates and opening certain channels so that the bloated corpses might float freely past their walls and not bring the pestilence upon them. Right to the Delta on the Sweet Sea the corpses would drift. Then they would rot and decompose and so give sustenance to the lands fringing the coasts of the sea.

So it was inevitable, when the last news of the plague said that Endal, although weakened, would survive, that Odan should decide to make the pilgrimage to Shanadul. He would visit the birthplace of Nadjul the Quick, and offer a sacrifice and set up an inscription.

The day before he told the king, Asshurnax, who had remained at his eyrie in Yellow Lotus Street, called on him. Odan had given orders to the guards that the old thaumaturge was always to be admitted immediately. He saw his old master to a seat and had a slave pour wine and called a water-wench for water to bathe Asshurnax's feet which were somewhat blistered. He regarded the old wizard with great favor.

"And, my lad—that is, my prince—I have a thought I would not impart to you; but one I feel I must, for you have wisdom past your years, and will see the true path."

"Speak on, Asshurnax."

"You are the son of a god. That is beyond dispute. Both Master Kidu and I can testify to that truth. It explains much; why you resisted spells, why you have the powers you have—powers you may expand and cause to grow." He looked up, like a crane, twisting his neck, as the water wench laved his feet. "You have been studying, still?"

"Yes. Master Kidu spends an hour a day with me. And I

have been working on Balniodor's invisibility. It is coming. I work. It takes away the boredom of this life."

"Yes, well. It would seem, Odan, that you are only half a god." Asshurnax mumbled about, taking a long time to come to the nub of what he had to say. And, then, and the words broke in glory about Odan's ears, he said: "I think if you studied and found the right masters you could become a whole god."

"A whole god? A real god?"

"Aye!"

"By Odan! Is this possible?" Odan started up, his face flushing, his eyes starting from his head. "You do not mock?"

"It is a chancy business, mocking even a half-god, Odan, as I have heard and you know full well."

"Then this thing is possible?"

"It is possible. There are ancient scrolls. But there is danger. The gods might hurl you down. But, then, again they may not. You know of the Myth of Abak?"

"I know of the Myth of Abak."*

"Then you know the truth. I can point you in the right direction. After that it will be on your head. Your destiny is your own."

But Odan's thoughts had winged far beyond his master's words. He saw—in a flash as of the lightning striking between two peaks in the mountains of Zumer—he saw.

The unholy hunger burned in him. Sacrilegious, illicit—it might be all these things. But Odan the Half-god saw the promise, he saw the prospect opening before him, and his mind was made up even as old Asshurnax spoke on.

"Odan the Khuzuk. You can become a god. I warn you—the blasphemy is possible, always possible. The dangers will imperil your ka. You may fail and be chained in the deepest depths of the seven hells for all eternity. I faint at what I may have brought upon you. But—it is possible. It is a thing you can do."

"Yes. I can do it! Odan the Khuzuk can become a god!"

* 'The Myth of Abak' is to be published as Appendix A to Book Two of the Odan Trilogy, *Whetted Bronze.*

Chapter Eighteen

Worms

"Shanadul!" said the king, waving away a courtier who brought a petition traditionally inscribed on a clay tablet and baked into hardness. "Later, later—Shanadul," he said again to Odan who stood with compressed lips beside the broad table of state. Morning sunshine slanted in through the window of the tower and from far below the scurry and bustle of the palace reached them with a muted bee-song droning. The chariotry were due for an airing across the desert this day and Ankidu had insisted he take Odan with him. Odan's chariot-work needed to be sharpened up if he was, one day, to be king.

"Aye, king—father. I have a debt to pay there. And I am sick and tired of the hollowness of life in the palace."

Neb-ayin-Ke leaned back in his charismatic seat. He frowned. "Now, by Zadan the All Glorious! Do I not know that life is often boring. But, my son, if you would be king there is much you must learn. And one is to dissimulate unpleasant information."

"You would wish me to lie to you?"

"No, no!" The king stroked his chin. He still refused to grow a beard and donned the various official tufts of hair with their variegated gold and jewels for each necessary function. "No, you imp—you are the son of a god and you do not have to chop words with me. Why do you wish to go to Shanadul?"

So Odan lied.

"I have a debt to pay to an old friend, an inscription to raise, a sacrifice to make. And, too, it is needful, if I am to be a king worthy to follow you, that I should know what lies beyond the Eastern Gate, along the Golden Road to Shanadul."

"You learn, I observe. But an inscription and a sacrifice—they are profound reasons. But I like your second better."

So it was arranged.

Chasing in sheets of riven sand across the desert, Odan managed to stay in the bucking bounding chariot and lash on the two horses. He enjoyed this chariotry. Later, bathing the sweats and stinks away, with the bath-wenches scrubbing their backs and the sweet perfumes in their nostrils, Odan said to Ankidu: "It is settled. I am for Shanadul in three days."

"And I, too!"

"I welcome you, Ankidu. We will be a small party, incognito, and inconspicuous."

"They say the belly-dancers of Shanadul can enchant a man."

"Girls mean nothing to me—" began Odan. Then, cautiously, he changed that, and said: "I await the perfect girl, Ankidu."

"I have found mine, my prince. But she is far beyond me, and so I grieve not; but enjoy myself and carry her image in my heart, pure and undefiled. Although, should any man not worthy of her attempt her or, even marry her against her will, I shall surely slay him—and with joy."

Odan was far too intemperate to bother his head about Ankidu's unhappy love affairs. They busied themselves in the next two days in preparations for the journey, and then they set forth from the East Gate of Eresh upon the Golden Road to Shanadul.

Odan kept a careful watch in the place of assembly for any man with a large and ugly wart upon his left hand. He did not see man or wart.

By now his purely automatic look at the left hand of every man he met was a mere part of his life; but when he saw that wart and recognized it as the same—then routine would take a new and frightful form.

The way stretched across the golden desert. Their chariots rode easily and lightly, for strings of asses carried their dunnage, and of water they carried many skin bags, the hair turned out and the water a rich wine-red color from the tanning. The stars burned with a fat and closer luster. The air burned during the day and bit at night. But, here in the desert, Odan found a strange and trance-like easiness stealing upon him. There would be a life for him. Once he was a god he could—and then his blasphemous thoughts coiled inwards, and he would go to sleep with a fierce and savage rictus of his lips. No, he was not a happy man—but, then, he was not a man. He was only half a man.

Shanadul proved to be a city entirely different from those with which Odan was familiar. Cities of The River were shaped by the broad watercourse. Here on the coast of the Sweet Sea the city of Shanadul occupied low hills around a bay. The views were breathtaking. Odan joyed in everything, because he came every day nearer and nearer his goal. He did all that he had promised. He found Nadjul the Quick's birthplace and sorrowed to learn his family were all passed away. He set up a fine stone inscription, which read in part: 'The Greatest Swordsman to travel The River, beloved by all he met, faithful unto death.' And, again: 'This is erected in memory of his friend by Odan, Prince of Eresh. Hail to Anki! Hail to Zadan! Hail to Ke!'

Looking on, smiling a sympathetic smile, Ankidu said: "You do not have the stone mason inscribe the name of Odan En-Ke, my prince."

"I thought—I did not wish to presume on Nadjul. He was a very fierce swordsman and gave me many bruises."

"He would have wished it, Odan."

"Then, as I am a Hekeu, I will risk it! Ho, Mason—take your tools and inscribe, there, Hail to Odan En-Ke." He frowned, very fiercely. "And mind you include the En-Ke. That is important."

"Yes, master," said the mason, scared half-witless.

The scribe for the masons was summoned in all haste, and told, and marked with his chalk the way the words should go. Then the mason started in to cut around the lines. He could not read. But he could chisel the most perfect line in stone. Each to his skill.

Four bullocks were sacrificed, one to each god. The place in its little dell on a green hillside overlooking the bay would have pleased Nadjul. Odan did all that was necessary, and prayed the gods that Nadjul enjoyed much beer and wine, many pretty girls, and a good skirling sword fight every now and then to keep the muscles young and limber. He stood up. He stepped back.

Smiling, Ankidu followed him down towards their chariots.

"And now the fleshpots, my prince! The belly-dancers! The wine!"

There was no doubt the prospect tempted, for Odan was still a hot man with the lusts burning in him strongly. But the lust to be a god overbore any other.

"Do you go on, friend Ankidu. I have a certain business. And, mark me well. No word of this is to reach the ears of the king or the ministers or the priests. Understood?"

That last barked word brought Ankidu up, quivering.

"Aye, my prince. Understood."

"Then I shall meet you in the palace in the morning." The King of Shanadul had welcomed them, as was proper. Odan would find his way back, after he had fought to a new destiny.

So he took himself off, away from the city, driving his chariot and pair with a reckless disregard for his safety and for the welfare of the travellers he met on the road.

Ankidu looked after him, and sighed.

"He may be a prince and he may be a half-god; but he is a man driven by demons!"

The necromancer Sjalu of Shanadul possessed but one eye. His left ear was shorn. His scant white locks dribbled about his grey scalp. But he held onto the bucking chariot with a firm enough grip, clasping a scroll under his other arm. Odan had picked him up at the spot he had expected, Asshurnax's grifting having arranged the meeting with perfect ease.

"You turn off into the forest here, prince," said Sjalu. "The way is infernal dark."

"It is with darkness that you traffic now, Odan the Half-god."

"I will traffic with all the demons in Endal to gain my heart's desire!"

He had sense enough to let the horses find their own way among the trees. All the bright sunlight seemed cut off, as though hesitating to enter the gloomy spaces beneath the trees. Sounds grew thin. Odan saw none of the familiar woodland creatures he expected. A dankness grew clammily in the air.

"A far cry from your deserts, prince."

It was a far cry from the forests of Zumer, also; but Odan maintained silence. He had learned how to retain a dignified silence during boring proceedings in the multitude of enormous functions his return had conjured forth in Eresh. He had sat through speeches, ridden his chariot in processions, listened to priests chanting. The life of a king would have to change, when Odan, if he ever did, sat on the throne of Eresh.

"It is not far now, prince. The Oracle may be summoned if the spells requisite are known. This I can do for you, out of friendship for Master Asshurnax. Once I have performed my part you must walk forward alone."

Whilst perfectly ready to go into the mouth of hell to gain his godhood, Odan turned a frowning face upon Master Sjalu. "You do not accompany me?"

Master Sjalu closed his one good eye. "No, prince."

Well, it was of no moment. And what Odan wished to ask was better asked in privacy. His plans must be kept a close secret until he could burst upon the land of Ea with everything fulfilled.

The trees thinned a little up ahead; but there came no corresponding lightening of the shade. Rocks struck through the soil, harsh and grey, grotesque, twisted by unthinkable forces into shapes that made Odan's eyes water. The horses blew and curvetted, and stopped, and would not go on. Sjalu hopped down from the chariot. He squatted down and made his preparations and then opened the scroll. His one eye fixed on the papyrus. He looked like a crouched gnome, dark and evil and beyond the knowledge of this world. But, Odan reflected, the necromancer was working for him, and would be paid in gold.

This was the famous—or infamous—Oracle of Shajemish-tu. Mortal folk dared patronize her powers only at the last extreme. She trafficked in the main with sorcerers, wizards who sought her out for the puissant powers she conjured, thaumaturges who consulted her in matters of mind-warping horror. She was known as the Raven.

As Odan walked slowly forward, with Sjalu continuing to weave his intercessions at his rear, three large and heavy black birds rose silently into the air from the rocks. The ravens flew with strong wingbeats, their feathers dull in the shadows, vanished. Odan strode on. He came to the narrow cleft in the rocks Sjalu had told him to look for. Here stood a tripod on which balanced a golden bowl. Odan took the purse from his belt and dropped it into the bowl. Gold chinked against gold.

As Sjalu had instructed, he cried out: "Raven! I, Odan, stand before you and seek the favor of your supernatural guidance! Hear me, Raven. Hear me and condescend."

One story told how a man had done all these things, and a tongue of smoke and flame had hissed from the rocks and consumed him utterly.

Odan stood, his powerful form half-stooped, his hand on his sword hilt, his magnificent head lifted, glaring into the slot of darkness.

Movement writhed in the darkness. A sparkling luminosity that coiled and vanished and grew and smoked upwards. Pale smoke like ivory shavings gyrated in the darkness. The smoke thickened. Odan caught his breath. A beautiful woman stood on the threshold of the rock. Dazzled, Odan gazed. Yes—yes! She was like Zenara! That face, that graceful form, that hair—yes, this was a ghostly simulacrum of his beloved Zenara—A voice whispered.

"I hear you, Odan the Khuzuk. I incline to your request."

Odan swallowed down. The darkness thickened about him; but the form of the woman who looked like Zenara but was not Zenara limned in a crystalline light. The voice whispered, syrup sweet, cajoling, reminding, demanding.

"You come to me seeking that which is forbidden."

"Not so, Raven, not so." Speaking was difficult. He knew a mistake, a fault on his part, could result in an agonizing death. These were the risks he ran. Sjalu would not—could not—help. "I am the son of a god. This is proved. I would learn the secrets of attaining full godhood. I am—"

"You are a god-less fool to meddle."

"I am a fool, yes. But I am not god-less. Can you unravel to me the secrets?" And here some of his Hekeu training made his voice lift, his head jut arrogantly. "Yes or no?"

A hiss greeted this. "Softly, softly. You speak as a man speaks who seeks to have his ka parted from his body. Do you not know of my powers?"

"I would not be here if I did not. Can you give me the knowledge I must have?"

"You have brought gold. But you have brought no humble spirit, craving benediction."

"I am humble before the gods. You are no god. I am a—"

"You are no half-god, Odan the Khuzuk!"

Stunned, Odan stared. He licked his lips. "What say you?"

The hiss was unmistakable. "I am old, older than you can

imagine. Yet there were those before me, long and long ago, and I know their wisdom. There were men in the land of Ea, great men, near divine in power and wisdom. And then other men came, little men, men like apes, hideous, malformed. These new men believed in the powers of stones and trees, of birds and beasts. They feared the dark and they peopled the heavens with the feeble gods of their own invention."

Odan listened, grasping at the meanings.

"And the great men of whom I speak struck down these puny newcomers with their weapons of flint. And then—and then on a day of woe and grief, a day of disaster for Ea, gods came, real gods, gods in their Dream Chariots. These gods are real, these gods gave to the foul and feeble little men new weapons and new knowledge, so that the great older men were banished from their bright cities, sent to hide and cower in the outer darkness."

The voluptuous white shape of the woman moved sinuously. Odan could see shards of the rock through the phantasm. The smoke thinned and coiled, and then thickened as the voice hissed on.

"And among the new gods, the real gods, came Nirghal and Zadan, came Anki and Lufali, came Tia and Sakhmet." The evil hiss shrilled so that it became almost a laugh, a mocking trill of thin sound, like a swordblade, rustling from the slot of darkness beyond the phantom white figure of the woman. "And the old gods that were the inventions of frightened people—Ke and Setto and the others of whom you know,—you know!—linger on only as the childish superstitions of children in the land."

And Odan the Khuzuk understood. He remained standing, although his limbs were turned to water. He tried to speak, and gasped, and tried again, and said, hoarsely: "And Odan En-Ke! Odan is an old god—"

"You credulous fool! Odan En-Ke does not exist!"

"No! This I do not believe!"

"Your witless beliefs mean nothing. The truth is."

Shocked, Odan reacted with the instinctive, vicious, frightening speed and violence of a Khuzuk. He sprang forward and his sword flamed from the scabbard. Instinctive, his movement, but not thoughtless. And, as he flung himself at the ivory coil of smoke voluptuously writhing in the shape of the most beautiful woman in the land of Ea and the woman denied him, so he felt a vibration through his whole being.

He was barely aware of formulae parading in his thoughts. He just wanted to slash and bash at whatever gruesome form was projecting the illusion of Zenara, was denying him his right to be a demigod.

This blasphemy against his whole life must end.

The hissing voice keened higher. Was there alarm? Alarm at a mere half-god hurling himself forward with lifted sword?

"You vanish from my sight, Odan the Half-god! But you are no true son of a god, you cannot be—and yet I cannot see you!"

The bronze changed color eerily as Odan slashed it through that mocking seductiveness. Zenara, Zenara . . . The smoke wavered and did not resist his blows. He planted his feet wide and thrust through, determined to slay whatever evil lay beyond.

"Now I see you, Khuzuk! You are mad—you cannot stand against my power. You will be sucked down and devoured—"

"You have not blasted me yet with smoke and flame and I do not think you can. I *am* a demigod. And I *will* become a god!"

"And I am old and wise past your comprehension—stand still so that I may see you!"

For Odan, holding himself from the berserk anger that sought to topple his reason in this place of ghosts and shadow, flung himself on with all the primeval power and speed of a savage of the mountains of Zumer.

"You vanish, Odan—and yet—" The hiss shrilled. Now Odan felt a gush of confidence that that old hateful voice betrayed a real and terrible fear.

"Stand still! You have mastered the arcane arts of Balniodor's invisibility. You may run and avoid my eyes; but you must stand still in the end, and then I shall have you."

There was no time for any joyous surge of elation in Odan that he had at last mastered the metaphysical arts of Balniodor. He had time to reflect that it would be useful for the future—assuming he had a chance of escaping from the Raven and having a future—that he could assume invisibility when he moved, only becoming solid to sight again when he remained still, and then he had broken past the ghostly pseudo-Zenara into an ebon bowl among the rocks. He stared about, as the dagger-tooth lion stares about when he is hungry.

"Perhaps," came the Raven's voice, still ahead of him

against the far wall of dark. "Perhaps you are indeed a half-god. Nirghal claimed to have fathered a son, in pursuance of his destiny. Are you Nirghal's son?"

"And you, Raven, do not know?" The mocking taunt in Odan's voice rang with unmistakable scorn.

"I know many things." The wraith-form of Zenara wisped away and vanished. There was need no longer for that phantom between them. "I know the new gods contend perpetually for the supreme power, the highest position. Fools! They struggle one with another, and they use the poor puny tools of mere mortals. It is said that a god will father a son upon a mortal woman and through him will become the supreme god. This is believed by the new gods themselves. But the half-mortal son must die, for the god his father will maintain his power only if his son is ritually sacrificed."

Now the mockery lay all in that hissing bubble of the Raven's voice.

"You would be a god, Odan the Half-god. I have told you the fate reserved for upstarts, half-god, half-human. Do you still wish to seek out your father and be sacrificed for his dreams of grandeur?"

"Nirghal is not my father!" Odan shouted the words, defiant, his mockery stripped from him. "In that you lie, hag!"

"I do not lie. My people have no need of lies with your likes."

Against the far darkness a blue radiance wavered, pulsing, throbbing. Without questioning his knowledge, Odan knew the light as it rippled and squirmed upwards was shot through with evil forces. He knew. He felt his lips rick back from his teeth.

"You bifurcated creature of scorn!" The Raven's voice lashed. "You do not relish the thought that a god spawned you for his own ends. He will use you to take a city or topple a throne or dupe a multitude. And when you bask in your little blaze of glory and he is supreme among the pantheon, he will put you down utterly, and sacrifice you as is ordained, for his own power and glory. Fool!"

"Yes! That is what Nirghal, the god of the devils of Endal, would do! He is the devil himself. But my father is Odan En-Ke and he deals honorably with his people of Eresh. My father will not sacrifice me."

The hissing increased. The blue radiance squirmed and wriggled against the wall, casting a corpse-light upon the rock. Odan hunched forward, his massive head jutting, glaring madly upon the hints of blasphemous forms within the radiance.

"You may believe what you will, human. Nirghal may not be your father—the truth of that is unimportant. But you have had your sport. You have boasted and called down insults—now—" and here the bubbling hissing belched like the sulphurous lakes below Mount Wusuv, bringing Odan quiveringly alive to his own peril. "—Now, human, you must pay."

And, in that moment of supernatural horror when in the next instant demoniac forms and eldritch blasphemies might burst about his head, Odan felt the strong resurgence of his human half. In that terror-filled moment he seized upon the notion, ludicrous and satiric beyond casual dismissal, that many gods might have sired sons upon human women. There might be a whole squadron of Half-gods roaming the land of Ea, searching for their absconding fathers, ready to rush out to glory and death!

No hint of a smile moved his harsh lips. His massive hunched shoulders made an attempt to square themselves, a convulsive rictus of enormous muscles, pulling his back up and thrusting his head out. From under brown-bar eyebrows Odan the Half-god stared challengingly at the goblin blue light.

"You are no human being," he said, his voice grating with the pitch of the moment. "Demon, hell-spawned bitch. I do not fear your sorceries." He spoke in knowledge that Master Asshurnax and Master Kidu had tested him in matters thaumaturgical and found him resistant, like the harsh rock all about.

"It is not upon feeble sorcery that I rely, human." The Raven spoke with that irritating scratching hiss, a fibrillation upon the nerves of a mere mortal, an offence to a half-god. "Prepare yourself for your doom!"

More than ever, with this rhetorical shilly-shallying, Odan became convinced that the Raven had been attempting to exert her powers upon him, and had failed. He could turn around and walk away as though he walked the battlements of fabled Eresh.

There was nothing more to be learned here. He had learned much. He still was not sure what to believe about Odan En-Ke—after all, the reports which he had listened to assiduously had all unanimously testified to the divinity of his birth and of the appearance of Odan En-Ke and his Dream Chariot blazing in the heavens. But, if he was not the son of Odan then he was the son of some other god. He could feel this as a testament in his blood and bones. He was a demigod!

So he turned to leave and he did not move.

There had been no tingling. Nothing to indicate he was in the grip of sorcery had come to warn him. But he could not move.

The hateful laugh bubbled up again like a biliously bursting sulphur pool. There was no smell of sulphur or saltpeter; the Raven had no need for showy blandishments of that kind. Odan bulged his monstrous muscles and did not move. Sorcery came in all manner of guises, he had learned. The little magicians wove their small magics and many of them used up a spell and could not repeat it, constantly searching for new spells to keep in business. Other griftings lasted, for that was one of the subtle distinctions between a common spell and a master's grifting, although they were confused in the lay mind. Had the Raven mastery of the higher thaumaturgies? Odan, struggling futilely, became convinced she had.

"Meet your doom like a man—or a half-god—or a god! It is all one to me." The blue radiance pulsed with the words. A ring formed on the rocky ground around Odan. He stared down. Revulsion caught his stomach. He did not retch; but he felt his gorge rise and he gagged on bile.

Squirming on the rock in a wide circle about him—maggots!

Hundreds—thousands—of wriggling slimy worms, encircling him. At once Odan realized—as he had all along suspected and refused to acknowledge—that the Raven was possessed of gramarye beyond the scope of knowledge he had laboriously forced himself to learn and grasp and seek to understand. Much had come easy to him—this was going to be difficult.

The worms pulsated, slipping and sliding about one another, looping tendrils of glistening pink flesh, slick and slimy, oozing in coils and ropes and squirming masses. He stared, fighting down his revulsion at their sheer numbers, as though all the worms from all the corpses in Ea had wriggled into this constricting ring about him.

Their sizes varied from tiny maggots that rolled and fell and coiled to long sinuous worm-snakes that reared and swung tiny bead-black eyes at him. Their mouths formed suckers, round tubes fibrillating with hunger.

They were legless and armless; but only men needed arms and legs for magical purposes. These worm-people fashioned the higher sorceries with their own arcane knowledge, old before man swung down from the trees.

The worms ate at the rock. They ate inexorably, and rock casts formed beyond them, growing as the rock was gnawed away. A round plate of rock and Odan at its center and the ring of worms biting steadily in towards him. The solid rock under his feet lurched. They were cutting through and when they had freed the plate of rock he would pitch down and down—down to where?

Struggle as he would he could not break the enchantment that gripped him in invisible savage bonds as strong as Zadan's metal.

He wrenched frantically at his thoughts. The worms were not real. They were illusions. They were mere phantoms conjured by the Raven. And she, the bitch, was old, old beyond belief, and yet she had a life span that must end. Her beginnings lay far back in the past. Her people—the worm-people—had owned all the world before humans arrived. She had called him a bifurcated creature. Yes, this Raven, this great Oracle of Sha-jemish-tu, was a worm-woman.

Supernatural horror struggled to grip Odan utterly. The worms were mere illusion, yet they ate at the rock and the rock tilted beneath his feet, lurched and fell away. He plunged down into a smooth walled shaft and as he fell so the worms poured down over him in a regurgitating mass of bloated flesh.

His trapped powers flailed insanely. He conjured gramarye and as he fell, rigid, like a bar, his heart battered his chest. He felt the bonds snapping. He was abruptly changing place—he was in the body of a worm, staring with bead-like eyes upon the massive hunched figure of a man sliding down into the feeding pit. A worm! Odan the Half-god infesting the slimy body of a worm! He fell, tumbling with a hundred, a thousand, of his fellows, falling with a pittering pattering of squashy bodies to the chamber below the rock.

The feel of the sinuous bodies sliding and roping upon him struck through with the shudder of the damned. How each slimy body roiled upon the others! He was a worm in a mass of worms driven blindly by remorseless hunger, driven on to devour and suck away all the rich juices of this body dropped down into the feeding chamber. He would suck! He would eat! He would gorge himself on flesh and blood!

A tug at all his senses shocked through his squirming, coiling, seeking worm body. He understood. The Raven had sensed what he had done and was sending to drag him back to the body in which he would be eaten. Well, he was a man, a half-god, and he would fight with what weapons he had.

He opened his eyes. He was back in his own body.

Did he have any weapons?

Blue radiance illuminated a corner of the chamber. Obscene carvings decorated the walls, parodies of men and women and beasts, pictures of unholy sacrifice, pictures of worms triumphant.

The worms recoiled. He lay breathlessly on the rock and felt his body lift into the air, and transferred by invisible hooks he was deposited upon an obsidian block. He stared upwards as the blue radiance wavered above him.

"You are fit to be eaten, Odan who calls himself the Half-god. But you are too good for the mere servants of the Raven."

Odan saw the blueness pulse, as though evil laughter consumed the Raven. Although he knew, now, her name was never Raven.

"You may kill me, you may devour me, Raven, worm-woman. But you will never reverse history. Your foul people have been beaten and banished. You cannot survive—"

He stopped.

Survive! How Ke would regard him with a sad frown. How Hekeu would snarl and urge him on to make a last supreme effort. Could he, a savage primeval Zuman, meekly lie on an obsidian slab and allow himself to be devoured by a monstrous worm?

For from the blue radiance the worm appeared.

The Raven was enormous. Fat, pulsing, bloated, pink and blue flesh glistening with ichor, the giant worm advanced.

The worm body towered over him, black eyes glittering in the radiance.

"I shall not eat you, human." A snout advanced towards him, a protuberance from the worm's body. The tip glistened black. As he stared the black pointed tip opened like a sphincter and he glimpsed the white glisten of eggs within.

"Oh, no, Odan the Khuzuk. You will feed many as they grow within you."

"So this is why the gods destroyed your people! You are an abomination in Ea!"

"Ea is ours! We are the rightful owners of the world! Bifurcated devil! It is your very bifurcation that gives me ingress, so that my eggs will grow and break out and feed. A husk, Odan the Half-god, a husk is all you will be!"

The sphincter closed. The hard and shiny pointed tip moved closer. A single drop of ichor glittered at the point of the black cone, ridged and ready to puncture.

"We used your kind in the long ago, when you were mindless animals. But you grew proud in your feeble strengths, when you picked up a rock, when you chipped a piece of flint, when you caught and captured fire. You are our property and were and always will be."

So Odan understood that the worm-people needed human beings in which to implant their eggs. Other animals would not suffice, as so many dead-ends of the animal kingdom specialized too far and were destroyed. He could not laugh. But he spat at the worm creature.

"Your day is done. Humanity will never bow down to you again. Your breeding chambers will gather dust and dry leaves. Spiders will crawl and spin their webs where your fat worms crawled. I despise you, Raven, for a worm!"

He still gripped his sword. He could feel the hilt hard and ridged in his grip. He could feel the blood in his body, singing in his head. He could feel—but he could not move.

This enchantment binding him was not the simple spell of Abimalaikal's Paralysis. This gramarye harked back to an older and darker time. Odan tried to recall what Asshurnax had told him, what Kidu had said, the scrolls and tablets he had read. Of one thing he was reasonably confident. The Raven worm would attempt to thrust her sphincter up him and he would attempt to prevent her.

Whatever happened he would not supinely allow her to flesh him with eggs. No, by Hekeu!

The horror of the situation, the terror in the blue radiance, the writhing masses of worms revoltingly alive and wriggling, the enormous worm-woman herself, towering over him, glistening, tumid, ichor-running, the black hard point of the close sphincter probing towards him . . .

An inch from his body the black point stopped.

The coalescing rivulets of color ran and divided over the worm and cast a brief rainbow light. The color-changes must be the spell summons. Even as he realized this Odan guessed the rest and so was ready.

To cover what she was doing the Raven hissed again and taunted him, the point hovering ready to drive home into his body.

"You are rich and fat with flesh and blood. My eggs will thrive in you, Odan the Fool! Prepare to fulfil your destiny, the destiny which fate ordained for your humanity to the eternal well-being of my own!" The word she used to describe the worm-people passed over Odan; unpronounceable by human vocal chords and tongue, it drove a shudder through him.

He felt the departing shock. He saw the black cone-point thrust. He knew that the caul of Paralysis about him would prevent ingress of the sphincter; the worm must release the Paralysis before she could implant her eggs. And Odan was ready.

An ordinary mortal might never have reacted. A simple human being overcome by the horror of the moment and by revulsion as the worms writhed and swarmed might simply have stretched out beaten and defeated and allowed what seemed inevitable to occur.

But Odan was of the Hekeu. He might or he might not be a demigod. He had been thrust out of the Hekeu of Zumer; but he was a true Zuman, a Khuzuk, a dagger-tooth lion in all but name.

The black point struck.

Odan moved.

The bronze blade slashed in a single shearing bolt of bronzen light in the shadowy chamber.

The worm shrieked.

The sphincter-tipped proboscis dropped away, a foul ichor smoking from the severed end. The worm drew back, colored rivers of glisten thickening across the skin. Odan gave her no chance. The sword lifted, slashed, lifted, slashed again.

Chunks and gobbets of worm spattered against the rocks.

The mass of writhing worms vanished. The radiance dulled to a painful purple.

The rocks opened. Odan breathed the fresh air. The descent to the feeding chamber had been an illusion along with the rest. Only the worm was real.

The Raven, the worm-woman, was real—and she lay in scattered bloody chunks about the space in the rocks. A few of the gobbets twitched still with evil life. Odan went methodically about slashing every piece to ribbons. He did not think the eggs would find sustenance in that place of horror.

Then he cleansed his sword on the grass and so stepped back out of the cleft and retraced his steps to seek Sjalu.

He found the necromancer sitting still in the same position, the scroll open upon his knees.

He was dead.

Upon his one-eyed, one-eared face was stamped a look of utter horror, a child-like terror that had frozen with death.

Odan took up the scroll and rolled it carefully.

He walked back to his chariot.

He paused.

He stared up through the interlacing branches of the trees. On his face the look stamped there was not one of horror or of terror. Odan the Half-god's harsh face held a look of anger, and malignancy, a look of vicious primeval hatred.

He bellowed, raucously, intemperately, up against the sky.

"You gods! You who play with men as children play with ants! I am Odan! I am Odan the son of a god! Which one of you is my father? Have you no courage, no guts, are you all craven, weak, furtive fumblers in the night?"

A peal of thunder rolled ominously across the heavens.

Odan mounted up and drove the chariot furiously out of the trees, out under the sun, out under the sky of the gods.

"I despise you, gods! I would be a god and I would know my father so that I might give him the respect which is his due. But if he hides behind a false name—*Odan En-Ke? Do you exist?*"

He halted the chariot and stood, head lifted, his hunched body strained back. He stared up into the arching blue.

"I am the son of a god! Who will own to me, to Odan? Come, you powerful god, whoever you are, come and answer to your son!"

Against the sun, high, a second sun grew in the heavens.

Chapter Nineteen

The schemes of godhood

"I am Nirghal En-Theus! I am Nirghal of the Fire! Who are you who calls on me as father—declare yourself, mortal! Stand forth so that a father may see his son!"

The god-voice resonated from the dream chariot. Fire coruscated, magnificence showered the air, the whole earth lit with the blazing apparition of the god of fire.

"I am Odan! I am Odan the Khuzuk. Do you own me as your son, Nirghal En-Theus?"

"You speak with the tongue of a blasphemer! Down on your knees, dog!"

"If I am your son, am I a dog?"

The heavens opened with fire. The sky dripped a radiance that fell and scorched and what was scorched was made whole again and what was burned remained unconsumed. Through the wavering heat mirages Odan stood, his hunched body stiffly drawn back, his massive head uplifted. Snarling, he challenged his father to declare himself.

"I am Nirghal and I spawned a son to serve me. You are he—you who call yourself Odan. There is no Odan En-Ke."

"If I am your son, then am I half a god. I would be a whole god!"

"You, a crawling puny mortal—a god! This is a jest for the table of Hoveuz himself!"

"I know of the Myth of Abak."

"You may know; you do not understand. Leave it, son, leave it. You have been created for a purpose—my purpose! Together we may lay low the greatest and exalt the meekest. Together we may bring the proud walls of Eresh crumbling into the mud of The River, and so take all for ourselves."

About to yell that he had heard from the Raven of the end

of that dream, Odan held his tongue. He would keep some information privy to himself. He had absolutely no intention of allowing himself to be used and then sacrificed. That would outrage the rigid codes of Hekeu.

He knew he was a demigod. An ordinary mortal would be still shaking from the experiences in the breeding chamber of the worm, the reaction weakening, the horrific memories crowding in to shatter the human heart with terror.

"And what must I do to become a god—father?"

"Do as I command!"

"Well, then command!" Odan felt the flare of temper and repressed it. His neck ached. "Can you bring your chariot closer to the ground. Looking up makes my neck ache."

Thunder rolled across the sky. Odan took the clashing sound of divine cymbals to be a god's laughter. If the gods ever laughed.

The coruscations hurt his eyes. The chariot swung lower. He could barely see and put up an arm to shield his face.

"My son, conceived in secrecy and now sent to serve me. You must do as I command—Eresh—the army of Eresh must be crushed and washed utterly away."

"I can contrive that. By treachery. You will send the chariotry and the infantry of Endal against Eresh at the time?"

"I will. I will summon all the force of Endal. The devils of Eresh are due. The chief devil, Zadan, must be cast down and set in chains. And we shall not use chains of bronze."

"No," said Odan as though discussing the best point for a new arrowhead. "No, you will use Zadan's own metal."

"In the eighth hell, the hell below the seventh hell, will Zadan be chained. In his time. And to this end, my son, you will throw open to my chariotry the gates of Eresh and deliver up to my people all her people."

"All this I will do. And in return you will make me a god."

"You will be requited as is proper that a son of a god should be requited."

"That is a word that may be read any way. I will keep faith if you will keep faith—"

The thunder billowed about him, rocking him, sending him reeling back. The words battered.

"You dare to bargain with a god?"

"I do not bargain. I state terms."

Odan could barely see. The light blinded. Tears squeezed

past his eyelids. His ears ached. His head rang. But if this agony had to be endured he would endure, adhering to the fanatical codes of the Hekeu. Nirghal who had always been the devil to the folk of Eresh must keep his word once given. Odan believed that, although he had no proof. Gods were divine, and their words were divine. He had to force himself to stand up and face this demoniac being who was his father and who plotted the destruction of Eresh—the city of Zenara.

But, for Zenara's sake it was he did all this.

What was going on within the radiance of the dream chariot Odan did not know. The light diminished. He could see again. The great god-voiced battered his eardrums.

"I will treat you as a god if you keep faith. Throw open the gates of Eresh as my chariotry and infantry come up. Do this thing. Slay the king, Neb-ayin-Ke. Slay all who would oppose me. Open Eresh to my people of Endal and I will do with you as a god may do with another god. I will treat you as a fellow god."

Was this all Odan could hope to win at this time?

"And this you swear?"

"I do not swear to a mortal—but you may rest assured that I, Nirghal En-Theus, will do as I say."

The dream chariot rose into the air. The light brightened, pulsed, the sound of thunder parted the air, the light winked out and the dream chariot and the god were gone.

Nirghal must keep his word to treat Odan as a god. The gods were immortal. If Odan was immortal he could not be sacrificed. The prophecy spoken by the Raven, the worm-thing, would not be fulfilled.

Odan the Khuzuk whipped up his chariot horses and drove in his usual reckless smashing way back to the palace of the king of Shanadul.

After Shanadul—the Golden Road,—and Eresh.

Civilization had had little hand in shaping Odan the Khuzuk. The strict codes of the Hekeu and the banditries of the bazaars, these forces had fashioned him. He thought—just once—of his betrayal of Eresh, of Neb-ayin-Ke, of Kidu and Asshurnax, of his friends, of Ankidu and of his mother Momi—and then he put that thought from him. He knew his path and what it was necessary for him to do.

A god might do anything.

Odan the Half-god was obsessed in those days. Drunk upon the visions opening before him, he thought of nothing save his dreams of godhood.

He had been welcomed back in vast kindness, the people of Eresh flocking into the streets to cheer as he passed by. Already as a result of his measured words the false sorcerers had been taken up by the king's guards. The bazaar pirates festered still and his friends continued to scratch a living. He wished no ill to the Tigers. He kept, as he had promised, a watchful eye out for Tansi, pleased that she had found another bandit to assuage her grief at his parting. The city prospered. If the thieves wore hungrier looks, they were welcome to try any other of the jewel-like cities of The River, each with its own god.

Odan Crookback found many and devious excuses to avoid the religious ceremonies in honor of the god of Eresh, Zadan of the Sword. The power of Zadan was real and immense. He might look into Odan's heart and descry the treachery seething there.

Odan gave anything at all to do with Zadan a very wide berth.

In those feverish days as he used his new powers of invisibility to spy out every gate and to plan how he would act on the day the signal came from Nirghal, he was aware of a strange barrier between himself and Master Asshurnax. He did not see Kidu and was content to avoid the king's wizard. But Asshurnax—his old master wore a preoccupied look. Odan realized the old wizard would not meet his eye. Did Asshurnax suspect? Had he sent a grifting to watch over his protégé who was now the prince of Eresh, and therefore seen all that had gone on? But, had he done so, if Asshurnax knew, then surely he would warn the king, warn Master Kidu?

Perhaps he had.

Perhaps they toyed with him. Perhaps, when he made his move and opened the gates to welcome in the chariotry of Endal the wizards would strike and undo all his planning. A godhead rested on his right reading of the riddle.

And, beyond the godhead—Zenara.

How much did Zadan know? Odan's loyalty lay to his father, not to the god of the city to which he had been brought masquerading as the son of Odan so as to become all in due time a traitor to that city. Nirghal's plan was simple and obvious and by those truths effective and workable. He had introduced his own half-mortal son into the city of the god he hated, the city that once destroyed would give Nirghal power enough to seize the puissant power. At a stroke he would make the King of Endal powerful enough with the vassals he would accrue to subdue the other cities of The River, one by one. An alliance of gods was at best a fragile thing. But the conquering god, the god who threw down an opposing god and took his power to himself—there lay the base for success and the pre-eminent position in the pantheon.

By these same truths—did not Nirghal the god of Fire deserve success? Had he not planned? And, as well, had he not promised to treat his son as a god, and thus keep faith with him and break down the prophecy of doom? Surely, to Nirghal lay the palm.

In those days as he planned and waited for the sign Odan Crookback had no doubts.

Odan had learned much of the economics of The River and there was much yet to learn. Traffic up and down the stream paid tolls at each city. The richest traffic went via the long central arm between the Two Seas. Eresh and Karkaniz controlled the traffic. But the Golden Road to Shanadul could start from Endal, to the south of Eresh. The distance was a little greater by some twenty miles; but the traffic going to Karkaniz from Endal must pass through Eresh.

No wonder envy gnawed at the heart of the king of Endal and every merchant of that great city! They had destroyed Tubal and razed it utterly. Now Eresh must go the same way.

No help would come from Anki of Shanadul or from Tia of Karkaniz. That powerful god and goddess would caution their kings. The merchants at each end of the traffic between the Two Seas would deal with the city in power, be it Endal or Eresh. Geography favored Eresh; but if Eresh was reduced to a heap of blackened brick, then the merchants would bring their trade and their wealth to Endal the Victorious.

Smaller irritations vexed the people of Endal. When a crawler brought its wares downstream for onward transmission along the Golden Road, the timbers of the vessel would be taken apart and broken up in Eresh so that a constant stream of fine wood found its way into the city. Downstream wood became scarcer and scarcer. Every mile downstream added value to wood and stone. These common factors counted in the economy of The River in the land of Ea between the Two Seas.

Practicing his invisibility, Odan had to face the unpalatable fact that he could not rely on his art. Balniodor's invisibility worked for him perfectly satisfactorily for the most part; and then suddenly and for no reason he could fathom out, would desert him so that he would be left stranded, bereft of the power, visible to all who cared to look.

On the day the signal came Odan completed the last section of his plan.

Out of nowhere in his chamber within the Tower of The Armory a little flame broke from a papyrus outspread on his table. Odan ran across. The papyrus burned. The flames licked up, wavering, thin, but real. The papyrus was consumed to a small irregular scattering of ash. Odan looked closely.

The ash formed the perfectly legible pictogram for the word: 'One week.'

A week.

The door opened unceremoniously and Kephru-Ket, the high priest of Zadan, and Master Asshurnax burst in. They looked deeply perturbed.

"Have you seen aught to startle you, prince?" Kephru-Ket had overcome his feelings once Odan had been revealed as a demigod. He served Zadan, and Zadan the god of the Sword was of far greater power than Odan En-Ke. But, still, this Odan Crookback was acknowledged by the king. "Anything to cause alarm, my prince? There has been a sending within the temple, the omens fall wrongly. Dark forces have been loosed."

Odan leaned forward and gently blew the ash into a meaningless scatter of dust.

"Nothing, Kephru-Ket. I have not been disturbed."

The two looked agitated. Asshurnax stared at Odan. Odan returned the stare levelly.

"You are sure, my prince?" He no longer called Odan 'my lad' in the old familiar, forgetful, friendly way.

"I have said, Master Asshurnax. Nothing."

They retired, bowing, and Odan went to find Ankidu.

They had foregone much of their practice with the wooden swords of late, although Odan kept up his chariot work. Ankidu greeted him, showing him a new bow just fashioned, desiring his comments and expert advice.

"A nice weapon, Ankidu, finely balanced, sweet in the draw and like a tiger in the loose. And now I must ask you a favor."

"Anything I can do, my prince—"

"The inscription we set up for Nadjul the Quick. I have had a dream. The stone has been defaced, cast down—something has disturbed it. I would that you took the Golden Road to Shanadul."

Ankidu nodded. "We can ride tomorrow!"

Odan paused. Now why did the mention of Nadjul the Swordsman cause him a pang? Nadjul hired out his sword and his skill and he kept the faith of his fee.

"Not so, Ankidu. I particularly wish the Princess Zenara to accompany you—why, man, what ails you?"

For Ankidu had turned as white as a cotton bud.

"Nothing—nothing, my prince." He said the word in the way Odan had said it, answering the priest and the sorcerer. "I shall be honored to escort the princess."

"Then that is settled. She has expressed a desire to see the inscription to Nadjul. He was a good friend to me and through him the princess saw her brother again."

How bitter, how filled with gall, those words!

But he had successfully got Ankidu and Zenara out of the city. He did not think his mother Momi would leave; but he would be with her when the tigers from Endal broke in. They would not harm her. He, Odan the Half-god who would be a god, would see to that, by Hekeu!

Now that he was Prince of Eresh, money, wealth, vast riches, were Odan's for the asking. He selected a rare and valuable gorytus from the armory. The bow and arrows case snugged neatly abaft the wearer's left hip. The small compound reflex bow of horn and wood and sinew would usually be kept fully strung, the arrows in their separate compartment ready to hand. This rich gorytus was taken by Odan up to his room where he traced certain magical formulae upon the back and had a slave needle-woman stitch tiny red and yellow beads in exact correspondence. Carrying the case with its silver medallions and silver representations of chariots and horses and scenes of war and the hunt, Odan Crookback went to see Ankidu off.

He had resolutely refrained from any contact with Zenara.

Now, in privacy, before Ankidu left, he handed the case

over, saying: "Here is a gorytus for your new bow, my Ankidu. It is a poor piece; but I find it of worth—"

"It is magnificent, my prince! It is fit for a king."

"Well," Odan did not smile. "A king had it fashioned and it was stored in a king's armory. But now, my friend, it is yours. Guard it well and it will guard you well, in return."

This meant more than merely a gorytus was a man's best friend. The cabalistic signs would exert a measure of protection over Ankidu and thus by correspondence extend to Zenara.

"And now, fare thee well. Ride safely and in the care of Anki and Zadan."

So they parted, Odan and Ankidu.

Wrapped in a long grey cloak, ready with hand on sword to deal with any ambitious slavers, Odan stood by the East Gate of Eresh and watched the caravan start upon the Golden Road. He saw Zenara, muffled against the desert sand, and his heart lurched. He kept his harsh features composed. But his brown eyes betrayed all the bitter emotion in him, the gall of treachery, the uncaring and desperate drive for his own dark ambition, the savagely repressed feelings he would not own.

Soon, the day after tomorrow, he would meet the chariotry and the barge-borne infantry from Endal, and help in the ruination of Eresh and, thus, come into his destiny as a god.

Once he was a god there would be no one to say him nay.

Chapter Twenty

The chariots roll

The white plumes of the two horses nodded in sprightly fashion as Odan, Prince of Eresh, drove his chariot out along the dike above the irrigations, heading south. Odan stood in the car, braced in that cunning diagonal charioteer's stance taught him by Ankidu. He held the reins with a firm yet gentling hand. He was alone in the car.

A group of ditch-men working up to their waists in water plying pick and shovel went on working as he trotted past. Their foreman leaned on his stick, watching his charges in bored fashion. He did not stir when the Prince of Eresh trotted past in majesty.

A black-haired woman hurled her basket of freshly dug mud up and over, so that gobbets flew perilously close to the gleaming six-spoked wheels of the chariot. Odan flicked his whip and the horses trotted on.

The water shimmered in the sunshine. The brilliant viridian of the new-growing vegetation cut the land into squares of bursting life. Water fowls cried as they sailed past in their high wedges, or dived in a great splashing after fish. A party of slaves marched past carrying enormous bundles of papyrus stems. They marched stolidly, one after the other, and neither they nor their overseer heeded the chariot of their prince.

So Balniodor's invisibility continued to function. Odan felt the pleasure at that. If that cloak of invisibility failed him at a crucial time he might not know until it was too late.

Gathering speed Odan drove recklessly south. He passed the last of the cultivations and headed out into the brassy desert. He felt the heat striking him like the buffet from a bronze shield. He threw his chariot-scarf around his face.

Sand blew up from the horses' hooves, stinging, bitter on the tongue, fire in the eyes.

He passed an isolated ruin, once the retreat of a hermit, where now only scorpions scuttled beneath the shade of the broken walls and the three drooping palms. So ended all mortal dreams, he reflected, drawing fresh sustenance from the melancholy sight for the dream that drove him on.

He drank sparingly from the goatskin bottle. When he reached out again for the bottle he checked himself. He was growing lax and slothful. No man of the Hekeu needed water in the enormous quantities civilized men consumed. He drove his horses on over the burning desert and he watched the southern horizon for the first sight of the army from Endal.

They would be well protected by spells. Griftings would cluster thickly before them. Nirghal En-Theus himself his father, would provide further protection, for he was a powerful god. Enquiries in Eresh would reveal that Zadan was the more puissant god of the two; in Endal they would shrug and say Nirghal was the god of Fire, fully equal to the god of the Sword.

In the old-fashioned sorcery it was once believed that there was only a limited amount of the substance of magic in the world. Once that had been used and was consumed, there would be no more sorcery and magic and no more thaumaturges. The first hesitant doubts had been thrown on the theory when learned men asked: "But surely if that were so how could there be any of the substance of sorcery left after Ke created the world and the heavens and all that are therein?" Further researches showed that, in all truth, the ignorant, the clumsy, the careless sorcerers were using up their own magics, reducing their stock of the art. But the skilled, the knowledgeable, the conscientious, knew full well that their art added to the pool of knowledge and strengthened as they practiced the store of the substance of magic.

Odan hoped his own skill was equal to what he demanded. Still he had not properly mastered the permanence of Balniodor's invisibility; but his plans did not call for evanishment this day, after he had quitted the city.

A bird passed high overhead. Squinting up, Odan saw the wide-winged desert vulture and instantly projected his ka towards the bird. It would make a capital observation point. He soared; he felt for a fleeting instant the wind under his wings, the high glare of the sky, the desert spread far below in ochre and blazing yellow—and then he was thumping and banging along in the chariot, cursing the horses as they broke into a stumbling run.

Something had knocked him away from the bird.

Some force, a paraphysical force of irresistible authority, had simply swept away his mental projection.

He stared up malignantly at the bird which tilted and planed away to the south. It vanished in sun glare and Odan was left cursing futilely.

Driving fast but within the capacity of his horses and stopping to water them from the pannier filled from the goatskin bottle, he at last made out the long dun and dusty line marking the advance of the army of Endal.

Soon outriders were up with him, bows drawn and arrows nocked. He lifted his empty hand in signal and, together, the chariot from Eresh and the chariots from Endal dashed back to the center of the host.

Odan Crookback held himself as upright as he could. He was impressed by the magnitude of the army. Dust rose in clouds. Men in armor swarmed everywhere, marching on with a steady swinging tramping tread. Chariots lined out it seemed to the horizon. The noise of a great host filled the air.

Anxious to press on to the assault the King of Endal did not halt, instead he sent word by an over-dressed courtier for Odan to ride with him in the regal chariot. This was the travelling chariot, with four wheels and a canopy, drawn by eight horses, all a midnight black, glossy and polished and with tall nodding multi-colored plumes upon their arrogant heads.

Odan saluted the king gravely. He felt no repugnance. The king apeared to him a mere mortal man, heavy-fleshed with triple chins, swathed in cloth of gold, festooned with ornaments, dangling with jewel-hilted weapons. His dark eyes were set close together beside his fleshy nose. He sweated and he smelled of costly perfumes and unguents. And yet in him there was perfectly visible the bronze core of hardness and authority, the overweening pride, the desire to smash all opposition, to humble Eresh, to make King Svettu of Endal supreme along The River in the land of Ea.

Odan looked for the master mage of Endal, Master Sebekghal, but could not find him close to the king, where he would be bound to drive his own dark chariot. Probably, the thought struck Odan forcibly, the wizard's ka had been riding that desert-vulture whilst his mortal body lay at home in his eyrie in Endal.

"You do well to follow the orders of your father, the great god Nirghal En-Theus." King Svettu's voice was hoarse, cracked like a well-pitcher left to rot. He sweated. "All is prepared?"

"All is prepared. If your army fights well, then you will be king in Eresh."

"And the arch-devil, Neb-ayin-Ke?"

"His time is numbered."

"Make it so."

The shifty look in the king's eyes puzzled Odan. Surely the great king was not affrighted of a hunched-over half-god? But something disturbed the equanimity of the king.

A chariot noticeable for the gaudiness of its finish and the brilliance of its gilt and paintwork drew up alongside. Its four horses were as midnight black as the king's, drenched with favors and plumes, feathers and brasses—although the brasses were all of solid gold. The young man who was the sole occupant of the chariot looked across and Odan caught the bright gleam of his teeth. He wore a dark chin beard, and his face promised much agony for those who slipped beneath his chariot wheels.

The king took no notice of the newcomer and Odan, not to be outdone, resumed his grim converse with the king.

The youth's brave chariot rumbled alongside that of the king. The king's charioteer pulled a little to his right to avoid a long dune, taking no heed of the other car. The young man, who would most certainly have exhibited petty spite had the chariot encroaching on his way have been any other than the king's, pulled his horses aside.

"And the devil in Eresh will be humbled and fall low. His blasphemous image will be taken from his ziggurat and brought in triumph to Endal and there paraded through the streets, and contumed and defiled will be ceremonially burned. The priests of Endal shall gloat upon that day! The devil in Eresh will be no more and the great god Nirghal, may his name be praised, will rule all!"

Well, Odan owed nothing to Zadan the All Glorious. Perhaps, grudgingly, Zadan might be allowed a little gratitude for allowing Odan-en-Ke—as he so mistakenly thought as the plot began—to bring his half-mortal son into the protection of Eresh.

But that merely proved the superior survival capacity of Nirghal his father. Zadan could blame only himself when his image was taken down from his ziggurat and insulted in Endal and then burned utterly away to the greater glory of the god of Fire.

With a few last salutations, Odan whipped up his horses and sped back into the north.

As he went he kept his face half-turned back, fixing his eye upon the king's black horse nearest his chariot. The beast wore a wicked look, with a blood-red nostril, and his eyes rolled as he lunged onward over the shifting sand.

Well away from the host, with the last of the outriders wheeling their chariots in spinning dust, Odan Crookback lashed his reins about himself, fixed an unbreakable grip upon the ivory rail before him, braced himself in that cunning diagonal charioteer's stance. He sent his ka racing back, directly at the king's great black horse.

The sand beneath his hooves, the dust in his mouth and nostrils, the straining onward lunge against the harness all told Odan that he was in the body of the horse. His own body, securely fastened, hastened towards Eresh. In the noise and confusion of men and armor and chariots he could hear well enough. He pricked back those glossy black ears. The king was laughing, a great gut-rolling belly laugh of pure enjoyment.

The youth who had ridden his foppish chariot stood now in the chariot with the king, stood where Odan had stood, and he, too, laughed in unholy glee.

"The simpleton! My father has gulled him—but he opens the gates of Eresh to us. All hail to Nirghal En-Theus, father to Nirghi the demigod!"

"We have them in our hand," said the king, thickly, joying in the moment. "And our vengeance shall fall upon them in moaning and sorrow, in impalement and slavery. And the great and glorious Nirghal, god of Fire, will reign in humbled Eresh!"

"And I—I, Nirghi, the son of Nirghal, shall reign in glory at the side of my father, with you, King Svettu—all hail!"

The words penetrated the black ears of a horse; but they shocked through to the inner being of Odan the Half-god.

Then he saw the horror. If Nirghal was not his father, if he was being duped, and this jackanapes Nirghi was Nirghal's true son—and never mind the prophecy for Odan would joy to see this loathesome Nirghi impaled—then all was lost to Odan the Half-god.

There would be no godhood for Odan, no immortality.

There would be nothing.

As he struggled to retain a semblance of sanity a desert-vulture swooped down upon the chariot. It screeched. It flapped about the king, who stared up, heavy face concentrated in sudden comprehension.

The master mage Sebek-ghal possessed great powers. His griftings were of enormous potency. The vulture spoke with the voice of a man.

"King Svettu of Endal! Beware! The being called Odan spies upon you!"

The pain struck Odan then, a searing blast of whiteness that scorched his being.

He was tumbled out of the horse, staggered to the lunging plunge of his own chariot. Instantly he snatched the reins and lashed the whip. The horses responded. They bounded across the desert. So Sebek-ghal would tell the king, and the king would send swift chariots after him. The people and army of Endal were too far committed to turn back now. Barges of their infantry must already be near to Eresh. The combined assault would still go in.

Eresh!

He did owe things to the proud city.

Momi—and the king, Neb-ayin-Ke, and Ankidu and Asshurnax and the Tigers and—and Zenara—no! Ankidu and Zenara might be on the Golden Road to Shanadul; but it would be their city that was destroyed.

Furiously, Odan Crookback lashed his horses on.

He reached forward to ply the whip again and a monstrous dagger-tooth lion, as big as a crawler of The River, leaped at him. He threw up his arm—and even as he reacted so he realized the lion was a phantom. Sebek-ghal was throwing grotesqueries at him to halt him, to stop him so that the pursuring chariotry might come up with him and slay him. He pushed on, driving the idea of the hekeu from his thoughts. Other phantasms crushed down upon him, wolves, dragons, mammoths, tigers—he drove through them all, as though they were not even there, despite the evidence of his eyes, for his heart and his art knew they were not really there.

Serpents rose hissing from the desert sands. Scorpions of a size to gobble a horse curled their tails and struck. He held his composure and drove on. His harsh face drew down in lines of vicious force. Against the wizard he felt he could barely hold his own—if Nirghal took a hand he was surely doomed.

When the radiance grew about him throwing a long distorted shadow of the rushing chariot and the laboring horses forward onto the sands, Odan threw back his massive head and bellowed a defiance up at the sky.

"You are foresworn, Nirghal, the devil of Endal! I, Odan the Half-god, despise you! You are no true father to me!"

And the light grew and there were two suns in the sky and then, lo! there were three suns in the firmament.

Odan could not stare up. He was aware of frightful heat, of a buffetting scorching wind. He continued to lash the tiring horses. Ahead appeared a strip of green, low upon the horizon rim; he could barely make it out through the tears swelling beneath his eyelids. The light became intolerable. Gigantic noises burst down from heaven.

There was no need to be told what was going on up there in the heavens.

Stupidly, he was staring at an arrow sprouting from the front board. It must have passed by his body, closer than a finger's width away. He turned. Chariots! Spuming sand, their horses straining, they came on in a glitter of bronze.

The gorytus snapped up, the bow came out. With the reins wrapped about his body, Odan turned and drew an arrow, set it to the bow, pulled, aimed and loosed.

He saw the leading chariot veer abruptly away. A quick glance ahead showed the green no nearer. Could no one there see the battle in the desert, the flashing highlights from the chariots, the spinning wheels, the riven dust?

If only he could use a grifting! He had read the scrolls and the arcane tablets. He had the words. But he had never mastered the art of projecting his ka beyond his immediate vision.

He shot again and did not see where the arrow went. The pursuing chariots bore on, their horses fresher than his. Arrows spat about him, spitefully.

"O! you people of Eresh! Are you all blind! Eresh! Eresh! Your doom rushes upon you—rise—rise and stand to arms and fight!"

He shot back again and again. The chariots trampled

nearer. He strained all his fiber of being, everything that made him Odan the Half-god. He must warn Eresh!

He yearned to be there, in the palace, running up the long flight of marble stairs where the painted enameled figures of the king's guards stood their lonely vigils. He could feel the marble beneath his feet. His legs were thin and trembled with age. His eyes were misty. In his hand he grasped a great staff, a staff of ivory and ebony with gold and silver medallions, as he tottered up the stairs, and so he knew who he was—rather, he knew into whose body his ka had been projected out of the sheer desperation of his need.

Narpul the Staff burst into the king's chambers.

"King! King! Endal is on us! Call your men! Arm! Bring your chariots to the south gate and your archers to the jetty walls! Hurry!"

And, then, he felt the burning strike of pain along his shoulder and knew a devil arrow from Endal had at last found a mark. He was back in the chariot. He looked back. They were close, close . . .

Whilst he had been away and his body no more than a corpse in the chariot, they had swung in and were about to pour in their final shots. He drew and loosed with all the skill of the Hekeu. Men shrieked and fell over there, their bronze helmets toppling into the sand. Two chariots collided and exploded into a smothering jumble of smashed timbers and bloodied rags. The horses ran neighing wildly.

Another arrow pierced his arm. He tore it out, breaking it, flinging it away, and forced the pain back and away into that small chamber of his feelings where the Hekeu imprisoned pain so that it might not interfere with their survival.

He used the arm to shoot again. His shots struck home now with precision and skill. These men of Endal were merely very highly-trained charioteers, chosen to be outriders for their superior qualities. They had not fought a Khuzuk before. They could not understand how a man might not only fight but continue to live with the arrows feathering his hunched and fearsome body.

The lights in the sky had all gone, all vanished. Now only one sun shone there, the same old Zamaz that Ke had placed to give light to the world he had created.

Greenery fled past. The horses fled along a raised dike. The pursuing chariots hesitated, hovering. With a curse from his bloodied lips, Odan lifted the bow and sent a last shaft at them. He saw a charioteer rear up, the arrow through his throat, before the others wheeled away, their wheels neat and shining, and spin away from the irrigations back into the desert.

But, beyond them, coming up as a dun bar along the horizon—the chariotry of Endal!

Dust spumed, the flick and glitter of bronze ran along the line like fire. The chariots were driving up to crush Eresh before her chariotry could roll. The infantry of Endal would come up to finish the work and then the impalements would begin.

All was finished, as Odan lashed his exhausted horses on, all was done for he could see no succour for Eresh now.

"Eresh! Eresh, the proud city! What have I wrought to thee in my dreams! Eresh—I mourn for thee—"

He whipped past a stand of palms and out of the corner of his eye saw a chariot, waiting quietly. The bow came up and the arrow notched back and he had almost loosed when a strong voice bellowed: "Hold! Hold, Odan the Half-god!"

And it was Ankidu, and there were other chariots, hidden behind the palms, squadron after squadron, quietly waiting, their white plumes nodding, their bronze all dulled so that no betraying gleam might warn the oncoming host.

Stupidly, Odan said: "Ankidu?" Then: "But you are in Shanadul."

"The inscription to Nadjul the Quick has been seen to. I sent a trustworthy chamberlain. But I am here, and you have brought the might of Endal down upon their destruction."

"The king—"

"Is with us. Archers line the jetties—now ride on to the city and have your wounds seen to. The devils of Endal ride upon their doom and I will joy in their slaying."

"No," said Odan the Khuzuk. "No, Ankidu. And you are my friend I will stand in line with you this day."

"My prince—Odan—you honor me by calling me friend. You should go to have your wounds attended by the doctors—"

"Wounds? Since when have wounds bothered a Khuzuk?"

The chariots moved together, wheel to wheel as Odan brought his horses about. He saw they would be able to run little further.

"Another chariot—" he began.

"A chariot for the prince!" bellowed a bluff officer who

might have been Bluff Seljak's son. The look Ankidu bestowed on the warrior made his face blench. He repeated his words, this time in a whisper that merely rasped the eardrums instead of near-rupturing them.

A brisk professional bustle resulted in a spanking chariot rolling up, driven by a warrior rather than a driver. White plumes nodded in a cluster as the high officers conferred. The horses waited. The chariots with all their gleaming decorations dulled rested in a long hidden line behind the palms, a screen of lower vegetation along with the papyrus stems affording perfect concealment. Odan vaulted into the car and, gripping the forward rail which was of bronze, stared through a chink in the green.

The desert appeared covered with the mass of onrolling chariots. Dust smoked. Plumes of many colors waved. The sun broke back in splinters of fire from bronze and gold. Fire! Yes, Nirghal the god of Fire rejoiced on this day—and yet, and yet—that third sun could only have been Zadan in his dream chariot battling with Nirghal. That contest had been finished and the gods had withdrawn. Now the battle lay with the mortals of Endal and Eresh—and with two demigods, Nirghi and Odan.

Ankidu, who looked more hard and competent than ever Odan could remember him, gestured.

"Once they enter the irrigations, my prince, we have them. We shall smash them and drive them back to the desert. Then the chariots will be unleashed."

"I will drive with you Ankidu."

"Then pray to Zadan the All Glorious to be with us this day."

There was no coherent answer Odan could make to that.

Just before the moment of contact when the arrow storm would burst upon the surprised chariotry of Endal, Master Asshurnax appeared and stood, one hand on the chariot, looking up, talking quietly to Odan the Half-god. Asshurnax wore his finest robes. He wore his cap of potency. He wore, also, a short stabbing sword of bronze, inlaid with designs that made the eye water.

"So, Odan, prince of Eresh, you return to us."

"Return, Master Asshurnax?"

And, in that instant, Odan saw and understood.

Asshurnax smiled his long rueful smile.

"Much of your art is veiled from me. I could not remain

easy in your presence. Kephru-Ket and I, we suspected; we did not know. But my grifting saw the desert-vulture, saw through Balniodor's invisibility—Odan—you would go to great lengths to seek your godhood."

"I will. If you know me at all, then you know that."

"The army of Eresh has been prepared all day. Yet I saw your attempt to warn the king—Narpul the Staff has not yet recovered from your punishment of his old body—your warning was unnecessary. Yet in making it at the risk to your own body you prove yourself—"

"It proves nothing! And so you suspected and spied and the army was ready. And Ankidu—my friend—said nothing—"

"A stricture laid on him by the king and Kephru-Ket which he could not disobey. But he sees your true worth, Odan the Half-god. You did not betray us. As Ankidu truly says, you have lured the army of King Svettu of Endal on to their own destruction."

"They will fight hard. The day is not yet won."

"We shall win. Zadan fights on our side."

"As Nirghal fights on theirs."

Now, carried unmistakably on the air from the desert, the sonorous sound of many horses and chariots brought every warrior alert. Hands grasped reins, hands grasped bows, eyes grew brighter. Odan, looking upon the host of Eresh, felt a quick and betraying sentiment. These were the men of the city to which his father had brought him still in the womb. Although much had happened afterwards, this was in a very real sense his city.

"You made a supreme effort to warn Eresh, my prince." Asshurnax took his hand away from the chariot, for it was time. "In that are you absolved."

Looking down, reaching for the first arrow, Odan said: "I need Eresh. Without the city I have nothing. Had I, in truth, been Nirghal's son . . ." He could not finish the words.

"But you are not the devil Nirghal's son. You are the son of Odan En-Ke. There is no doubt."

"The Raven doubted. But the Raven is dead—the slimy bitch."

And with that harsh down-to-earth, common expression of contempt, Odan joined with the men of Eresh in bringing war and death upon the army of Endal.

The bright rays of Zamaz the sun fell upon the solid flights of arrows and the shadow passed over the land beneath. The chariots of Endal, caught as they defiled along the irrigations, reeled from the onslaught. Men screamed and, screaming, pitched from their cars to roll on the mud and so splash into the ditches. Horses ran shrieking, trailing bloodied corpses of drivers, their reins still lashed unbrokenly about their bodies. In a panic at this abrupt and awful ambush the chariotry of Endal broke and turned, horses screaming, men yelling, a shower of arrows rising from them—rising ineffectually for they had no clear targets—and then in a mixed and surging mass breaking back for the desert.

Along The River the corpses floated from the barges of Endal and the waters roiled red. The infantry clung on, stubbornly, and the fight there hung for a space.

The silver trumpets pealed. High, shrill, beating at the blood in a man's head, the trumpets of Eresh unleashed the flood of chariots with the white plumes flaring. Over the ruin they drove, out past the irrigations, and on the wide openness of the desert, deploying with martial mastery, they poured forward to the slaughter.

The sun beat down and Odan jolted to the onrush of his chariot. In the onward rush of the army he lost Ankidu. Chariots banged and clattered all about him. Horses screamed as shafts pierced their glossy coats. Excitement burst all along the line.

The devils of Endal stood here, for a space, wheeling their gleaming chariots into line, ordering their prancing horses, shooting clouds of arrows. Multi-colored feathers nodded. The wink of bronze blinded in the sunlight. The dust rose, the noise bellowed, the taste of blown sand clogged mouths and eyes.

Like the closing jaws of a crocodile the two lines of chariots smashed against each other.

All was noise and confusion, the raw bright stink of spilled blood, the screams of horses, the spurting sand driving up as hoof and wheel raked the desert floor. His massive body hunched over Odan seized up the javelins arranged slanting beside the chariot. He threw with all the awful force that amazed even the primitive savage tribesmen of the Hekeu. The chaos of chariots locked together, wheel to wheel.

The mass surged across the desert, trampling, spinning, fighting, bloody, enormous.

Odan hurled his last javelin and saw it burst through the

bronze and leather of a warrior of Endal. His own driver screeched and flopped down, an arrow through him. Odan cursed and seized the reins. The movement in the mass spread like the scummy surface of a volcanic pool. The chariots were rolling again, the chariots of Endal recoiling and the chariots of Eresh leaping after them like tigers.

"On! On!" shrieked Odan. "On for Eresh and Zadan!"

He flogged the horses on and the sky was under him and the chariot above him, he saw a wheel spin away like a child's toy, he saw a maze of legs and hooves battering past, the dusty flickering whicker of spoked wheels, he saw the white plumes all upside down, and then he was flat on his back on the sand with all the breath knocked out of him.

With two grasping lungsful of air he sprang up. The pain must be pushed away. The dagger-tooth lion did not acknowledge either pain or defeat. Death alone would never defeat a Hekeu.

The chariots smoked away into the desert. Defeat and victory were bringing blood and death and glory and triumph. They were smashing the devils of Endal. The battle here in the desert was over—save for this last warrior of Endal who rose from his wrecked car. Odan watched him as the wheel-less wreckage of his own chariot vanished fast after the host.

The two were surrounded by the aftermath of a chariot battle. The shambles looked as though a timber yard and a butcher's shop had fallen together. The devil of Endal recognized that he must slay this warrior of Eresh before he could escape. With a shout he advanced.

Odan drew his sword, that leaf-shaped bronze blade that symbolized so much of life in the land of Ea between the Two Seas.

"Die, pig of Eresh!" The fellow was confident. He bore a shield as well as a sword. He came on at a run.

Nadjul the Quick had trained Odan well. Many a time he had made him fight with sword alone against sword and shield. Nadjul the Quick, the Swordsman—Odan did not shout. He simply ran on, twisted that powerful body, dazzled the bronze blade to deceive the shield, slid the sword and so slashed his own blade across the fellow's throat. The blood stained along Odan's brand.

He stepped back. He was not even panting. The man of Endal fell.

"As you will all fall, you devils of Endal!"

So Odan the Half-god stood alone in the desert amidst the shattered panoply of war. He stood with his legs wide apart, sucking in mouthfuls of the hot desert air, his head thrust viciously forward as he surveyed the scene of death and triumph.

He had achieved much. There was much left to be achieved. By Odan! By the god who might exist and might be his father and who might not exist and might not be his father! He felt the blood in him. By whatever god who would own him! He would win through the impossibilities ahead, he would win Princess Zenara, his own half-sister. The worm-people were old and shrivelled and what they mumbled in their arcane gramaryes could hold no meaning for the future.

So he stood, blocky, hunched, monstrous. Blood covered him in a shining coat. His limbs trembled, and yet he stood, firm and square, hunched over, his massive head thrust arrogantly forward.

He was Odan! Odan Crookback, Odan the Khuzuk—but, most of all, he was Odan the Half-god.

He shook his bronze sword at the bright sky. The blood gleamed freshly wet along that leaf-shaped bronzen blade.

"You gods! You gods who toy with men as playthings. Look on me! I am Odan—and I will be a god. This is a fate that cannot be denied me. I will be a god."

He brandished the bronze sword against the sky, a hunched and majestic figure, alone in his might.

"I will be a god!"